C L A N   N O V E L :

Ravnos

KATHLEEN RYAN

author	kathleen ryan with john h. steele and stewart wieck
cover artist	john van fleet
series editors	john h. steele and stewart wieck
copyeditor	anna branscome
graphic designer	aaron voss
cover designer	talon dunning
art director	richard thomas

More information and previews available at
white–wolf.com/clannovels

White Wolf Publishing
735 Park North Boulevard, Suite 128
Clarkston, GA 30021
www.white–wolf.com

First Edition: January 2000

10 9 8 7 6 5 4 3 2 1

Printed in Canada.

To my dad, for his birthday

Ravnos

part one:

master

Wednesday, 28 July 1999, 7:54 PM
Inside a small space
At an unknown location

Khalil Ravana woke to hot, cramped, noisy darkness. As the day's stupor faded, he became aware of pressure confining him from every direction—of his arms pinned tightly to his sides—of legs bent, frozen, and unfeeling—of his neck forced down toward his chest—of toes and twisted hands supporting the weight of his body—of the friction of bare skin on some rough substance—of a hard, unyielding knob thrust uncomfortably against his chin—

Outside the tiny prison, he could hear thumps and thuds, muffled voices, and a gentle creaking sound. Khalil stretched himself, expanding to fill the last free space available. The knob in his face ground uncomfortably up his jawline, and he recognized it for what it was: his own left knee. The Ravnos shrank himself down again, trying to feel his hands. They weren't tied…they could move, a little….

Suddenly, the gentle creaking stopped. Khalil felt himself come to a halt with it, realizing for the first time that it had been moving him along. He had roughly one second to think on that before his body, and the shell around it, tipped and slid down a long, skidding drop. He seemed to half-fall for an eternity, and the dried-up memory of his stomach complained.

The impact flipped him over. Instead of being hung limbs-downward in his shell, his head was now bottom-most. Jarring, shrieking vibration traveled up through the corner—he was coming to feel that his casket was oblong—and into his ears. Khalil shrugged off the jolt and noise. The shift in position had freed his hands a little more, and he groped eagerly around the confines of his world. There were rounded, bristly, soft protrusions covering the "walls." He pulled on one and the tip of it tore away in his hand. Foam…. He let the little fleck drop and explored further. Farthest from him, in a small clearing of the spongy bumps, he discovered a tiny handle, a metal latch, and a button. He pressed the last, and a soft light came on. A wave of relief poured over him.

He was inside a suit- or guncase, packed comfortably enough in gray eggcrate padding. He wished, fleetingly, that whoever had done the job had had a real trunk or a coffin handy, but considering the hurry his new ally had been in to leave Calcutta, this was first-class travel. Khalil peered up at the latch—yes, it opened from the inside. Hesha Ruhadze's men were clever. Smuggling corpses from nation to nation— no trouble, apparently. The Setite had gone to sleep at the same time Khalil had—Hesha's mere retainers, then, were competent to move contraband on a global scale and jury-rig accommodations for unexpected travelers at the last minute. Calcutta to Delhi, Delhi to London, London to Chicago…he added in time for layovers, and decided it was just now turning night in middle America. He nearly laughed out loud. The inexplicable rocking, the long drop, the squealing metal, the heavy noises from without—he must be on the baggage carousel in O'Hare already, bumping around with all the other luggage. Something fell on him from above, and his own case settled onto its edge. Both bottom corners shrieked now, but Khalil relaxed almost cozily in his foam cocoon.

Just a little longer, and one of the old snake's boys would come pick him up, cart him through Customs safely, and take him out to join "partner" Hesha in some luxurious suite stocked with plenty of blood. Cold blood, Khalil thought wistfully, but free…

Blood…

Khalil was hungry. It went almost without saying. He'd nearly starved to death as an honest gypsy boy in India. He'd been merely hungry and poor after his family died and he turned to thievery. When the *shilmulo*—the vampire—adopted him, he'd had a month or two of real food and regular meals to fill in his ravaged muscles and hollow face. When the change came, when the *shilmulo* took him as a son forever, then he knew *real* famine. He'd learned every trick of dodging it, feeding it, taunting it, hunting for it, filling it up with promises when there was no blood, filling it to bursting when there was. The hunger of the past four nights was desperately different.

He wanted family blood. He could taste it in his mind. Memories of his "father" and the first sweet wine of immortality rose up in him. A girl he had loved, twenty years later, and traded kisses with—an elder whose strong blood had closed wounds Khalil had taken defending him—a living Rom with *shilmulo* blood flowing through his line, fought and conquered and destroyed. Every Ravnos he had ever known…the demon inside him lusted after them as it had never lusted after any lives before. Three nights now, he'd felt this…ever since the earthquake…and the desolation of Calcutta…the impulse, overwhelming, to run out and devour his own kin. Each day he dreamed of their legendary ancestor Ravana dying, his giant body scorched black by the sun, his shadow looming over his children, his irresistible voice commanding them (Khalil shuddered) to undo all his works and wipe their race from the earth. The dead Rakshasa King flashed bright in his descendant's eyes. Khalil would rise up and find the others—he would take an honor guard to the hells with him—he would—

The small, huddled creature in the guncase shivered and blinked away the image. The hunger faded into the background. Fear flooded him instead.

Calcutta had been empty of other Ravnos (all but one, he reminded himself), but how did he know what had happened in Chicago? Had the founder's command been heard this far? Was there already some kin of his waking to the smell of fresh Ravnos blood in the city?

He cursed Hesha. "Hurry up, goddamn it," he muttered under his breath.

Hesha is not coming, said a voice in his head. Suddenly the case seemed twice as crowded as before. Khalil fought off the impression and recoiled from the intruding thought. He'd figured he'd left that thing far behind.

"Get out of my fucking head, you shit," he said aloud. The presence retreated slightly. The young Ravnos's chest expanded with pride. He'd made *it* do what *he* wanted, for once—maybe five thousand miles was enough distance after all. Then he felt the aftertaste of the thing's mind. It was smug. The old one was smug and satisfied and just as much in control here as it had been in India. It seemed to nod at that. Sullenly, Khalil dropped his head back. The tendons on his neck flared up. He spat out, "I was strong enough to defy you even in Calcutta. I told Hesha your precious Eye was in Chicago, not New York, you bastard."

The presence shook its head sadly. **You were not strong enough even to keep yourself from lying,** *you weakling. How do you hope to defy me?* The tone altered, became even more contemptuous. *And he saw through you like the water-carrier through the temple-dancer's robes. You are pathetic and I pray to Siva that through you I will find a worthier servant.*

Khalil felt the carousel slowing. It ground to a halt, the squealing noises stopped, and the few voices left outside moved away. More time passed. Khalil squirmed. It felt like hours going by, and he began to suspect that the old one was right. And if Hesha had abandoned him, he would have to start moving soon. Even if no *shilmulo* arrived to kill him, even if no unknown American terror jumped out of the shadows, someone might open him in the morning.

I am glad that you have come to see my point of view. Now you will go to New York City, and you will do exactly as I say. Wait...wait...now there is no one looking at you. Get out.

Khalil plucked at the latch and handle and cracked open the case.

Baggage from the late flight out of London had been sent to the last claim area in the row. The only people at that end of that bay were one elderly female cleaner, mopping up where passengers were least likely to be at that hour, and a near-teenage security guard sneaking a highly illegal smoke. Neither of them had been paying any attention to the sole remaining item from Calcutta, a shallow black trunk with nickel-polish hardware. When the top of it flew up and smacked into the conveyor plates, the noise hardly impinged on their tired brains. By the time either of them looked around, the sound was thoroughly explained: A dark and curly-haired, handsome young man held the strap of the rolling carrier. His clothes, slick and fashionable, were as wrinkled as those of any other victim of economy-class seating. If he seemed rather pale and thin, well, cheap air travel could do that, too. The guard turned away to hide his cigarette. The lady with the mop eyed the devilish face and impish black goatee of the passenger and wished herself forty years younger.

Khalil Ravana winked at the old woman and walked calmly through an unattended Customs station. "Nothing to declare," he murmured to himself, and smiled.

Saturday, 31 July 1999, 12:14 AM
Red Hook, Brooklyn
New York City, New York

The street was barren, poorly lit, marred with cracks and potholes, and stifled by a rotting summer. Water hung heavy in the air, and carried with it the smell of the upper bay and the mingled Hudson and East Rivers. Feeble, creeping breezes brought the stench of decaying garbage—food, drink, booze, bodies—from between old buildings, from abandoned lots, and from the project houses looming in the distance.

The street was surrounded by the ghosts of dockyards past. Squat, brick warehouses hunkered down on either side of it. Some lay empty; some sheltered those who could afford nothing better. A few had been converted to office space or artist's lofts, the rest plied their old trade—but stored the unwanted and inconvenient instead of the lifeblood of industry.

Halfway along the street's length, one building stood slightly apart from its fellows. It was four stories high and distinctively intact. Its first floor sported sturdy metal doors and bricked-in windows. Above the street, the windows were barred and darkened, but very few were broken. The place had an air of habitation; someone would see to any cracked panes. Someone kept bulbs in the streetlights, and replaced them as they burned or were shot out. Now the landlord's carefully tended lights picked out movement at the main door. A lone man emerged.

He was black and clean-shaven. His scalp was smooth and bare as an eggshell. Angular bones and wary lines complicated his face. He had character. He was not handsome in any analyzable fashion; his appeal—strong and magnetic—had less to do with his looks than with his personality. He was above the average height, but not noticeably tall. His body did not, at this moment, intimidate. His beautifully tailored suit hid enduring, powerful muscles and sinew, but it *could* hide them. Even rags could hide them, if he carried himself to match tatters. The role of beggar served him more often than the role of bully…but tonight he wore a light, expensive trenchcoat over his silk suit. He carried an ebony cane with a solid, sterling-silver handle. His platinum watch gleamed dully. The golden rim of his monocle winked from its place in his breast pocket. The bag at his side, however…

Hesha Ruhadze put a hand on the flap of the rough canvas sack. It was not in his public persona as financial wizard to carry such a thing in the city— the rubberized cloth was plain, dirty, heavy, and slightly damp despite its protective coating—but he would have risked far more than mere mortal reputation to keep the bag in sight and at hand.

It held the Eye of Hazimel.

It held the greatest prize Hesha had ever gained, attained only after the longest quest he had ever undertaken, and at the highest cost—in lives, time, sin, and service—he and his had ever paid.

The heavy, windowless portal swung shut behind him, and Hesha listened to the steel bolts click into place with a sense of satisfaction. There was—there had been—a woman, an obstacle to his success. She had troubled him; she had distracted him from the true path. Elizabeth (the name rolled softly into his mind, and he nearly spoke it aloud). Elizabeth Dimitros (he added the last name and felt a clean sense of distance between them). She had been an inconveniently perceptive, interfering, traitorous mortal. *And now we atone, Lord*, Hesha prayed silently to his god, Set. *She waits for the sun, and I sacrifice her to your will. I am yours, and she is yours, but Ronald Thompson will never be…and that is my fault. Compassion is a sin. Accept this offering and forgive me. Speed my steps in your service.*

The devotion brought the need for haste to his mind. He had been waiting for almost thirty seconds. A touch of impatience grew behind his face. It was not permitted to mar his features, but it lay in his mind nonetheless. With Thompson gone, the other servants writhed like a headless snake. The old retainer's replacements were less punctual, less professional, less accustomed to Hesha's needs. Competent, of course—he and Thompson had handpicked them from a host of well-trained guards and detectives—but untutored. Hesha knew there would be no time to teach them properly until the business of the Eye lay complete.

If Vegel had survived… Erich Vegel had been Hesha's lieutenant, his junior partner. He could have seen to the staff. He would have shared the heavy burden of this victory. He might have interpreted correctly the signs that had led to the murder of Elizabeth…. Hesha cut the thought short abruptly. Shortly he would know whatever could be known about the fate of Erich Vegel. He hoped the information would be worth the risk he would take for it.

He felt the bag beneath his hand, and mused. The mud inside no longer sloshed; it had the consistency of pudding, smelled worse than the harbor, and weighed far more than it had any reason to. The ancient inscription that had given him the knowledge to contain the Eye stated that the relic would be safe and undetectable once caked in the mud of a holy river—the Ganges, in this case—but said nothing about the time before the casing dried.

Hesha's deep brown eyes watched the street carefully. If others could still sense the orb, or knew by other means that he possessed it...

Hazimel himself was said to be a Ravnos. The "gypsy" clan might come seeking to parley or to trick him out of the thing. If the legends were right, the *shilmulo* had the most claim to ownership and the best chance to find it. He thought of Khalil in Chicago, and wondered how the little Rom had fared.

The Nosferatu were most likely to know he had it despite all precautions for secrecy; they were the most likely Cainites to know anything. Two months ago he would have counted on them as allies—would probably, with Vegel and Thompson gone, have asked their aid in guarding the treasure. But Vegel had lost contact—had been destroyed or captured by the enemy—at a party in Atlanta which the Nosferatu had insisted that Hesha attend. Perhaps the attack that night had been a surprise to them. Perhaps not. If it had been a trap, it had caught the wrong man, and the Nosferatu would try to net their prey in another snare. And if it had been a trap... Hesha would reckon with them in time. The Setite disdained revenge for its own sake, but recognized its beneficial effect on observers.

As for the rest...the Tremere possessed the occult knowledge to realize the Eye's potential, if they knew of its existence. Any warlock would trade his or her teeth for it gladly—or strike in force. The Sabbat and the Camarilla had their hands full fighting a war for the East Coast; but the first battle had been for Atlanta, and the Eye had surfaced there. Someone might know something. It might even have been stolen from one group or the other. He thought of the reports that the Tremere's Atlanta chantry had been destroyed at the solstice, and wondered.

A black sedan careened around the corner. It sped toward him quickly and rolled to a guilty stop directly before the door of the warehouse. Tinted windows hid the driver, but Hesha knew that she could see his face, and he allowed the shadow of displeasure to cross it. He turned on his heel and walked, pointedly, three yards farther along the pavement. The sedan crept up to park in the new space, and the right rear door opened automatically. Hesha slid silently inside and waited, perched on the edge of the seat, watching the sidewalk. The driver pressed the door controls. The discreetly armored, bullet-proof, flame-proof, insulated panel closed, and the Setite settled himself comfortably in the exact center of the passenger compartment. He placed the heavy canvas sack on his lap, and his eyes fell on the woman in the front seat.

For an awkward moment, the mortal behind the wheel did nothing. She seemed to be waiting for her employer to speak. Her head turned tentatively to the rear—Hesha caught a glimpse of smooth olive cheek, of uncertain coal-black eyes, of simple silver studs in the woman's ears, of the empty pierced places in her nose and brow. After a second, her training kicked in. The sleek, jetty head checked itself. The chin-length bobbed hair swung back into place around her jaw.

Better to make the car a moving target, Pauline Miles thought, *even if I have no idea where to go.* She took her foot off the brake and let the powerful engine pull the car forward.

The dead man in the back of the car observed all this with care. He followed quite clearly the progression of his bodyguard's mind from confusion to conclusion; he had trained servants for centuries. Hesha opened his mouth to speak, noting her tightening jaw muscles and white knuckles. There had been a coachman, in England, who had begun this way....

"Miles."

"Sir." Pauline's voice trembled only slightly.

"You are late." Hesha's carefully modulated tone expressed no disapproval. It expressed nothing at all. His driver blanched further. "In the future, do not stop at manholes, sewers, or steam grates. I will not cross them to come to you."

"Sorry, sir."

"Not at all." Half a laugh accompanied the curt reply. "I had not mentioned it to you before this," he went on, tolerantly. "There are some uncommon safety measures you will need to acclimate yourself to...certain new skills to be picked up." Miles's grip on the wheel relaxed, and Hesha heard her breathing slow down a little. "I expect you need more practice with the car, for one thing—

"I have business in the Bronx," he said resolutely. "Pay attention. Use the Brooklyn Bridge. Head north through SoHo and Greenwich Village. Pick any route you like through Midtown...." Hesha reached out and opened a phone line. "As we go north, maintain, at all times, a distance of at least three cross-town blocks from Central Park. Pass that," he said, pressing a button, "on the west side. There is limited space between Barnard College and the Park's northwest corner—do your best to keep an equal distance from both. Then proceed northeast to the Grand Concourse. I will give you an address once we have left the island. Is that clear?"

Pauline Miles's lips moved slightly, and her left index finger traced a crooked, imaginary line up the center of the steering column. "Yes, sir," she answered. With clear eyes and sharp movements she made a right turn and started on her chosen course.

The Setite noticed and nodded. The woman's memory seemed to be everything Thompson had claimed. Hesha picked up the handset and finished his transmission. A bell tone rang once.

"Hello, sir." Janet Lindbergh's voice sounded thin and brittle over the tiny transmitter, but it had force. Hesha smiled to think of the old woman, secure in her safehouse in Maryland. Here was one of his tools still strong and unbroken.

"Good evening." He realized there was more warmth than usual in his greeting, and a touch of gratitude. He found both inadvertent emotions disturbing. "Report," he barked.

"The ordinary business runs as usual, sir. Would you care for details?"

"That can wait until my return, I think."

"Very well." Janet mentally turned a page in her notes. "Baltimore," she began seriously, "is experiencing a slight increase in homicide and deaths from "exposure," "hemophilia," and "anemia." No direct confrontations appear to have broken out, however, and neither your close relatives nor the rest of the

Family have tried to contact you through my chan-nels since we last spoke.

"Your new man—" *Matthew Voss*, thought Hesha. Janet scrupulously avoided the use of any real names over unsecured lines— "arrived safely, and our boys"—*The Asp*, filled in the listener— "are briefing him on his new duties. The doctor sent a message for you from Alaska—"

"I doubt I wish to hear it."

"It was complimentary, sir." Hesha could almost see Janet's puckered, lined face grinning.

"That has nothing to do with the matter." It was familiar, comfortable banter. A surge of temptation washed over him to leave New York immediately— to take his retinue and his prize and go.

His secretary's recital lapped at his ears. A thin part of him took note, and saved the information for later, but his real thoughts lay deeper: This trip to the Bronx was a terrible, fantastic gamble, skirting the edge of enemy territory on all sides, carrying what might be the brightest (*no*, thought Hesha suddenly, *the darkest*) arcane beacon on the continent. In Bal-timore, he had a haven, he had security, he sat at the center of his web and knew precisely the movements of everyone within it, he could finish the Hazimel project and be done with the matter. Every instinct urged him south, to safety….

On the other hand, if Vegel had been captured, not killed, that safety was pure illusion. The Sabbat could have interrogated him, wrung all Hesha's shared secrets from him, and made the farm in Maryland a deathtrap by now. The younger Setite had been (and perhaps, still was) strong in body, mind, and faith— but the Sabbat had ways and ways.

The week of the battle for Atlanta, he had made a journey east to Queens to enlist two young serpents, Orthese and Bat Qol, in his investigation. He had given them a private plane to take them to Atlanta, money, support, information, technology, police contacts, and all the weapons their chilly hands could hold. The local temple spoke highly of the team, and Hesha knew them personally. They should have been up to the challenge. Both were smart enough to slither out of tough spots without fighting. Both were capable of understanding that their patron wanted information from them, not a rescue, not heroics, not more disappearances. On the 24th of June their message suggested they had found a holding area for prisoners caught in the art-museum attack. On the 25th they failed to report in. Hesha cut his losses and sent no one after them; he assumed them destroyed at the hands of the Sabbat.

And tonight, of all nights, Bat Qol had resurfaced, left a message, and asked to meet him at a different rendezvous, nearer the Setite temple grounds…and closer to known Sabbat territory. It could be a trap. Baltimore could be a trap. Every haven Vegel had known of could be a trap. But if the girl had information about Erich or Atlanta, Hesha *had* to know it.

A slight catch in Janet's speech brought his full attention to her.

"Two other things, sir, which I thought you'd wish to attend to yourself." Janet hesitated. "Amaryllis Rutherford called again, trying to reach Elizabeth. I put her off, but it's becoming more difficult to do.

"Second, Rutherford House has sent a bill for Miss Dimitros's services this week. How would you like me to spin this?"

Hesha's answers were quick and ready. "Go on delaying Ms. Rutherford. Pay the partners. We will devise a suitable, public disappearance for Miss Dimitros when the dust of the current crisis settles."

Pauline Miles's hands tightened on the steering wheel. She pinned her eyes to the road, and tried in vain to keep her mind on her job.

Somewhere in the back woods of Maryland, Janet Lindbergh shook her head. She gritted her teeth and swallowed all the things she wanted to say to her employer.

Hesha took notice of the silence. "After my appointments," he began, "I want every available resource devoted to taking us out of New York. Use the agency for protection and decoys. Have a flight go west...to O'Hare, I think...with my name on the passenger manifest. We are going underground until the Family's squabbles have been decided one way or another. There is a great deal of work to do to put our own house in order.

"See to the arrangements," he finished, pressing the button to slide the privacy panel up. He connected the phone through the driver's intercom and shut off the speaker in his own space. Janet and Miles could coordinate the details just as well without him, and he had other things to worry about besides their feelings. Whatever the two women thought of the issue left behind in Brooklyn, they had their orders, and they *would* carry them out.

Saturday, 31 July 1999, 12:14 AM
Riverside Park, Middle West Side, Manhattan
New York City, New York

Green grass, well-tended, lay dimly gray on either side of the gravel path. Old trees grew black and tall overhead. The waning moon shot feeble rays through gaps in the canopy, wresting the memory of color from beds of flowers all around. The filthy, emaciated husk of a man made his way feverishly up a little hillock, desperately striving to catch a patch of light. He clutched in bewilderment at the silvery space, then moaned in disappointment and hung his head like a beaten animal. His eye (he had only one) closed on bloody tears. Brackish, black fluid rolled down the seamed and ravaged face, making a furrow in the grime and…other things…dried there before it. Wearily, the head came up, the eye opened again, and the wretch pulled himself together and charged off, as best he could, for another bright spot in the distance.

There had been a time—ages ago—when the creature's name might have been Leopold.

What lurched after the moonshine had no word for itself anymore. He moved through formless darkness and recognized nothing. He knew only an unbearable pain deep within, and a vision—a divine and glorious vision—without. Ahead of him, dancing wherever the moon found a way through the thick summer leaves, there was the girl—the ghost—the goddess—his muse.

Each time he reached his goal, she slipped away from him an instant before he could touch her.

His left foot tripped and twisted beneath him. He had slipped before—often before, as the scraped and ragged skin of his shins could testify. He had caught himself, as he did now, on his torn palms, his raw, open elbows. Road dirt and gravel had embedded themselves under the papery skin. The lover never noticed the pain; he felt only irritation. When the horizon jolted and tilted he nearly lost sight of *her*. His feet looked after themselves, the spindly legs scrambled back under their body out of habit, and the gestalt propelled itself up again.

To his dumb surprise, he found he had gained on her.

It would be another trick…how cruel she was to flee him, never to speak to him as she had in that other time, never to lean over his shoulder and help him…she stood perfectly still now (she could do nothing that was not perfect)…and that was cruel, too…she teased him and taunted him unmercifully….

Suddenly, he was at her feet. She graced the center of a pedestal, white as stone under the moon.

He touched the base—

She stood there yet—

He placed a foot beside hers—

She ignored him completely—

He flung his arms around her beautiful, beautiful body and pressed his lips to hers—

The goddess accepted him! At least, she stayed where she was…he caressed her flesh with his callused, cracked hands and knew it to be cold, like his own…he kissed her with abandon….

And wept.

She returned none of it. Slowly, reality filtered through his broken mind. This thing before him was not his muse, not his goddess. He held stone between his two hands, and she did not yield to him because she never could. He sagged away from the statue, and looked at her face. Pure, innocent, youthful, cold, but full of grace…beautiful in her own fashion, but lacking the burning half of his idol. The sculptor had left cruelty off *this* face.

He heard the sweet, knife-like, chiming laughter of his mistress riding the wind behind him. Sweet, bitter, acid…his eye closed again, and more blood flowed from the crusted lid.

The yellowed beam of a flashlight struck him from behind. It cast his stark black-and-white shadow on the girl, and her saintly stone face took on an fleeting, illusory, horrified grimace.

"Excuse me, sir," said the voice of authority. The thing on the statue flinched. "Yes, I mean you. Turn around, slowly, and climb down here, mister," said the policeman. "You can't stay up there, and you don't want me to have to come up and get you." In a lower tone, to his radio: "Dispatch…Zamojski? Yeah. Schaeffer here. I've got a probable drunk and disorderly down at Joan of Arc." The handset buzzed back at him. "Looks like the one. Send a car around."

Slowly, the tramp clambered down off the pedestal.

The beat cop kept his distance, and brought the light up to shine directly into the suspect's eyes. He saw the blood, the wasted body, and shook his head. "Dispatch, send an ambulance along with the car. Looks like someone's been beating the shit out of this guy." Schaeffer, warily, with one hand on his gun, stepped forward to offer the sick and wounded man a little assistance.

Stop.

Khalil looked out the passenger window of the car and picked a name off a sign. "Bond Street. This is where I get off, darling. Slow down, won't you?"

The woman driving fluttered her made-up lashes at him and made a dime-stop in a bold, red, no parking zone directly before a fire hydrant. "This good enough for you?"

"Perfect, darling." He gazed into her eyes and shook his head sadly. "If only it weren't the end of the line." Khalil leaned in over the stick shift and kissed her.

"It doesn't have to be—"

"I have business—"

"Here." She reached into her purse and pulled out a silver card-case. She selected a light-blue card and held it out to him with long beige fingernails. "Take this. It's my work number. Call me." Khalil took the card and the hand together in his two palms and kissed her again, biting into her tongue this time to distract her—

"Hey!"

He pulled back. "Too rough?" His voice was tender.

"You took my wedding ring."

Khalil smiled ruefully. "I did. I'd steal you, too, if I could. I just can't bear to think that a woman like you has a husband chaining her down. Don't be mad…just another of my little tricks, darling."

Be gone.

The *shilmulo* reached for his door handle. "My bag."

They met again behind the car, she unlocked the trunk, and Khalil lifted his case out from beside her grocery bags. He walked her back to the driver's seat, whispering cheap love in her ears. "One more kiss?" he asked playfully through the open window, and took it—and a good deal of her blood—and her wallet—and her watch. He stood by as she drove off, and then turned down a side street, counting her cash.

Leopold walked north through the park on the river's edge. He knew his name. He knew the grass beneath his feet. He felt the earth beneath the grass, the stone in the earth, the mushiness of buried wood, the obstinacy of old house foundations, the echo of tunnels, the mixture of rock and water, the solidity of living rock, heat, and the plastic, malleable stuff underlying everything...soft, like clay.

More personal awareness returned to him. He saw his rags and determined, idly, that something should be done about that. He saw the muse in the corners of his eyes, but he neither rushed after her like a madman nor forgot her nature. She was angry. He had lost a gift she'd given him. His thoughts spun around recovering the gift, the tool that he needed to fulfill her inspirations. He looked down at his hands—healing, now, for some reason—and wondered a moment at the piece of metal they held. Vaguely, it came to him that the little shield was a policeman's badge. He worked it in his fingers, trying to shape the cold metal as he used to shape wax...and had shaped stone.

Leopold wandered away from the water, and his clearing brain took stock of his situation. He understood that a piece of himself was missing—not merely the eye that should have filled his empty, torn, and distended left socket. He felt blood flowing to try to heal that, though he would rather have left it open, ready for the great Eye as soon as he might find it.

This loss…not his eye…not *the* Eye…not mere hunger…. He seemed really astonishingly well fed, considering that he didn't remember feeding for a long, long time. Not the muse…she was lost, but still with him, blessing him; she would return with all her favors as soon as he found the Eye again. No, the loss that plagued him had to do with *memory*. His last clear recollection was of the finished statue in his cave. A flood of pride caught him up. That was worthy of the muse, worthy of the material, worthy, at last, of his talents: a masterpiece. Leopold swore. That masterpiece would be his last unless he found the Eye once more. *When* had he lost it? The thing had disappeared with the forgotten time and *in* the forgotten time. From the Adirondack Mountains to New York City…surely there had been many nights and effort spent in travel…why couldn't he remember any of it? Why was the time before the cave so dim? *Atlanta*, he thought, and there was a picture in his mind to accompany that.

Absentmindedly, he glanced down at the scrap of metal in his hand. The badge had melted beneath his fingers and become a woman's head in miniature. Leopold smiled. *Victoria*. She was part of what was lost. He flicked the contours of the cheeks and hair, and another face emerged. *My muse*. The tiny lips and eyes opened. Leopold found this quite natural. She called him—she urged him onward.

The power to *shape* had returned to him. Joyfully, he broke into a run. His feet hardly touched the ground—up streets—around corners—across traffic, when that was shortest. Cars crashed around him, and some poor mortals cried out—cursing, jeering, warning each other about the madman in the middle of the avenue—Leopold neither heard nor cared. The Eye had returned. The Muse had led him to it and it to him, as surely as lovers meeting. So close, now...he darted between two buildings and felt the last obstacles pass by.

A final sprint—like a bow from an arrow—faster than the corner-lurkers could follow. He saw the prison of his prize—a black sedan—and leapt after it.

He lifted a finger, and felt the Eye jump toward him.

He opened his mind to the power and brought the essence of the earth up from the asphalt to hold the fleeing car in place.

Pauline Miles checked her rear-view mirrors roughly every five seconds as part of an automatic pattern. It was her training. It was completely reflexive. It rarely resulted in anything more than slowing down—if the scan showed a patrol car—or a change of lane, speed, or direction, if a too-familiar vehicle encroached on her comfort zone.

Side, side, center—Miles squinted. There, on the right side. Not a car...she turned onto a larger street, and the figure showed itself again.

"Sir," she began. The privacy glass started its glide down. "There's a man chasing us on foot. Unarmed, but...unusual."

Hesha pulled a convex mirror down from the upholstered roof. He watched their follower for a moment, and then said, speculatively, "Drive faster."

Miles laid her foot to the gas pedal and wove forward. She found a gap in the cars around them, and managed, by ignoring two lights, to bring the car up to forty miles an hour despite the weekend traffic.

The headlights of the cars she'd left behind glared in her mirror through the window tint. She saw the silhouette of the running man eclipse the nearest, and frowned. "He's keeping up with us," she complained, and slammed her foot on the gas.

The black sedan shot ahead.

Hesha felt a movement in the bag on his lap. The canvas pressed sharply down and back, into Hesha's abdomen. He lifted the bag by its strap and watched it swing just once, like a magnet on a string, toward the rear and whatever monster chased them. A baseball-sized bulge formed in the fabric, in the spot closest to their pursuer. Hesha frowned. The Eye within had been pulled (or had it burrowed?) out of the center of the soft mud. Hastily, apprehensively, he flipped the sack around and put the bulk of the river muck between the Eye and the force grappling with it.

Instinct overtook him. "Stop!"

His driver, confused but obedient, tried to comply. The brakes squealed and then ground with the effort—the pedal shuddered under Pauline's foot as safety systems kicked in. Beneath the metal shrieks something else began groaning. Miles cocked her head to one side to get a better listen. A second later the rumbling was ear-splittingly loud, and she grimaced against the pain. She remembered artillery making noises like that, thought of earth-cracking shellfire, and gripped the wheel more tightly.

Slowly, without an explosion or shrapnel, the blacktop in front of the car rippled and slanted up like a crashing wave. Hesha stared, alarmed, at the phenomenon, and plied his memory in vain for anything like it in the whole history of the Eye.

Miles yelped and swerved. Her left foot slammed down on the emergency brake pedal. The car skidded sideways down the median for a moment, then banked against the lower slope of the ten-foot wall of tar and gravel. For an instant, the black sedan shot along like a surfboard, and its driver fought for control of the wheels against the slippery, uncertain surface. She jammed one arm through the steering wheel to brace herself, reached for the emergency brake's hand-release, yanked the cord up, stepped on the accelerator again, and regained traction again in time to take the car out from under the "breaker." In grim silence, Miles outran another growing hill of asphalt and drove up onto the sidewalk. The sedan passed through a crowd of pedestrians without quite hitting any, and tore around a corner.

"Stop," repeated the voice behind her. Pauline checked her mirror in disbelief. Her employer readied his hand resolutely on the door latch.

"There's another one coming—"

"Good. I'll use it." He gathered himself in the corner of the seat. "Get yourself away. I'll call you when this is over."

Her hands and feet went to work on the controls. "Sir!" In evading the wave, she was forced to slow down, and she saw his door open.

"You cannot help me against this, Miles." He disappeared in the curve, and the door shut automatically behind him. Pauline bit her lip, surged over a dying wave, prepared herself to wrestle with the road again…

…and found herself alone in a silent-running car on a perfectly ordinary city street.

•

The tar swept after the sedan for only a moment once its quarry had left. It moved hungrily but blindly, subsided into low ripples, flattened out, and then vanished.

Hesha Ruhadze didn't see it.

From the instant he hit the pavement, his precious bag cradled in the center of rotation—couched between his stomach and his arms to protect it from the impact—the Setite had neither looked back nor stopped moving. He put as much distance between himself and the car as possible—partly to protect his fleeing servant, partly to experiment with what he had begun to think of as "the disturbance." He heard wheels spin, then nodded in satisfaction as the engine-whine sped away.

The listless breeze picked up, bringing the smell of burning rubber with it.

Downwind, thought the Setite, *as good a direction to take as any...better than most...and it's northward...toward the temple, if I need it.* He emerged from the sidewalk-narrow alley he had taken and fell into a loping stride that ate space but gave him time to react to the pedestrians. Women dressed for commerce called out to him shrilly. Men in shabby clothes cried scorn and hooted at him. Ahead of him, a group of young bucks in expensively ill-fitting costumes turned to check out the noise. They sported strips of bright cloth on their heads, necks, arms, or legs, and despite the flamboyant differences between each one, they were frighteningly similar to each other...carbon copies of themselves and of sword-rattling children Hesha had known in Africa, India, and Europe. The same pairs of eyes looked down the sidewalk as had looked out of the *wadis* of Sudan in his youth.

The boy in the lead—*not* the leader—stepped aside to give his betters a chance to see more clearly and shoot first, if they cared to. Short words flew between them, and hands crept to pockets, waistbands, and sporty little packs slung low over their guts.

Hesha called on Set to lend him divinity, and never broke stride. He watched the gang's group face turn from belligerence to uncertainty to uncomprehending respect. He darted along the suddenly clear path amongst them like a god—ignoring them completely, as modern gods do—and their ranks closed behind him in awed silence.

The boys recovered cat-fashion, pretending to themselves, as one, that nothing had happened that they had not allowed—hell, *wanted*—to have happened. They began to talk again. They drifted north now, instead of south, and were unconscious of the reasons why. No one mentioned the rich brother who had passed through them; the closest anyone came was the most ambitious, who put forth, tentatively, the idea of hooking up with a higher echelon of organization—if and when they found someone worth their time. In all their minds, the running man in the long coat and dark suit rose as the very type they might be willing to oblige.

Full of speculation, the ambitious one kept his eyes on the fleeing figure. It crossed the street at high speed and disappeared into a crowd. He frowned and glanced back. What made *that* man run?

It was an apparition. He had to blink and look again before he believed in it. There was a tall, stick-thin white tramp coming down the street at a walk that was faster than an all-out run. When the boy slowed the image down in his mind, he felt a familiar contempt: The bum moved like a real junkie right before the last crash. On either side, the boy's friends began to notice. The first one shook his head. The speed…it must be some nightmare effect of the new batch of stuff they'd tried tonight. He stared as the thing came closer. He could see now why this freak had caught his attention. It had one eye unblinking on the right, and an open hole the size of a baseball on the left. The skin where the lid should be flapped in time to the thing's pounding feet. And the color of his skin…stark white, paper white, glowing by the streetlight…with dark, dark streaks everywhere. Red streaks. Red clothes. Soaking wet red clothes, and shining red arms…. The teenagers watching the oncoming mystery had seen blood before; they had killed other people. They had had friends shot away from beside them. They had brought hamburger in to emergency rooms, and they knew how much fluid the human body gave up on bleeding to death. This man chasing their man must have swum through a pool of the stuff. Long stiff hair wrapped around his arms, and flecks of gory tissue spotted his death-colored rags. The gang stepped out into the road to face down the thing coming through their territory, killing where it was their prerogative, hunting *their* people.

Hesha found time to survey his surroundings. So far, the ground lay steady under his feet, but a faint rumble from the south warned him that the disturbance, whatever it was, had followed him, not the car. When the asphalt closest to him began to ripple, he leapt and made the next sidewalk. *It comes for the Eye*, he confirmed in his own mind. The slab beneath him began to tilt, though the concrete and cement didn't flow like the tarry street had.

He caught sight of the gang in a window. They had moved to the center line; they radiated the arrogance of ignorance, numbers, and guns. The Setite ran on, following the glass storefront west.

The young men fired at the intruder.

The screams of bystanders filled the narrow road.

The hoarser agonies of the young men, not quite dying, tore through the shrill wails.

More shots, more screams, more death cries...

In dim, jumping, mirrored images, Hesha saw the bodies of the boys melt and run together. Silver-gray bone sprouted from the horror. Twelve shades of black skin swirled and blended. Foamy, yellow fat erupted and ran down to the...ankles...of what was left. Rifts opened near the top of the gestalt, and blood spurted twenty feet into the air. The fountain sprayed buildings on either side, and rained down fine red mist on the frozen or fleeing Saturday night crowds. Hesha watched, stunned—his feet ran on of their own accord—his mind caught up an instant later.

Fleshcrafter. The Setite's brain rolled the implications over as he chose a new route—one paved with sturdy concrete, not soft tar and gravel. *Fleshcrafting means a Tzimisce.* Hesha set aside for the moment the creature's ability to shape the earth to his will. *And a Tzimisce means the Sabbat. The question is, how many Sabbat?* He knew himself to be capable of destroying entire packs of the sect's rabid, thin-blooded shock troops. He felt sure he could master a handful of such cannon-fodder, even with the interference of the thing behind him.

A fleshcrafter of such power itself...

Perhaps, in a fair fight, on good ground...if the Eye were not an issue. He prayed fervently to Set that his enemy not be an entire war-party of elders with inexplicable powers like that thing.

The sidewalk took him past an empty lot, and the earth heaved. A shower of trash, dirt, and rubble fell around him. Hesha thickened his skin with tough scales and ran faster. Whatever power his pursuer used, it affected the bare ground even better than the asphalt. The building ahead...no...the foundations of the new, cheaply built shop were shaking open under the stress. Hesha looked to the street—just here, there was a median—concrete—he jumped even as he saw it, and landed on the opposite corner while the shaking cinderblock façade collapsed into the road and the ground beneath it swarmed up through the cracks.

Earth moving...tar moving...but the cement holds together...safer on stone? The Setite twisted north and caught a glimpse of spires and scaffolding in the distance. A cross jutted up from the tangle, jet black and unlit against the smoggy orange night sky. A *cathedral...holy ground....* The man chasing him looked European. Yahweh's blessings had never hindered Hesha, but they might have some effect on the other man. And Christians built their larger temples out of rock....

He rushed forward while the road sloshed sluggishly after him. The stuff was fast, once it was under way, but its—Hesha searched for a word—*reactions* were slow. Corners bothered it a little, and swift changes in direction confused the thing's blind mind even more. Hesha made as many switchbacks as he dared, then fled straight for the block on which the huge church was being built.

He hurdled onto and over a low shed. From the top, as he lunged forward, he surveyed the cathedral in front of him. The closest corner, a tower, nearly brought a smile to his thinned-out lips: Four finished stories and a foundation at the least…a ground vault and extra basement reinforcements, if he guessed correctly. It was perfect. If he could reach even the second level—he dropped off the roof of the shed and into a small quarry-like area—he would be above the height of the tallest 'waves' he had seen so far—he leapt from stone to stone in the little enclosure—with a staircase…two, at the most…to defend from within, and breaking glass to warn him if any adventurous Sabbat minions tried to attack him from the outside. His boots crushed marble chips underfoot. Small puffs of stone dust swirled in the small breeze of his trenchcoat's passing. From the tower, he decided, he would call the Setite temple, and gather reinforcements. Morningside Park would be full of snakes this time of night. He sprang up a stack of yard-high arch-stones as if they were stairs, and vaulted to the top of the fence.

Hesha looked down on good green earth, and cursed.

The mason's area was an island of rock in a large, open garden. He could cut across it. He could run to either side and try for the sidewalks (thin ribbons of cracked cement…no use). Or he could fight where he stood.

He hurled himself without hesitation at the closest bend of the garden path. His boots clicked comfortably against the hard slate. He followed the stone flags between white rose bushes and through an evergreen hedge, and found a grotesque figure blocking the way forward. It had flaky, red skin, twiggy limbs, and nothing that resembled, even remotely, a face on its near-spherical head. Hesha dropped into a crouch, ready to fight the Tzimisce's war-creature....

It remained peacefully stock-still.

The waning moon cleared a cloud, and Hesha saw the twisted form for what it was: modern art—iron rebar welded into the shape of a woman, left in the weather to rust and illustrate...reverence? It gave the impression of bowing or kneeling before something greater.

Hesha's gaze flicked away and he rushed round the little group of worshippers. He'd lost time. He was only halfway to the church when the squares beneath him started tilting. The Setite jumped straight up, narrowly missing having a leg swamped by rolling turf. The path floated on the green grass like scum on a wave. Hesha landed on one foot and pushed off the spongy morass onto a concrete platform. Two sculptures flanked him—the silhouette of a man, and the slab of metal the artist had cut him from. Part of his mind recognized the image of the blast-shadow of Hiroshima; most of it concentrated on the next solid structure in line with the tower, a tall, multi-tiered thing whose meaning he couldn't even guess. It was close enough to reach, if he could trust one step on the drifting slates for a single push. The earth rose like a wave—a flagstone washed up the hill—Hesha sprang to it, jumped up, and caught himself on the upper bowl of a waterless stone fountain. A mockery of the sun looked down at him. He grimaced back at its ugly face. The strange statue was covered in small, anemone-like projections that made excellent handholds. The Setite wasn't sure what he held, but he used them to gain better footing, pulling himself higher, scanning the billowing garden for another stable perch on the way to his goal.

All around, the hills rolled in. If he were going to jump, it would have to be—

Hesha's neck muscles twitched as though someone were watching him. He whirled round, and got his first good look at his pursuer.

No.... The Setite's eyes widened in shock. This matchstick man was the creature he had left in torpor in the mountains. This was the Cainite who had possessed the Eye before him. This was no elder, no Tzimisce...this creature had been so weak that a mere mortal had taken the Eye away from him. He should have lain unconscious for years. He should have been caught in the rockfall....

Hesha abandoned what "ought" to have happened. The earth-waves closed in around him; in another moment he would be swallowed or mauled or crushed. Hesha launched himself from the tip of the grotesque sun. His hands grew long talons; he arched them, ready to dig into the heart of the stranger. Needle fangs slid down from thin gray gums. The Setite's tongue transformed itself into a thin, forked, razor-edged whip, and coiled to strike. His elongated, serpentine body drew together and poised for the impact. The long coat fluttered and snapped like a flag in high winds, and everything Hesha bore fell free with him...even the weight of the Eye was lifted in the everlasting second before he reached his prey.

Hesha landed heavily. His claws tore in and down along the hollow chest of his opponent—the man's ribs were better than a ladder to him, and his curled legs found purchase on a folding knee. The snake tongue flicked out and sliced open the only cornea the Cainite had left. The bag holding the Eye slammed into Hesha's back, and the trenchcoat swirled treacherously around his enemy's shins.

The matchstick man staggered.

Hesha let the momentum take them both rolling across the grass—suddenly stable, flat, unmoving grass—and gave an extra tug and shove with the left side of his body, ensuring he landed on top. He felt his face sag as one of the Cainite's claws tore through the muscle above the cheekbone. It began to heal immediately; it was a scratch with no force behind it. He took his right hand out of the thing's chest, splayed his fingers as wide as possible, and pulled them through the unprotected abdomen and bowels. Atrophied organs spilled from the wounds, and where the five little scythes came together and scissored out of the body, large chunks of dead flesh tore away. He kept his left hand firmly wedged between the slats of the ribcage and twisted the claws to be sure nothing mended around them.

The matchstick man flailed about and shredded Hesha's clothes. In one arm and one thigh, he dug deep enough to breach the slippery scales and rend muscle.

The Setite let the flickering claws go by unchallenged. His opponent was such a novice as to strike flesh and leave tendons intact—to ignore the eyes, and try to wrestle for control of hands—to try to rip the throat of a dead man open, instead of tearing away the spongy blood-storing tissues of the torso. Speed could win over skill, but it would not tonight. Hesha licked open a wound in his enemy's left shoulder and severed the sinews. The limb hung loose and twitched for a second, the opposing muscles contracted, and then the matchstick man's forearm curled uselessly under.

Hesha heaved the useless carcass off the ground. It was in his mind to talk to the poor leech, to give mercy and utility a moment. The creature must know something valuable about the Eye, and the question of that earth-power nagged at the Setite. Hesha cut through the other arm, and considered whether the matchstick man would survive being hamstrung or perhaps staked for a day….

Accomplices, thought Hesha, and then wondered why the danger came back to him so abruptly. Was it movement? The garden seemed empty, except for the prisoner, himself, and the statues.

Something nudged him gently from behind. He turned—still holding his man by the ribs—and saw another cut-metal piece, a good one, standing there. Nothing else.

The statue… A moment ago, he would have sworn to the position of every obstacle and bit of cover on his battleground. *Know the field*, he remembered the priests teaching him. *But it was two feet further back. I was sure….*

The Setite, disconcerted by his mistake, turned and scanned his surroundings. He saw other pieces, still on their pedestals, but all seeming, from his angle, to be placed off-center. Closer to him. *Wrong.*

Hesha backed toward the stone fountain uneasily.

Something brushed softly against his coat.

Hesha sprang forward, too late. Jagged bronze caught at the rough canvas sack on his hip. Tiny cotton threads parted, the waterproofing stretched and tore, and mud oozed out of a hole the size of a dime. A thick stream spouted from the gap.

The canvas sack burst apart under the pressure, and a gummy sphere dropped to the ground at Hesha's feet. The matchstick man opened the eye he didn't have—a pale, cold light emanated from the lid of the still-shut Eye on the path—

—wrought-iron fists pounded into Hesha. His long bones broke and tiny slivers cut through his flesh in an agony of needles; he damned the pain and forced blood to the limbs to heal them. He darted sideways on shaky legs to avoid the rusty stumps the worshipping sculpture had for hands. A third enemy—a fourth, a fifth—and evasion was impossible. From the corner of his eye he saw twisted steel swinging toward his face; he dropped and turned. His skull caved in across the back, from ear to ear, and thought itself became torture. The force of the attack wrenched the prisoner's body away, and Hesha watched it sail through the air with only faint regret. The matchstick man landed on the grass two yards from the Eye. As Hesha crab-crawled, dully and stupidly, to the safety of the stone fountain, his enemy lay motionless.

Iron and bronze and copper closed in. Through the hail of blows and the thick, mobile, statuary veil, Hesha thought he saw his enemy roll closer to the Eye. It meant nothing to him.

A blast of something unrecognizable—not acid, not flame, not poisoned blood—flew up from the ground. It moved like a bullet; it was slower by only a blink. Hesha saw a livid blue-white bolt like lightning rushing toward him and closed his eyes automatically; the stuff hit, and he *could not open his eyes again*—either the lids had fused shut, or his face was simply no longer there. Pain and fury clamped their fangs into him and stole what remained of his mind.

Beneath Calcutta, there was a sense of inevitability, and a determination to fight.

Beneath Manhattan, a murky intelligence stretched itself and ceased to care.

In Atlanta, a lone Malkavian stood up with the unexpected but unquestioned certainty that he should go for a walk.

On the lowest tier of the Tree of Life—a sculpture voted Ugliest in New York City by the Morningside Heights residents' association—Hesha Ruhadze came out of oblivious frenzy. He listened to the echoes of Calcutta and Manhattan through a white stone he wore around his wrist. With a red stone around his neck he knew precisely at what moment the Eye stood up, and he felt it turn away as though it were part of his own body.

In the garden of the Cathedral of St. John the Divine, Leopold finished patting his skin back in place and let himself rest quietly for a moment. His arms and body knitted together nicely. He watched the sky pass by, and amused himself by looking at it winking left, winking right; with both lids wide open; and even with both tightly shut.

Leopold, fully healed and quite complete, walked down the path toward the sidewalk. The fight was dimming already for him; the doubts he had held died as his vision restored itself. What was missing? Nothing: He knew where she would be as he turned the corner....

The muse stood in plain view, in the center of a circle of yew hedges, simply waiting.

For him.

Journeys end in lovers' meetings... a snatch of some song old and sweet ran through his head.

Perfection held her hand out, and Leopold's grisly face lit up. His expression reflected her beauty for an instant, the way ruins reflect the palace that died for them. In total rapture, he stepped forward. A soft bar bent beneath his foot. A bone twisted out of shape in the corpse that lay there. Leopold took his muse's delicate fingers and touched them to his lips. She led him—demurely, without her devil's tricks—away from the battlefield and into a world of her own. The earth disappeared, and the two walked off into the silver mist.

The watcher saw this differently:

A lone and wounded vampire stumbled out of the garden of the Cathedral of St. John the Divine. His mismatched eyes were terrible, and he carried the broken stone hand of a martyr ahead of him like a dowsing rod. It writhed as though it lived.

The watcher came out, much later, and dragged a blasted heap of necrotic flesh from beneath a pile of twisted metal. The watcher examined the body carefully, as it did all things, and after a moment's thought, pulled the blackened corpse down after itself into the gutter from which it had crawled. It needed haste; the sun was crawling out of its own hole. Half an hour after the watcher collected what it wanted, bright and deadly rays crested the skyline of New York.

Khalil Ravana sauntered pleasantly down the back streets of Brooklyn. Two nights of real travel—catching buses, cadging lifts from sympathetic lorry drivers (*Truck drivers*, he corrected himself), telling the tale to lonely sales reps driving late, picking up women who ought to have known better and just couldn't resist him—had settled the Ravnos's nerves. He'd fed well, he'd amused himself, he'd come up in the world. His clothes broadcast money, and class of a sort…though none of them fit him as well as they had their original owners. Amazing, these Americans. They'd give you the shirt off their back just for asking (he smirked), and even the clumsiest Calcutta cutpurse could make a good living off the unguarded wallets in this country. A clever *shilmulo* like himself could make a fortune.

He swung his 'casket' happily. It had been a convenient prop for his pose as a stranded tourist. When the traveling-musician idea came along, he'd conjured the image of a broken saxophone into it, and picked up sympathy and a little cash from fellow "artists." Bus passengers needed luggage. Business types carried cases. It held his wardrobe and growing cache of valuables by night, and his sun-shy body by day. What a gift Hesha had given him…he'd have to thank the Setite properly.

As soon as possible, Khalil decided grimly. He began whistling.

A sudden urge drove him down a dark alley and

out onto a clean-swept, well-lit little patch of sidewalk. "All right," muttered the walker. "You don't need to hit me with it."

I wasn't sure you would hear me over your own boasting. The voice felt dry as drought tonight. *This is the place.*

Khalil slowed casually. He set down his luggage without a glance around, and felt in his pocket as if for keys. With one eye on the lock and one on his bag, he pulled two bits of wire from his right coat pocket, and from his left, the forcing pin. All three entered the keyhole at the same moment. Any ordinary observer would have sworn the young man, coming home very late, or to work remarkably early, had grasped his keyring with both hands and was having trouble with a rusty, cantankerous lock.

"You'd better be right," he whispered. "The sun's rising any minute now."

Trust me.

Oh, yes, thought Khalil to himself. *I'm sure I will.* The old Yale gave way beneath his probing picks, and the door handle turned in his fingers. Beyond the heavy steel portal lay a dreary, uninviting corridor. That its ceiling was high only made it seem more narrow; that it was casually swept clean only made the dust neglected in the corners more evident. The Ravnos picked up his case and strolled down the hall with something like contempt. He studied the doors as he walked by, and his thoughts rolled along familiar paths: *Photographers…cameras…got to find a fence in this city…. Imports…"imports" covers a multitude of sins…wonder what they smuggle…. Lawyers…goddamn busybodies…. Egh…I can see the stairs. You son of a bitch…* His "employer" prompted him to steps going up. Tall, many-paned old windows let a little dirty light filter into the stairwell. A new hall took him down an outside wall. Raw brick and crumbly mortar faced him and the floor underneath was splintery old wood. *Tell me, old man, why don't I think rich snakes would live in this dump?* He came to another stair, and another window. So far, only the streetlamps shone through. Khalil looked up, and saw more glass: skylights in the roof—very nearly a roof made *of* skylights. He stepped out onto a metal walkway and tried not to clank along it. His borrowed shoes betrayed him; they were new and hard leather (the very best Italian leather, the donor had bragged), and clopped audibly at each footfall.

The Rom winced but went on.

The last item on the catwalk was one huge, rolling steel plate the size of a barn door. Khalil came to it and felt its edges, looked at the rusty wheels in the top and bottom tracks, and felt an inner pull directing him away. The tug would not be satisfied until he stood a few feet back, before a far less interesting object: a plain, unmarked door the mate of the one he'd picked through downstairs.

"Here?"

Here.

"The sun's nearly up. This place—"

Open the blasted door.

He set to work, and the thing swung open on a room (he couldn't help but notice) with two enormous walls of nothing but windows.

From the door, it looked as though someone lived in the big lofty space. There were books and chairs and other furniture, innocent of dust, and arranged into little groups as though separated by walls into rooms. *But there are no walls*, thought Khalil. *Damn you. If I have to sleep in that fucking box again…*

His rant came to a sudden halt as he spotted something—someone—of interest to him. Hesha's pet mortal, Elizabeth D-something…Dim-something…. Hesha's girl, anyway, sitting silent, frozen, and pale as death in the center of the place. She looked terrified, and Khalil lifted a diabolic little eyebrow and smiled. The girl said nothing, nor did she move. The Ravnos regarded her thoughtfully.

She was not only sitting in the chair, she was chained to it. Her hands rested peacefully enough on its arms, but there were shackles fastened to her wrists—Khalil's eyes scanned down—and ankles.

If Hesha were here, he was a long time answering the door. If Hesha weren't here…the Ravnos licked his lips.

"Hello, sweetheart," said Khalil Ravana. He grinned evilly. "Did you miss me?" He shut the door with two lazy fingers and stepped down into the room. With a definite swagger, he approached the fettered girl and gloated down at her. He stopped just close enough to make her twitch, which, gratifyingly, she did. At this range he spied out more detail than he had before. There was blood on her neck. A human being's frightened pallor should have changed by now to something pinker—red rage, flushed indignation, even ugly mottled fear. This Elizabeth's face remained white.

"Been promoted, I see," Khalil bent over her condescendingly. "Welcome to the Family, darling."

The girl's lips and throat writhed as though she would be sick. "Thank you," she managed weakly.

Khalil took advantage of her immobility by walking out of sight. Three oval, peg-work boxes lay on a slim table directly behind her chair. He picked up the largest, and it gave a promising, monetary clink. The Ravnos dragged a dirty fingernail through the coins: British…German…small change, and no good to him here, anyway. "So," he asked chattily, "where *is* Hesha this evening, little Lizzie?"

The second box held a mismatched lot of loose buttons, keys, pins, and clips. Khalil fished among them. He recognized two friends among the junk: a Yale that appeared to fit the warehouse door, and a Schlage that matched the apartment's. He slid the spares into his trouser pocket. On the other side of the steel support column, Elizabeth Dimitros stared east. "I don't know," she answered.

"Is that so?" he murmured, taking the lid off the smallest container. "Why don't I believe you, sweetheart?" Gold and silver flashed back at him: earrings, a bracelet, a pocketwatch. The Ravnos emptied the lot into his jacket, and looked about for more.

"He's gone," replied the girl. Her tone grabbed Khalil's attention; he knew genuine despair when he heard it.

A note abandoned on a sofa caught his eye: a quick scrawl with 'Lizzie' dashed out at the top, on a pile of letters addressed to her. *This is her own apartment,* he realized with a shock. He frowned. There was only one other door in the great room, and it clearly led into the water closet. There were no signs of a struggle or a break-in (besides his own, of course). What in hell's name was a freshly dead Setite doing alone, unguarded, and trussed up for the sun? Khalil glanced outside and decided he had enough time to ask a few questions and dig up what he could. It would mean sleeping in the case today, but—

"Really?" he said aloud. "That's very odd. You were thick as thieves last time I saw you…and you've obviously grown—" he laid a feather-light finger on the bloodstain at her neck, and she shuddered— "closer since then. It *was* him that did this, wasn't it?"

"Yes…"

It was.

Khalil examined the thick chains where they crossed the column. The girl had fought—once it was too late. There were deep scratches in the painted surface, and her straining muscles had knocked the rust off some of the links.

"And these chains?"

Elizabeth said nothing.

Yes, confirmed the voice in Khalil's head. Another question sprang to the young Ravnos's lips. He stifled it and walked away. Out of the girl's hearing, he whispered irritably:

"Where is Hesha?"

Unavoidably…detained.

"Then why in all hells am I here?"

For the woman.

"You knew he wasn't going to be here, and you didn't tell me a damn thing—" Khalil lowered his voice again. "You didn't tell me anything. I'm getting tired of that."

She is bound to him. The voice spoke as though Khalil had not. *She will be useful to you in tracking him.*

"Wait a minute. I thought you knew where he was. You could tell me, right now, where he is—"

Do not interrupt me, whelp. Of course I know where he is…but Hesha may dispose of the stones at any time if he realizes their other powers. Why should I exert myself to hunt him down when you will do so just as well with the proper tool in hand? More importantly, I have neither desire or leisure to lead one demon to one snake by the hand. I have other affairs besides this to attend to, dog.

Khalil's back hairs stood on end, but he managed to keep silence.

You are going to ask her about her "true love," and you will threaten her to find out what she knows. Then you will suggest to her that she can know Hesha's whereabouts, if she tries, even though she has not been told. Get this information from her and I will tell you if she lies. Go.

Khalil knelt beside the girl. His hands crept spider-like along the chain from link to link. He followed the fetters up her arms. Elizabeth's skin tightened to gooseflesh, but she held steady. His fingers reached her wrists and caressed the heavy metal bracelets; he crooned into her ear with less breath than a whisper:

"Tell me…are you still in love with him? Worship him? Adore him madly? Do anything for him?"

Elizabeth gritted her teeth and hung her head. A dark red tear crawled down her cheek. *Her master is late,* thought Khalil, *and the wretched slave is lonely….*

"Cards on the table, darling. I am looking for Hesha. You help me find him, I bring about the joyous reunion of two star-crossed lovers. You lie to me, you cheat me, you try anything, and I leave you for the sun. Deal?"

"But I don't—"

"But you *do* know, and you will be able to help me find him, *because* you love him."

Elizabeth's eyes opened wide, then her face fell back into frightened lines. Her voice trembled. "What will you do to him if you find him?"

"Let me ask the questions, darling. Not many minutes left in the night." Khalil reached into one of his pockets and pulled forth a plain gold ring set with one cloudy green stone. He opened Elizabeth's right hand and placed the gem on her palm. "Tell me the truth, and the stone will turn clear. Lie to me," he said menacingly, "and the stone turns black." The Ravnos squinted hard at the green cabochon, and prepared himself for a little easy illusion.

"Hesha loves you, doesn't he, sweetheart? Even I could see that in Calcutta. So—why would he do a thing like this to you?"

Elizabeth stared at the ring and said nothing.

"It's going to be a beautiful morning. Why don't I just leave you here to enjoy it?"

Elizabeth opened her mouth quickly—and bit her lip again just as suddenly. Khalil watched a struggle go on behind her eyes. Her expression…what was it? Not fear, entirely, though she checked the windows just as often and as apprehensively as he did himself. *Good god, the light…*. Was it pride? In what? Why? Was she fighting to conceal her feelings? No—Khalil knew there was enough on her face to read. He simply didn't understand the language.

"He didn't want me to follow him!" she cried out, finally and desperately.

True, the voice confirmed. Khalil wrapped the stone in a clearer, paler vision of itself. Elizabeth, gazing into its depths, looked shocked. The Ravnos, surprised at her surprise, fought to keep it from showing. She went on:

"He...he had something to do on Long Island." The gem lightened further, and Elizabeth stared at it in apparent astonishment. Khalil preened himself, mentally. This little lie-detector had been a spur-of-the-moment idea, but evidently a damn good one. "He wouldn't tell me what, but I knew he was going to do something dangerous. He had a look on his face—a hopeless look," Liz nearly sobbed. "I didn't want him to go alone...but he didn't want me in the way. I...lost control. He had to...to put me down...like he put you down in Calcutta."

True, said the unseen listener. Khalil dropped a flaw or two from the image of the emerald, but grumbled, "I remember that a little differently."

Elizabeth laughed in near-hysteria. "Why waste a stake when you have such nice shackles handy?"

"Yes," The Ravnos agreed pointedly. "Very nice."

"He took the key with him," she began hopefully.

All true. Now release her and get under cover.

"And I think something terrible must have happened to him—he hasn't come back yet, and there's no time left—" She swallowed hard, and gestured with her chin toward her workshop. "There are bolt cutters under the bench. I keep them for old locks, but they might do for this."

Khalil jumped up and tore over to the table. He looked at the long-handled steel blade and drop-forged anvil of the cutters, thought for a moment, and then he seized a coffee can of pliers and watchmaker's tools from the shelf above them. "Oil?" he barked sharply.

"On the top shelf in the blue tin. Hurry!"

He set upon the locks with his own picks and a few useful things out of the girl's stock. In two minutes he had open the fetters on her left ankle and wrist. Shaking, she pulled herself free of the chair. The Ravnos unwound the chains from the column and the wood. He put an urgent hand under her shoulder and propelled her toward the bathroom without waiting to free her other limbs.

Elizabeth hobbled along painfully, and Khalil had to help her across the floor. What little light dawn had begun pushing over the horizon stung and drowned their eyes; it seemed to strike her harder, and he was glad his own first nights were far behind him. He slammed the door closed and twisted the knob locked. With a door between himself and the morning he felt a little better. Liz fumbled toward the light switch; Khalil brushed past her and shut it firmly off. He snatched down a hand towel and stuffed it frantically under the door. The blinding, inch-high strip of day grew brighter, and his skin itched. The girl made some kind of movement behind him—a large towel was pressed into his grasping hands. He shoved it into the crack and reached back for more. The washcloth, a T-shirt, the bath mat, the shower curtain—together Khalil and Elizabeth tore the room apart and built a barricade against the sun. It took thirty seconds; it took thirty hours. In the darkness afterwards, he laid his hands on her arms and dragged her down toward the floor.

Khalil slipped out of his jacket and rolled it into a pillow. Wordlessly, he put it under the girl's head, and she let him. He arranged his new companion's body under the sink and around the toilet pedestal as comfortably as he could. He dragged the shackle chains out of her way. He waited—fighting the urge to lie down where he was, as he was—until the girl's eyes had closed and her face slackened into the day's sleep.

Then Khalil passed the chains through the naked pipes beneath the sink and bound the girl hand and foot once more. He staggered and fell into the bathtub, and oblivion washed over him.

Saturday, 31 July 1999, 9:27 PM
The Cathedral of St. John the Divine
New York City, New York

Khalil Ravana paused for a moment on the path his master had set him. From the street corner opposite the looming, mountainous bulk of the church, he scanned it cautiously. A few upturned floodlights illuminated the carved stonework walls. They cast long and pitch-black shadows everywhere else. The Ravnos could feel his feet urged toward the darkest, most tangled and indecipherable place in sight, and his brief pause lengthened and became a true and nervous halt.

Pensively, he rubbed the stubble on his chin, stroked his beard and mustache, and glanced down at himself. He felt a bit better immediately. He'd changed the sharp suit for an outfit more to his taste. A flowing, wine-colored silk shirt with wide lapels and rolled sleeves was left wide open to show off his muscle-girt stomach and the curly black hair on his chest. Khakis, which he had always despised for their lack of color and military lack of imagination, had been turned around in America. He wore them in a style he had seen and coveted coming out from Chicago: unbelted and slipped nearly below his hips, revealing a bright and beautiful band of silk—fine, printed satin boxer shorts, slung low like the trousers. A short gold ball-chain graced his neck. The cloudy emerald ring swung on a longer, black leather thong. His shoes were cheap—suede as cheap as it came, with thin, nearly sponge-rubber black soles—silent, and without socks, nearly as good as bare feet to him. And the entire ensemble (the clotheshorse smiled to himself) had been bought with the money he'd got pawning Hesha's childe's jewelry. Khalil licked a finger, curled his forelock more tightly, and stepped across the street toward the churchyard.

"Talk to me," he muttered in the crosswalk. "What am I doing?"

The Eye changed hands here last night.

Khalil's eyes narrowed. "Hesha was unavoidably detained—here?"

Yes.

The young Ravnos gnawed his thumb in suspicion. He said nothing, but resolved to find a map of the city as soon as possible. This cathedral seemed a considerable distance from Long Island. Perhaps Hesha had covered a lot of ground last night. Perhaps the old bastard didn't know as much as it pretended to…. Khalil touched the pendant ring, and wondered.

More doubts rose like cankers. Why, if Elizabeth was supposed to be so useful, had the voice insisted she be left behind tonight? Khalil hated leaving his cache (which included the girl, now, in his own mind) unguarded. What if Hesha came back to gather her ashes? What if one of his men had been waiting in the wings last night…. The Setite had been surrounded by absolute gaggles of minions in Calcutta. Why not in New York? A shudder ran down the Ravnos's spine. Thompson—or worse, the Asp— could have been *in the apartment* while he himself slept. The thought stopped him in his tracks.

Move. Khalil's gut surged forward. He ignored it.

He had to find another source of information.

This reliance on the thing that called itself his master was intolerable.

Go, you filth-covered rat. The voice spurred him forth just like a horse. Khalil determined to stand still a while longer, if only to see whether he could. To the spurs was added a whip—pain in old wounds. The servant shook a little under the assault, but found it possible to resist. He smiled. The old thing's reach might go around the world from Calcutta, but its powers weakened with the distance. Khalil, deeply satisfied, let the force send him on.

As he reached the opposite corner, he blinked and scowled. There was a faint light in the distance that could not, quite, be accounted for by any mundane lamp or reflection that he could see. Curiosity took him toward it, in a circumspect and roundabout way—flanking it, in fact. A thin ribbon of pale blue, misty glow curved out of an alley two or three blocks down the other north-south street that bounded the cathedral compound. It traced an arc onto and down from a low building, and disappeared behind a fence.

"Are you putting that there, or is it really there?" Khalil asked his unseen master.

Your lack of clarity and articulation astounds me. I assume you refer to the residue given off by the Eye, not to the sky, the ground, or any other of the ten thousand things in your immediate vicinity?

"The blue glow," said Khalil, from between clenched teeth.

It is there. I merely enable you to see it. It would take a very rare pair of eyes indeed to mark it without my assistance.

Khalil paced along the outskirts of the holy precincts. He passed under the arching stream of light, and subjected it to the minute scrutiny he gave everything offered him by his clansman. It was only a few inches tall and deep. It described a very crooked and erratic path through the night, though the arc, from a distance, looked perfectly smooth. A hand thrust into the trail felt slightly chill. An eye peering straight into the light saw nothing but street and city, but sighting along the thread gave a better idea of the color of the phenomenon. It was a kind of venous blue, the tint of drowned skin or of a dead man's lips, but far paler. The Ravnos accepted it as real (with reservations) and walked to the other side of the fenced-in area to see whether the Eye had come out again.

It had, into what seemed to Khalil's untutored eyes a cross between a garden and a junkyard. The death-blue light moved down, up, across, back, and through the hedges and flowers on a clearly impossible trail. In one place, the will-o'-the-wisp plunged beneath the smooth, unbroken turf. In another, the Ravnos saw two arcs—jumps, he would have guessed—that were joined, presumably where a person carrying the Eye had landed and taken off again, twelve feet off the ground.

"I never knew snakes could fly," he commented darkly, and set out to follow the puzzle to its end.

A girl, dead, alone, and wary, watched him from underneath a thick yew hedge. She had darted into its black shadow and hidden her pale hands and face in the mulch the moment the stranger came to her notice. There had been the hope, for a short time, that he was an ordinary denizen of the city—that she could, if she chose, slip away through the garden, taking no more trouble than to avoid the few working lights local vandals had left.

The knowledge that he was *not* harmless, *not* human, *not* here by chance, grew on her with each step the stranger took. She could see, quite well, the ghost light in the air—and she could see that he saw it, and took a definite, sinister interest in it, as well. Now she dared not move. When he had first appeared, she had been doing a little tracking of her own near the ugly fountain-thing. The air around it was thickest with the glowing stuff, and so, at this moment, the stranger stood not a yard from her. When he backed up to look at the light-maze from a different perspective, his bare ankle came within six inches of her nose. He smelled of the grave, as she expected. She wished she knew whether sinking into the earth made a noise, and whether, once in the soil, her body could be dug out or staked or fired. She wished she knew how much longer the trace in the air—the fog that was no fog, not in this heat wave— would last. If it began to fade, she would *have* to come out. No matter who the stranger was, what he was working for, she couldn't let her only clue just melt away.

And if he's a clue? she asked herself.

The stranger stopped over a brighter spot, a patch on the ground. From there, the shine rose up—*To a man's height*, thought the girl under the bushes—and took a straight, uncomplicated line toward the street again—

And disappeared completely before it reached the sidewalk. The stranger stared at it for a good minute, then threw his arms up in flamboyant and furious anger. He said something, and the girl strained to listen.

"What the h-h-hell is g-g-going on?!" Khalil stammered with pure rage—close to the edge of his reason.

It has been taken and very cleverly concealed.

"What—even from you?"

The presence loomed large and threateningly in Khalil's mind. He cowered unconsciously. *Of course not. It is mine. I can see where it is. I merely do not know where it is.* Behind the stark tones, the young Ravnos felt something unexpected: admiration. *There is nothing in its surroundings to tell me its location, either. Someone has been intelligent.*

"So why the fuck did you let me trace this goddamned neon all the way to the end? Why the hell couldn't you drop a single bloody hint?"

You did not ask, said the voice maddeningly.

Khalil's hands began to twitch. With a supreme effort of self-control, he asked, quietly, "Who has it? There was a fight here. You said it changed hands. Therefore—" he took a breath for breath's sake— "Hesha hasn't got it anymore. So. Who has the Eye," and only the faintest emphasis on the next word betrayed his frustrations, "now?"

Leopold.

"Leopold."

The Toreador from whom Hesha and his household took the Eye. The voice paused, and a new note came into it. *Watch your back.*

It took a fraction of a second for Khalil's mind to change tracks—then he whirled around, frighteningly aware that an enemy could have taken that instant's delay to attack. Yet there was time enough to find his balance, and look at the lone figure standing near him, and take her measure, and still no blow fell.

She waited for him. Her hands hung loose and free, though with talons extended. Her eyes were on him, but her ears were obviously everywhere. The taut tendons in her neck flickered, moving her head to catch the slightest sound. She stood calmly enough, but for all that, her stance was unusual, casual. The feet turned out at right angles to each other like a dancer's, a sailor's, or a trained fighter's. Unlike the martial artist (long dead) she'd reminded him of at first, she chose to stand on up her toes. In fact, her weight lay so far forward on the tips of her feet, Khalil wasn't sure how she could still have her ankles bent, and useful, at all. That was wrong…he had a feeling for combat (though he rarely stayed to join in it) and he concluded that, however good she might be naturally, she was completely untrained. He felt a little—a very little—better.

What light there was counted against him; he knew she saw him more clearly than he saw her. There would be a better exit behind him, too, if he could change their positions a little. He stepped counter-clockwise, and was gratified to see her do the same. Again he circled slightly to the right, and the girl kept her distance from him. Another step, and she was just in the glow of a small flood-lamp illuminating a rust-colored statue.

The girl was dirty. She wore a tight, thin-strapped tank top, a pair of jeans that did nothing for her figure (except, perhaps, allow it to move). Dry leaves, burrs, and needles clung to her clothes and stuck in her knotted, curly, jet-black hair. Her face…dark, set in sullen lines…there was something about it…. Khalil chivvied her around the circle and into the full glare of the bulb. It struck her from below and cast macabre shadows up her face. A scar—no, an open wound—showed on the curve of her cheek. And the light picked out, in beautiful detail, the pointed tips of her inhuman ears.

A *Gangrel*, thought Khalil. What heart he had sank. *I visit the largest city in the world, and practically the first leech I meet is a jungle lover.* Between his clan and theirs seethed the oldest, fiercest feud the Rom had ever spawned—a quarrel he had never, in his entire death, understood. By all accounts it had spread to the new world with the Gypsies it centered around. Still, she couldn't know that he was a Ravnos just by looking at him, could she? He began to regret his change of clothes. Why dress to impress your living cousins when you aren't sure you have any and wouldn't know how find them in this city even if they were there? *Damn.*

The Ravnos realized he was now standing in the spot that had been his goal. He'd had his look at her. A fast and uncomplicated route out lay directly behind him. Now, he could back away, revealing that he was afraid of her—turn confidently and walk away, expecting the amnesty to last or hoping to force her into an attack at a time of his own choosing—or turn and bolt. He looked again at her misshapen feet. She was probably the faster runner. Khalil opened his mouth. Speech was his best weapon, generally.

But the Gangrel got the jump on him, conversationally speaking. "You can see the trail," the wild girl said in a sharp, urgent, and very young voice. She went on, insisting, "You were following it."

"Was I really?" Khalil forced as much BBC into his voice as possible. Fake British, fake Brahmin, fake

Babu…anything but a guttersnipe's Rom accent….
"What trail?"

"I watched you the whole time. I heard you, too,"
she added accusingly. "Tell me. Who the hell's
Hesha?"

"I beg your pardon?"

"You said Hesha had the…had *it*. Then you
asked, who had it now? And you answered yourself a
second later: Leopold." The Gangrel took a step in
Khalil's direction, and he shuffled back as inconspicu-
ously as he could. "So who's Hesha? Who's Leopold?"

Khalil licked his lips. "That depends on who's
asking, doesn't it?" Hells knew that was true.

The girl frowned. "Ramona." A bit of the tension
dropped from her, replaced by a somber pride. "Ramona
Tanner-Childe." She hesitated, as if about to add something else, but shut her lips on it decisively.

"Hesha is a Setite, Miss Tanner-Childe." Her face
didn't change. "Do you know," Khalil continued
thoughtfully, "what a Setite is?"

"It ain't a Toreador." And though the sentence
was undoubtedly a statement, her tone made the
faintest query of it.

"No," he replied, stroking his mustache. *And
why did you think it was?* he asked himself. "You're
quite right there," he said aloud, ignoring the doubt
in her voice, smiling as though she had told a faintly
funny joke.

The Gangrel's body relaxed a little farther. "I'm
looking for a Toreador. He had the…he had *it*, the
last time I saw either of 'em."

Khalil looked her up and down, then decided to
chance a little truth. "Your Toreador's name is Leopold."

Her ears pricked and eyes narrowed. "How the

fuck do *you* know?" she threw at him.

"I'm hunting him myself," said the Ravnos blithely, reverting to type. "I have come all the way from India to track this Toreador and destroy him—with my bare hands, if need be." A hollow little chuckle started in the back of his head; he ignored it. "I have," he lowered his eyes modestly, "a considerable reputation for demon-hunting and lupine-slaying in the cities of my homeland."

Her reaction caught him off guard. She laughed once, alarmingly, like a bark. "You? Alone?"

Lying idiot. She can see the trail; she has the mark of the Eye on her. She knows what it is capable of better than you do.

Khalil hid the bitter reaction behind his black eyes and smiled sagely at the girl. "Of course not." He took an ordinary, walking step toward her, and pretended that the possibility of a fight was over. It seemed to work. "I'm no fool," *whatever you may say, you old bastard*, "but I had to test you. Your wound—" His hand rose, still several feet from her face, and indicated the open gash. "May I look at it?"

"You can see it fine from over there," said Ramona.

"It's proof that you've been near the Eye." He paused. "And survived. And I might know a way to heal it…."

I know a way. What are you doing, boy?

Her face twitched in pain, but she came closer and let him peer at the mark. He brought his hands up, talons withdrawn, and touched the skin just above and below the open sore. "Sorry," he said as she flinched. Quite naturally, he put a hand to the side of her neck to steady it.

"Are you American?" he asked conversationally.

"Yeah."

"From New York?" Khalil kept his eyes on her cheek. He turned slightly for better light.

"No," Ramona answered shortly, then relented. "California. That was…before all this shit. Lived here about a year, I guess."

"You know the city well, then?"

"Sure."

"You know the Ravnos here?"

A moment's pause. "Sure," she answered confidently. "Street gang from Queens."

"Just so," said Khalil. He took his hands off the girl's throat and sat down a comfortable distance away from her. She followed suit, perching on the edge of a planter. "This Leopold—I really am trying to find him. I know things about the Eye and I have allies who may be able to help me, but I don't know this city. I have to find someone who knows the territory. That could be you. Maybe we can help each other."

For a minute, Ramona sat silent. She hiked her knees up and hunched her arms around them, staring at the stranger. A bitter frown crossed her face, and her shoulders fell in a little more; her eyes dropped to the ground. Khalil watched in fascination as the grimy hands stroked the stiff denim jeans, picking at the threads absently. She held herself together—she set her jaw, and the hands turned to fists—she looked up at him again, and he returned the gaze with his best earnest honesty. "'S going to take more than you and me to stop that thing."

"I know," he said. "I know. But someone has to."

Ramona stood up and came closer to her new

acquaintance. "What's your name?" she demanded.

"Khalil."

The Gangrel nodded as if in approval and stretched herself elaborately. *Just like a cat that's agreed to adopt you,* thought the Ravnos, *or a mark who thinks he's found a good deal, or a woman ready to take you home...still wary, but still mine....* He thought of his ride into town, of Elizabeth chained to the pipes—watched Ramona studying the track though the air—looked past them all to the city, and repeated to himself, *Mine.*

And the voice, too softly for Khalil to hear it, whispered also,

Mine.

Khalil Ravana gazed lovingly at the tiny computer screen. Its bright green face asked him politely
whether he minded, as this was not his own bank, an
additional charge of one dollar and fifty cents added
to his withdrawal. Khalil pushed the shiny silver button for 'No,' and the machine responded, "Please take
your cash." The Ravnos smiled and did. "Please take
your receipt." The Ravnos picked up the little curl of
paper and read the numbers on it with pleasure.
"Don't forget your card." The Ravnos plucked it from
the port as it came out. "Thank you for doing business with us, Elizabeth Dimitros. Please come again."

"Thank you," said Khalil happily. "I will." *Cautious girl, that Liz. Doesn't keep her PIN number in her
wallet like my musician friend…but she files it under
Checking in her records…* He grinned and walked on
down the sidewalk.

"Now, old boy. Tell me—'cause I just know that
Gangrel bitch is going to ask the moment she meets
me tomorrow—how do I heal Eye wounds?"

*I disapprove of your co-operation with this girl.
She will turn on you, like the rest of her clan.*

"Well, I disagree. She knows jack-shit about me
and the feud and, I gather, even her own people. So
this one thing, we'll do my way, yes?"

Silence.

"Yes?"

*I suppose it may be useful to me to have you
practice the necessary method on another person.
It may even give you the courage to use it on your-*

self should the need arise. Another pause. *Then again…I'm not sure that you have that courage within you. It will be best to have the girl learn the technique as you do, so that there may be a healer available when the*—here a low chuckle rumbled through Khalil's brain—*great demon-hunter and lupine-slayer tracks down the Eye's host.*

Find some turmeric. You will need at least one whole, dry root or large shavings from one.

"And how do I get that?"

Think. There must be spice merchants here. Witch doctors. Herbalists. That is your problem, boy. Attend to it later. I have business for you now. Hire your transportation.

Khalil stepped off the curb and hailed a taxi. A boxy yellow car pulled up precipitously beside him and swayed to a halt. Inside, on grimy plastic seats, the Rom felt a pang of homesickness. There was a Ganesha statue attached to the dashboard and dirty, faded silk flowers hanging from the rear-view mirror, knotted tightly together like offerings. The driver's name was posted on a little card: *Sarat Mukherjee.*

Tell the man to go to 2417-B—

Khalil listened with half an 'ear' to the voice as the cabman spoke, greeting him in Bengali: *"Nomoshkar?"* He went on enthusiastically in the same tongue as Khalil smiled and nodded. "Where to?"

"Harlem, 2417-B West 119th Street."

Mukherjee made a face. "That's not a good part of town for you, my friend. Let me take you to my cousin's place. He has a very good restaurant—very popular, very exclusive—but I can get you a table. You sound like a Calcuttan, he specializes in Calcuttan local dishes. Just like home."

"Sorry. I have an appointment to keep. If I knew how long I was going to be there…" He left the question hanging, hoping his master would answer it.

"Look," said the driver, fishing a card out of the glove compartment, "When you are finished, you call this number and ask for 758. I'll be cruising, and maybe I'll still be around that end of town—probably a little south, if you run late. You'll want a safe ride out of the barrio, I could use another fare…and maybe my cousin's café will still be open."

Khalil took the dog-eared pasteboard card. "Thanks," he said as the car started moving. He slipped the number into his shirt pocket. On a chance, he asked, "My brother, can your cousin the cook tell me where to get some good dried turmeric?"

"Curry powder?"

"No, the root itself."

"My uncle keeps a grocery store in Queens. He'll know how to find some. Do you want me to ask?"

Khalil smiled and handed the man a roll of twenties. "I'd take it as a personal favor, my brother, if you would presume upon your uncle's kindness. I'll call when I'm through."

2417-B rose three and one-half stories from the street. A half-flight iron staircase led up to a classical, brass-handled door painted pine green. A set of cement steps led under the stairs to a slightly shabbier, more utilitarian basement entrance. The windows of the first floor glowed softly, and showed trim and well-chosen curtains. The apartments above were dark.

Khalil mounted the stairs. A shining knocker in the shape of a pineapple presented itself at eye-level. The Ravnos rapped three times with his bare knuckles, instead, and discovered that the weathered wood of the door was a sham; tough and solid-sounding metal bit back and left his hand bruised and stinging.

Lights on either side of the stairs came on softly. Khalil shuffled his feet under their glow. Then the door opened, and a smiling, dark-haired, dark-complected woman in a neat gray suit and white blouse ushered him into the house.

"Please, if you'll follow me, sir—" she opened another door (the beige-colored hallway was lined with them) and led him into a small waiting room. "I'll let Mr. James know that you've arrived."

Khalil smiled to mask his trepidation. The lady (a secretary?) was alive, but these people could be…anybody. Anything. With his utmost charm, he nodded and replied, "Thank you, Ms.—?"

"Bernadette," said the woman, and left him. The Ravnos sat down in one of four green, tapestry-covered armchairs and surveyed his surroundings. The framed prints on the walls said nothing about the taste or interests of the owner. A television and remote control waited, unused, in a cabinet opposite his seat. In the center of the room, *Cosmopolitan* and the last week's worth of *USA Today* reposed on an oval table. On a bookshelf beside him, last month's *New Yorker*, *People*, *Time*, and *Life* magazines were strewn about, wrinkled and slightly torn. The address labels had been scratched away completely. Khalil stared at his feet against the abstract patterned carpet. Never had he seen a lair so devoid of personality. In India, you could tell the clan, at least—

"Mr. James is ready to see you now," said Bernadette, returning. Her voice had no marked accent. Khalil rose and followed her, and the foyer seemed even more neutral than before.

"Good evening," boomed a big man, standing at another plain and unmarked door. "Please, come inside, have a seat, take a load off," he rattled on heartily. The unfortunate Ravnos allowed himself to be escorted to another tasteful, emotionless seat (blue and salmon tapestry, this time) and waited patiently while his host settled into a rolling version of the same chair. The large desk between them was of deep mahogany glistening with polish. A white frosted-glass banker's lamp took up one corner of the essentially executive expanse. A brass stand occupied the other, its gleaming, carved nameplate proclaiming clearly that the man behind it was one Walter James, Ph.D. Between the two were scattered the pieces of a very fine desk set in saddle-colored leather.

Mr. James opened a folio he had been holding and glanced down at it, seemingly refreshing his memory about the case—Khalil felt more and more as though the offices were legal; the bookcases on either side of the desk looked vaguely legislative.

"Well," said Mr. James, closing and laying down his notes. "I'm very happy to report that our little commission was completely successful. I trust our mutual client will be pleased with the work." He added frankly, "It was a difficult case, as I'm sure you are aware."

Khalil knit his brows gravely and inclined his head as though he were entirely aware. "As you say,

Mr. James," he said, implying congratulations tempered by *savoir faire*.

"Please, call me Walter." The man seemed honest, seemed friendly…he was dead, of course, so he was likely to be neither.

"Our mutual client made his payment this morning—without any trouble, I'm glad to say—which clears the way for us to hand over the object to you." He smiled broadly. "And so we come to the terms of delivery…."

Khalil nodded and raised one eyebrow.

"I have instructions from our mutual client to ask you a few questions," Walter James's smile became quite clinical as he paused, "just to eliminate the possibility of misunderstandings, misrepresentations, impersonations—you understand."

"At your service, of course," said the Ravnos.

"Your name?"

Absolute panic washed over Khalil. Then the voice intoned, *Jarek Bhandara*. The *shilmulo* repeated it aloud, relieved that these people would not be walking around knowing his own name.

Walter James smiled encouragingly. "What color is the object?"

Sunset red. Say that exactly. And Khalil did.

"Now, what is the word, Mr. Bhandara?"

Khalil listened. His mouth twitched a little, and then the voice's answer rolled out over his tongue. "Sycophancy," *you bastard.*

"And the last question—"

"There is no fourth question," Khalil challenged promptly.

"Just so," commented Walter James. "Very good."

He pressed an intercom button. "Bernadette? Would you bring Mr. Bhandara's package in?" Relaxing into his deep chair, he regarded his guest with satisfaction. "My associates and I would like to express how much we've enjoyed working with you and your…agency. It's not often that we have the pleasure of being paid in advance anymore—some of our clients have simply no honor at all these days." The gray secretary walked in at this point in the speech. She laid a small package wrapped in brown paper on the table by Khalil's side. Walter James thanked her with a glance. "You'll wish to examine it, no doubt?"

Not here. He desires to observe your reactions. Stand and leave.

Khalil picked up the little box. He kept an eye on his interviewer. "Thank you, but that won't be necessary."

Walter James arched an eyebrow. "Very trusting of you."

A host of remarks, witty and otherwise, fought for Khalil's attention. With an enormous effort, he made one slight bow and exited as quickly as possible. Bernadette opened the outer door for him, and he murmured something polite and negligible in response to her cheerful "Good night." The Ravnos walked a block, and another, and another, until he felt the ants stop crawling up his spine. He blinked, stopped, and muttered:

"Where the hell was I?"

The local Assamite coven's business offices. The holy palace of death itself in this city.

"Assamites…" Khalil quivered.

It did not bother you so much to contract that girl in India for the murder of Michel.

"Yes, it fucking did!" The Ravnos's eyes nearly popped from their sockets. "I keep my goddamned distance from those bloody zealots. And you just sent me into a whole den of the devourers and didn't tell me?"

Of course not. You would have become as transparent as glass and twice as fragile. As it was, in your ignorance... They think great things of you now. Does that not make you happy, boy?

Khalil reached for the cab driver's card with a faltering hand.

For a reason Khalil could not quite determine—
and because of a vague sense of unease he was equally
determined not to realize—the Rom found himself
increasingly focused on the elephant-headed god
perched on the dashboard of his new ally's cab. Sarat
Mukherjee chattered incessantly. Until, that is, he
finally noticed that his fare was no longer responding. Khalil Ravana was finding unwelcome depths to
the bouncing plastic god Ganesha.

*Do not trouble yourself with false gods, boy.
Heed the one who gives you life by his whim, and
curtail this whim of your own immediately. See that
package safely to the apartment.*

Khalil shook his head, but the buzzing persisted.
Which should he fear more, a little god or a distant
god? A plastic god or a disembodied god? He waited
for the voice to answer or goad or laugh, but the old
one didn't stir. Maybe it was just distant and disembodied *enough*. Maybe Khalil needn't be a pawn
forever.

Or maybe he would be.

He leveled his eyes back at the statue of the
Hindu god. The glow of the city lights amidst the
looming towers of metal and stone that the Ravnos
detected in his peripheral vision gave Khalil the sensation that he was pursuing Ganesha into a cavern.
*Or following. Always following. Always under the heel
of another.*

It was perhaps inevitable that Khalil would find
little solace in this Hindu god, in Hinduism. He cer-

tainly hadn't as a mortal, but then he supposed that rarely did those assigned the bottom rung of life hail the decisions and decrees that placed them there. *Easy for the meditating fuckers at the top to sit around all day enlightening themselves when they have the means to decide that the rest of us should be doing their work.*

Khalil exhaled sharply and sank into his seat. Of course, if he had believed, if he had been a Hindu, then he'd have been in bad shape once he was Embraced. Not because the world was any different on the surface, because the caste system surely persisted here as well, but because his cycle of life would have been broken. He felt that being an undying vampire wasn't quite what the Brahmins had in mind when they spoke of *moksha*, release from the compulsion to rebirth.

Or maybe it was, and it was exactly what the Brahmins had in mind.

Khalil muttered aloud in Bengali, "Shit!"

The driver eyed the rearview mirror nervously but still said nothing.

Yes, I was a Brahmin, and more shame to me that I need stoop to use a piece of dirt such as you. But now, get yourself under control. All you are managing to do is frighten your friend and hence endanger my property.

Khalil wondered whether he or the package was the "property" in question. It wasn't really a question, of course, if the voice in his head was truly that of a Brahmin. The only difference between his unliving body and whatever was in the box would be the greater price paid for the contents of the box.

But Khalil had only survived his years in the rigid

society of India by virtue of the ability to set aside such bitter thoughts for the needs of the moment. Producing a smile for the benefit of the cab driver, Khalil once more became his usual confidently conniving self.

"Tell me, my friend, of your cousin's curry," Khalil said with feigned and confiding delight.

Sarat grinned and answered in Bengali, "It is too subtle to describe…or otherwise too hot to taste." He laughed. "It is as you prefer, but it will be the best you have tasted."

Khalil frowned, "Ah, but that is why I ask. And why I curse. Too much of this dreadful American food—I thought I'd shaken my sickness, but my stomach doesn't feel up to the task of real food or drink. But, my friend, I greatly wish to meet your cousin and see his restaurant. Besides, he may perhaps have turmeric root. Turmeric is very purifying to the body, is it not?"

Sarat forsook the rearview mirror and looked back with concern at his fare, despite the dense traffic. "Certainly my uncle is sending a root to the restaurant. We shall not let a brother of ours suffer, so far from home."

Khalil beamed, "Fine news, friend. You make me welcome indeed."

Khalil continued to chatter with the cabbie, a shallow brook babbling over his deeper thoughts. Yes, he'd been in Calcutta for the storm. Yes, he was a child of that city. No, he wasn't a Hindu. Yes, it was his first trip to America. The conversation wasn't as important as the result, which was the trust of this man. An adequate haven in New York was a necessity. Khalil needed people to trust, and another place besides the loft apartment to flee to if there was trouble. This cheerful countryman with his relatives and his transport would be a good place to start.

So preoccupied was he that he didn't notice the wariness in Sarat's eyes, or the note of a heartiness as false as his own in the cab driver's manner.

Some minutes later, the idle conversation and Khalil's ruminations were cut short as the cab slowed and halted, accompanied by two honks from the horn.

"What?" Khalil startled and looked around him for the obstruction.

"We are at the Nawab, my cousin's restaurant, my friend," Sarat smiled reassuringly as he opened his door and got out.

Then Khalil noticed that they were parked in a reserved space in front of a very tastefully and finely ornamented restaurant. Something had finally seeped in past his busy planning, and made him wary. "You always honk like that?"

Sarat smiled some more and motioned for Khalil to follow him. "So they will unlock the door. My cousin closes at eleven every night, even though he could draw after-theatre traffic on a Saturday like this. And, so they will know what food to put on my plate! Two honks means I want the special."

Khalil was dissatisfied, but covered it with affability. "And one honk?"

"My regular." Sarat laughed and patted his stomach.

Khalil stepped to the door. A young boy of perhaps eight had turned back the bolt and opened the door from the inside. From behind Khalil, Sarat said, "Now run along, boy, and get those tables clean. Even mine tonight. We have a guest, and he must not sit at a dirty table."

The boy scurried away and Khalil entered as Sarat held the door open. Then Sarat pulled up short. "But how rude of me. You are ill, so will not wish to sit at table. Will you be so kind as to join me in my home? It's the third floor, above us."

Khalil didn't answer immediately, and instead remained alert as he entered. Something didn't feel right. There was an itch in his head, although there always seemed to be one now, with his master's voice in his head.

There is another of our clan here.

"Great," Khalil said to both Sarat and Calcutta.

Khalil took quick stock of his position, sniffing for the trap. Sarat was behind him, and he seemed mortal enough. No whiff of Kindred blood that might be ghouling him, although that could be hard to detect sometimes. Maybe it would be easy enough to slip back out.

On the other hand, maybe the madness of Calcutta had passed. The burning, driving thirst for the blood of his kin had subsided since his arrival in America. Maybe that would change when he saw a clansman, but at this moment there was no special seduction.

Still considering his options, Khalil feigned weakness and stepped to the wall, resting his head lightly against it. To the left, the entry hall allowed a view of two window-side tables that were already cleaned and cleared. To his right was a four-foot-high statue of Devi, but not in her guise of the multi-armed and fearsome Kali. Khalil recognized this aspect as Lakshmi, the goddess of wealth, and he felt a little better about things. *A good omen*, he thought, *for a bad situation.*

He could work with those who worshipped gain more easily than those who reverenced destruction.

Sarat drew nearer, peering into Khalil's face. Was it true solicitude, or an attempt to block the exit? Exactly how much did this mortal cab driver know?

The other is Ghose. I know him for a fool. But do not let him make a fool of you in turn—though he is not very old, he is older than you, and therefore stronger.

Sarat put a sympathetic hand on Khalil's shoulder. "Perhaps the odor of the food does not sit well with—"

Khalil quickly turned, grabbed the man's forearm and twisted it behind his back. Now it was Sarat whose forehead was pressed against the wall.

"What—"

On tiptoe, Khalil hissed into the taller man's ear, "Silence! Just what did you have in mind for me here?" He nudged Sarat into the wall to emphasize the danger the man faced. "And do not try to cozen me, *my friend*, because I know who is here and waiting. Maybe even watching right now."

Sarat evinced confusion. "Who? What? I don't—"

"Your master is nearby. Where is Ghose?" Khalil quietly insisted as he pushed Sarat more firmly against the wall.

"No sense in whispering, brother," said a musical voice, too near by far for Khalil's comfort. Khalil convulsively pushed Sarat away. The mortal staggered down the hall, opening the path to the door. Khalil considered plunging toward it, but stumbled when the statue of Lakshmi next to the entry hall lost its golden hue and stood.

The other Ravnos was a tall and slender man. Lighter-skinned than Khalil, he was undeniably Indian as well. He wore a loose-fitting cotton robe so new Khalil could still smell the harsh dye even from several feet away. Simple leather sandals adorned his feet. Ghose's black hair was so short it made his round face look almost spherical. He stood with his hands open, palms facing Khalil, and slowly blinked, thick eyelids rolling and unrolling. "Have you any exceptional thoughts of murdering me?"

Khalil, regaining some of his composure, hesitated. "It seems not. If you thought I would, would you have let me come? Why *did* you have me brought here?"

Ghose smiled dryly. "I was partially curious to see how I myself would react. I delight to say the madness must have passed."

"Good news," said Khalil. "I admit I had not thought to find another of ours here, or your servant would never have caught me off guard in such a fashion."

"I am Ghose. You seem to know that already, but I will let you tell me later how my name has preceded me. Sarat and the others here are of my family. I shall make you known to them, that they may also be of your family. It is not easy to be without kin in the vastness of this city."

Khalil prepared for introductions even while madly scrambling for an innocuous explanation for his survival of the curse and his presence in New York.

The voice in his head did not bother to help.

That next morning, Khalil and his Setite prisoner sealed the door for the day (much more securely,
with foil and black plastic and layers of duct tape)
and settled down to sleep (much more comfortably,
with pillows and blankets and rugs for padding). Sa-
voring his relaxation after the truce he had made with
Ghose and his band, the Ravnos hung his jacket on
the shower head and remembered the plain brown
box. He clawed it open with lazy fingers and plucked
the prize from within: an eye, carved from stone the
color of sunset, with an iris black as jet. The back of
the thing was hollow; the front was smooth; the sides
cut in a curious spiraling pattern.

"Hm." Khalil passed the gem through his fingers—over, under, over, under—with an ease and
fluidity born of thousands upon thousands of shell
games. After half a minute of this, he glanced over at
Elizabeth to make sure that she was properly appre-
ciating the show. She was watching, but rather than
admiration or amusement, her expression was more
of…*recognition*.

The gem was suddenly still.

"*You* know what this is," Khalil said a bit too
enthusiastically—and realized that he might as well
have told her that he didn't. "You've seen it before,"
he said more calmly, in way of recovery.

Elizabeth stared silently at him.

"I'm just curious *where* you've seen it before. The
folks I got it from aren't exactly your kind of crowd, if

you know what I mean." Khalil flipped the gem into the air with his thumb. He didn't have to move his hand to catch it. He flipped the stone again. "I know all kinds of things to do with this little wonder."

"No you don't."

Khalil almost dropped the stone. "Why, you cheeky...!" He raised his hand to strike her. Liz flinched, but not enough to suit him.

Her sire possesses the stone's mate. Do you know more than Ruhadze, simpleton?

Khalil's hand quivered, but the blow did not fall.

She doesn't think so either.

"Can I find the Eye with this?" Silence. "Well, maybe I just need to *sell* this," Khalil mused spitefully, turning away from Liz and carefully inspecting the stone.

You will not sell it, worm. You will return it to me.

"I'm sure some jeweler would give me a couple hundred bucks for it. I don't see much point in keeping it...."

Ignore my wishes and you will never know.

There was silence in Khalil's mind—in the bathroom, too, until he started tapping his foot. "I'm *waiting*...."

Liz stared sullenly at the corner. Khalil ignored her.

Fill the hollow with blood—your blood—and you will be able to locate others of our clan.

"Hmph. Of course you couldn't have told me that a few hours ago, when I could have used some warning of where Ghose was lurking," Khalil muttered. He glanced around the cramped room. He rummaged through a drawer and found fingernail clippers, then took the small file and jabbed it into the palm of his hand. He tensed his hand and dribbled blood into the hollow space in the stone. When it was full, he licked closed the wound.

"Watch and learn, Miss Know-It-All."

To the surprise of both, the level of blood in the stone began to lower as if draining away. Khalil looked beneath the stone. Liz, trying hard not to seem intrigued, looked also. There was no blood dripping on the floor. A moment more and the stone was again empty. There was no hole within the hollow. The blood couldn't have drained into the stone itself.

Khalil held the dry stone.

He waited.

"Nothing."

Elizabeth, now smug as well as silent, crossed her arms and continued ignoring her crestfallen captor.

Do you see any other of our kin?

"I *think* I would *know* when I'm alone," Khalil sputtered through clenched teeth.

Inconsequential blood provides less range.

Khalil stuffed the stone roughly into his hip pocket.

Nevertheless, the stone is now attuned to your blood. When next our kind are near, you will know. Satisfied, the voice fell silent.

Khalil, much less than satisfied, kicked at Liz's foot and then settled down for the day.

The sun rose and the dead fell asleep.

Ramona Tanner-Childe clambered awkwardly out of the back seat of a small taxi. She looked around her with trepidation. The street was empty, and that was good. No one lived around here, and that cut both ways. This corner was well lit, which made her a target. She hadn't seen a patch of bare ground for three blocks at least, and that meant there was nowhere to sink into if she needed a hole in an emergency. This warehouse…it loomed up over her, and it had too many eyes. She didn't have a real reason—yet—to cut and run from this Khalil, but the half-reasons—the gut instincts—were piling up like flies on a dead rat.

After their talk by the cathedral, he'd set a meet for Sunday. He came to it alone, like she asked. But he hadn't said anything new, hadn't healed her cheek, and had been able to hail a cab (the cab she had just now stepped out of) in a part of town taxi drivers stayed away from if they liked their skins whole. "I know what to do for your wound," Khalil had said as he left. "Come here again, tomorrow night, and I'll have my man pick you up and take you to my new place." And he was gone before she could argue. Short, sweet, brutal choices: Play along and maybe be burnt, or miss the meet and say goodbye to the best hope of avenging your friends….

Suddenly she remembered what she was doing here, and turned to find the driver half-out of the cab. Ramona pulled some grubby bills out of her back pockets and stretched the money across to the man. He grinned and waved his hands at her.

"No, no, thank you. It has all been arranged for." He bustled around to the trunk and chattered on, "If you will just wait a moment, miss—" He lifted, with difficulty, a six-pack of housepaint shrink-wrapped into a cardboard tray. "This is for Mr. Ravana. Could you," he slumped slightly under the weight, "hit the buzzer for me, please?"

Ramona reached for the cans, but the driver was already stumbling awkwardly toward the door of the place. She darted past him and pressed the button, then slipped her lean, strong arms under his spindly, bony ones. "I got it," she said. After a token protest, the driver gratefully accepted. When the door clicked her in, he opened it and gave, in polite and heavily accented English, detailed directions to an apartment in the upper reaches of the warehouse.

With effort (the man had repeated some of the turns in his orgy of helpfulness), she found it. Khalil Ravana held the door open, looking past her both ways down the catwalk, and then gave her what passed for a welcoming smile. He slung an arm under the box and loped off across the huge room with his paint. "No trouble getting here? Mukherjee treat you all right?" Without waiting for her answers, he hopped up a step and dumped the carton unceremoniously on a battered old desk standing alone in the middle of upper level. "Just make yourself at home while I finish this coat."

Ramona shuffled farther in and looked around. The loft was large and airy—a pleasant contrast to the rooms she'd grown up in. It had tall, elegant windows, about a third of which now had black paint slathered over the glass. She watched a ropy strand drip off one of the top panes and splatter on the floor beneath it. At one end of the studio, sheets and sheets of coarse white fabric hung from a bar in the rafters. A few of them were torn away from their rings, and there were black handprints wiped messily onto the nearest. She turned away and inspected the rest of the room.

The Ravnos poured another blob of dark goo into an aluminum tray and picked up his long-handled roller. He squelched the fuzzy tube industriously through the matte-black latex and attacked the next sash. "What do you think of my flat? Ready for *House Beautiful*? Havens of the Rich and Famous?" Ramona's eyes flicked up at him, suspicious of levity and his impossibly British accent, but he went on without noticing. "The northern exposure is a bit much, I admit, but that's being taken care of." He dipped the roller again. "You're welcome to stay, if you want. The more, the merrier, particularly if unexpected guests arrive. Are there any looking for you, by the by?" Khalil half-turned to surprise her reaction.

She shook her head and stated flatly, "Nobody knows I'm here. Everyone who knew me's dead."

"Lovely," said Khalil thoughtlessly. "I mean, that you're the hunter, not the hunted. Much more comfortable position to be in." After a pause, the rhythmic squeak of the roller went on.

Ramona wandered away from her host's stepstool and behind the screen of a hanging blanket. Her claws itched at the man. There were odd little things strewn across the table by the quilt— torn up and ready for the trash can, she thought. She picked up a pen, idly, and uncapped it; it was a fountain pen, and she drew a jittery line across the top of a notepad with it. A dark metal tray, blotchy with tarnish, caught her attention. She peered at its engravings, and found it full of shields and animals and tiny mottoes in Latin, which she could recognize but not understand. *Vincit qui si vincit…Vocatus atque non vocatus deus aderit….* She shied away and heard Khalil's voice going on:

"I said, 'Want to help paint?'"

"No."

"Then is there anything I can get you while I finish up?"

Ramona ran a hand over (*through* was no longer possible) her matted hair. "I could use a shower," she admitted.

Khalil's grin became an effort. Elizabeth was still chained to the sink in the bathroom. Since this Gangrel didn't know enough to hate *him*, she surely wouldn't know enough to distrust the baby snake. He should have thought before he brought Ramona up here…but who expected a filthy outlander to want to wash? In Calcutta they seemed proud of their stink. He'd have to move the Setite, and… "A shower?" he repeated dumbly.

"Hell, I don't care," she snapped, flicking the air between them with an exasperated gesture. She muttered something bitter in Spanish.

"No." The Ravnos laughed half-heartedly. "No problem. Let me just move a few things out of the way, make sure the water is turned on…" He backed down off his stepladder and wiped his hands. Reaching for something from his back pocket, he headed for the curtains around the bedroom, cursing under his breath. The pipes continued out of the bath; there was a radiator bolted firmly to the brickwork. Khalil dragged the hangings closer to that end of the room and opened the door on Elizabeth in relative secrecy.

Ramona stepped over to some bookshelves. The titles disappointed her; myths, antiques, lost languages, histories of places she'd never heard of. The furniture was nice though, and there were candles and pictures. She stepped down to a group of comfortable chairs and sofas. *Nice*, she felt. *Home*, though the apartment was nothing like any of her own. It was all very comfortable and friendly, and it *smelled* right. She took a good sniff of the largest couch and paced wistfully around on the shaggy carpet in the 'living room'.

"Up," said Khalil. He whispered, but the Gangrel's high-tipped ears caught it. Dull clanking followed, and Ramona had a glimpse of the Ravnos muscling someone behind the screened-off section of the loft. Ramona stepped quietly to a gap in the curtains and spied inside. There was a girl—no, a grown-up woman—wearing chains on her feet and wrists like a convict, and absolutely silent. She noticed Ramona watching them long before her captor did, and the girl was struck by her eyes. They had dignity still, despite what Khalil was doing with her.

They made an appeal. The woman wasn't defiant and seeking to be smacked down for it (*Zhavon*, Ramona thought, *was looking for trouble...*). She was not a terrified, cowed prisoner, either (*Zhavon was terrified, at the end*, Ramona remembered guiltily). The strange gold-brown eyes simply said, "You are watching him do this." Without a word the woman made Ramona think about it, and when Khalil finally saw her, her feral face was black as night.

"What're you doing?" the Gangrel said menacingly. Khalil felt the room grow cold. He sidled out of reach of the radiator—and of Ramona—and strained to change his expression from guilty, red-handed panic to innocent surprise. He picked a piece of an answer at random.

"Moving her," he managed blithely. "You wanted to use the shower, didn't you? Lizzie and I have had to shelter in there the past two days." He indicated the windows with a flick of a finger, and explained, "I'm trying to give us more space, but there *are* an awful lot of windows to paint over. She may need to sleep in the tub again tonight."

"But why's she chained up?" Ramona pressed, a nasty edge in her voice.

Khalil licked his lips and moved confidentially closer to his partner. "Her lover, Hesha, is the man we're trying to find to help us get Leopold. He's missing," he murmured apologetically, "he may be dead—and she's having some trouble dealing with the loss." He glanced over his shoulder to the Setite. "She's new to all this, as well...liable to lose control. So to keep her from hurting herself, and others," he said, with a self-deprecating smile, "these things are an unfortunate necessity."

"Why in here? You were hiding her," she accused.

"I was trying to give her some privacy. She, ah...she's only two or three nights old...she was still being sick yesterday. Don't you think it's more polite to leave her to herself during that sort of thing?"

Ramona remembered her own first, lonely nights after her change...her body ridding itself of everything but blood...her parents pounding on the door of the bathroom...her flight to a culvert where she could avoid their questions.... "No," she declared emphatically.

Khalil whispered, briskly: "Look. Leopold has the Eye. Hesha Ruhadze can find the Eye, if he still lives. This is his childe. She can find him once he resurfaces. She's my bloodhound, and she's bait. All right?" He leaned further toward her, and spat out, "You're so hot to catch Leopold; she's a part of that." Angrily he shoved Elizabeth at the radiator, and picked open her left-hand shackle.

Deeply troubled, Ramona weighed her options. She wanted vengeance for her dead so badly she could taste its sweet sting at the back of her throat. But she could not be a party to slavery. She wouldn't stand for caging anyone the way Zhavon had been caged. On the other hand, she knew what she was like, herself, when she lost control, and there had been a time when she'd rather have been chained up than let the Beast do what it wanted. This woman might be grateful, later, for the restraint. She grimaced, and the expression opened the gash in her cheek again. Whatever happened, she had to have that wound healed. If the guy were telling the truth about being able to cure what that Toreador had done to her, *then* maybe she'd believe him about this lady. If he couldn't fix it, he'd pay for the lie with blood, and Ramona would set the woman free as she left.

And so revenge and uncertainty won over moral outrage. She had to look away from the lady's face as the cuff closed on the radiator. It slid down the shaft with a heavy clang that jarred the Gangrel's conscience. "Wait." Khalil turned and stared at her. "At least...she can sit out here with us." She snatched up a wastebasket and held it awkwardly. "She can watch TV or read or something. There's got to be a more comfortable place she could be and still have us be safe."

Five more minutes saw Elizabeth locked once more to the central pillar of her apartment. This time, however, she sat in state on the couch. At Ramona's insistence, Khalil agreed to leave the Setite one hand free. Reluctantly, anxiously, he warned the Gangrel over and over not to go within arm's reach of the snake. "Be careful!" He took up the congealing paint and watched his partner put little amenities by Elizabeth's side. "Not the pencils. She could stake you with a pencil," he lied. "She's dangerous, aren't you listening? Watch yourself." Sullenly he wet the roller again.

"Here's the remote," said Ramona. "And the trashcan down here." She shook her matted head questioningly. "Can I get you anything else?"

Elizabeth regarded the new warden of her prison carefully: dark, Hispanic, teenaged (to look at, she reminded herself—the thing could be centuries dead), self-conscious, dirty, fairly pretty under the dirt, be-draggled, misshapen, and possibly sincere. She thought hard and cast about for something to ask for.

"Hand me that writing desk?" The lady spoke in a low, pleasant voice. Ramona searched and found a kind of tray full of papers, pens, and little books on the coffee table. She pushed it within reach of the free arm, and the lady laid it on her lap. "Thank you," she said quietly. Without looking at Ramona again, she added, "There are clean towels, a washcloth, soap, and a spare hairbrush in the wicker cabinet next to my bureau. You're welcome to my closet."

Ramona watched a moment more. The older woman uncapped a pen and began writing something, and the Gangrel slipped away without another word.

Every window was the color of tar. The drying paint fumes choked the air but failed to affect the three creatures brooding in their midst. Elizabeth, curled around her sketchbook and notes on the sofa, hardly smelt it. Ramona, sitting bolt upright in the walnut desk chair, had sneezed and spat and tried to ignore the stink for hours. By now her nose was deadened to the solvent by exposure. Khalil rather enjoyed the effect the chemical had had on the Gangrel, and solemnly refused all attempts to open the door or ventilate the room.

The Ravnos switched on a gadget—a lamp with more arms than he had, and a great magnifying glass at its center—and positioned the glaring bulb directly over the rent in Ramona's cheek. From a pile of tools on the bench between them, he selected a curly dentist's pick and a rounded metal stick like a spatula. With the blunt object, he spread the largest part of the wound open and probed the inside, as gently as he could, with the other. His patient's grip tightened on the chair arms, but she kept motionless under the examination. Khalil moved on to the rest of the holes in her skin, studied each in turn, and then set his instruments down.

The wound looked, from the outside, like a narrow, curved, and superficial line—precisely as if the girl had been struck by a thin spatter of acid. Below the surface, however, the sore went straight down to the bone. Each dot on the outside had a large pocket of rotted, torn flesh beneath it, as though whatever hit the skin had burrowed on impact and eaten the larger area away after the first strike.

Khalil picked up a craft knife in his right hand. "Are you going to cut it out?" Ramona demanded.

"I can't." Khalil took the knobby turmeric root in his left fist, and set to work on it. "I could slice off that part of your face," he grinned merrily, "but unless the poison is gone you won't ever heal it. We have to destroy the residue and keep the rot from spreading." He shaved off good-sized stick and cut it wider at one end than at the other—he was clever with his fingers and very quickly carved a thick and wedge-like spoon out of the sliver. With the sharp, thin blade, he made a exact and tedious series of parallel cuts in the broad end. The result resembled a primitive paintbrush more than anything else.

"What's that?"

"Turmeric root. It's good for exorcisms." He laid down the Exacto and palmed something else: a lighter. Elizabeth, watching from the couch, raised an eyebrow and added another line to her notes.

"Can you stand a little fire?" Khalil asked archly.

Ramona's brown eyes locked with his. "Yes," she replied cautiously. "You going to smoke it out?" She considered she had experience with smoke and magic....

"No." All the jests fled his face, and he went on gravely. "Close your eyes," he said, "get a good grip on the chair, and," he looked slightly scared, "*try* to remember I'm doing this to help you."

It took five tries for Khalil to get the lighter flaming, and an agonizing seven seconds for the frayed bit of turmeric to catch. His twitching eyes watered as the smoke from the burning herb struck them. He waited while the dry root built up a good smolder. It bothered him to have to hold a lit object. The Ravnos was less afraid of that, though, than of what the voice had told him to do next.

With the knife, he cut a line linking all the Evil Eye's ravages together. He was painfully aware of Ramona's feral gaze pinned to every movement of his hands. He held the flap of skin open with the blunt spatula-thing, gathered his courage, and then plunged the fiery smudge-stick into the center of the wound.

Ramona shrieked and roared. Her legs flew up and her head jerked violently away. Khalil managed, barely, to keep the burning herb inside the Gangrel's flesh. He dug it further in. He twisted it deliberately, feeling out the rest of the path the acid had taken inside the girl's body. If the bones were breached, could he—

That is all at that location. The hurt was very small.

Khalil leapt back gratefully and dropped the turmeric into a bucket of water. He waited to see what the girl would do after the first spasms stopped. If he ran behind Elizabeth, Ramona might attack the Setite first and give him a chance to get away before the bloodlust took her further....

Ramona shuddered from tip to toe. Red rage boiled in her eyes, and the stench of her own body, burning, filled her nostrils. Memories of the sun, of a stake in her heart, of this same stink—sun and fire and death.... With an effort, she kept her mind clear. She clenched her fists and forced blood to her cheek as she had done so often in the past six nights—carefully, slowly at first, and then more eagerly. She caught the sensation, barely, of knitting edges. Her fingers crept up to her chin—no trickle of wasted life oozed from the wound this time. Ramona felt the area itself—the sickle-shape was smaller! It shrank beneath her touch, and she poured more effort into healing. At last, after ages of strain and what seemed gallons of precious blood, the skin of her face was smooth once more. She slumped in her chair, relieved and grateful, but suddenly sick with hunger. Even with the evil, the poison gone, that tiny cut had taken a lot of curing. Dull furies danced in her guts, and she knew she would have to hunt before dawn, or suffer worse, possibly uncontrollable pangs tomorrow.

Ramona rose, shakily. She tripped down the step toward the apartment door. Khalil hove into sight. "Where are you going?"

"Starving," she growled.

Khalil retreated. Her face was whole, he saw gladly. "Will you...will you want to sleep here tonight?"

"You'll see me when you see me," the Gangrel barked, fumbling with the locks. She lunged through the door.

"Are you coming back?!" Khalil called desperately after her.

No one and nothing answered, and the Ravnos bolted the steel slab, unhappily uncertain as to whether he would ever see the girl again.

Wednesday, 4 August 1999, 1:06 AM
Boerum Hill, Brooklyn
New York City, New York

They wore tight, shiny clothes that left their legs free, their arms bare, their muscles evident, and her chest tantalizingly half-covered. Gold flashed on their necks, on his wrist, and from her ears and fingers. Beads of sweat scented with tobacco, perfume, and alcohol glistened on bronze skin and on olive; the young couple had spent a beautiful evening dancing salsa with friends at their regular place. Clinging together, holding hands as they made their good-byes, they moved gracefully down the front steps of the one-room club. She kissed one last girlfriend on the cheek and promised to call; he gripped a friend by the arm and joked about work. Then the two stepped out of the circle of music and off down the sidewalk...north, away from the darkness of Red Hook...in the direction Khalil had expected them to choose.

The Ravnos sauntered down the uneven pavement roughly twenty feet behind his prey. Ramona's grunting talk of food had piqued Khalil; he felt rather peckish, as he put it to Elizabeth. She hadn't liked that. He smiled. She wouldn't like the rest of the evening any better.

His hearty appetite goaded him on, and he closed the gap separating the couple and himself. When the three of them reached a nice, shady spot, Khalil skipped forward and pinched the girl on the butt. She whirled on him, dark-eyed and angry, and her companion, after quick words passed between them, advanced on the offender with rippling biceps. A torrent of abuse flew from his mouth; his fists followed. Khalil dodged, winked at the woman, wished he understood more Spanish, and gut-punched the man so hard he had to stop speaking to catch his breath. Khalil jabbed and swung and dodged, and the fight backed its slow way into the real darkness between two faceless buildings. A bit of cunning footwork—the mortal was forced to retreat down the alley—his girl, realizing at last that her man's knuckles had no effect on the stranger, leapt on Khalil's back and tried to claw his eyes out. The Ravnos stopped playing, knocked out the male with one solid blow to the chin, tapped the girl unconscious before she screamed any louder, and dragged his prizes further from the street.

Two mammoth dumpsters flanked the back door of a little café, closed now for the night. Elizabeth sat chained to the nearest, her mouth securely gagged with duct tape. Legend had it no call for help in New York was ever answered, but the Ravnos took no chances.

Khalil laid the two victims down side by side and examined them judicially. "Dinner is served," he quipped, tearing the strips of plastic away from his prisoner's mouth. The man was stronger—he could take the loss a little better. Khalil pulled the girl over to his own side of the alley. He found a seat on a pile of decaying newspapers, tucked the girl into his lap, and shoved her boyfriend forward with his foot until the body pressed up against his prisoner's. He nodded at Elizabeth, saying, "That one's yours."

Khalil wrapped his arms around the girl. She wore a necklace with a charm engraved "Rosa," and the *shilmulo* whispered the name softly to himself. He kissed her red lips and smelt wine on her breath. He stroked her downy neck, found a pulse with his tongue, and sank his teeth in deep. *Beautiful, smooth, sweet darling,* he thought, before he ceased thinking and simply enjoyed. After a long time (*Never long enough,* cursed the Ravnos to himself), he wrenched his mouth away. He licked the wound clean and watched the twin holes seal themselves, weighed his belly, and checked the woman's color. She would be a white rose for a week or two, he guessed, but he was fairly sure he didn't have a corpse on his hands. *Good,* he mused contentedly, *she's a pretty one; maybe I can find her again a month from now.* Heavy-lidded and warm, he leant back against the wall and regarded his Setite childe. *Disgusting. She hasn't even made a move toward him.*

Elizabeth's nose, mouth, and throat burned with the smell of blood. Khalil reeked of it. The ally teemed with it. There seemed to be a red mist, even, floating behind her eyes, and her body—

Once, after a bout of food poisoning which kept her from eating real food for a week, Liz had experienced the first, faintest knives of starvation in her belly. She remembered how her hands shook lifting the spoon to her mouth, how applesauce tasted when the body had been eating itself for days. That feeling—doubled, tripled—had crept through her the last two nights. Now, with this solid smell in her nostrils, the hunger became a living thing lashing about her guts. *I will not,* she thought, without naming to herself what she denied. *This is wrong. Better to have died in the sun than to...*

"Feeling squeamish?" Khalil's voice touched her, unexpectedly full of sympathy and concern. Liz looked up with a kind of hope dawning on her face.

Her companion nodded consolingly. "It's tough the first time, sweetheart." He picked up a half-brick from the debris around him and reached out—Elizabeth froze—and Khalil smashed in the man's skull. The cranium caved in like an eggshell. Gray matter and bone sprayed up and flecked the torn skin and curly black hair. Blood began pooling in the horrific dent—and stopped. Liz stared at the dancer's unmoving chest. *He's not breathing.* She saw the girl's left hand outstretched, where it had fallen when Khalil finished with her. The third finger bore an engagement ring. *They would have been married…. She loved him. She tried to rescue him, and now there will be nothing. God grant that they've gone somewhere better, together,* prayed the new Setite.

"Go ahead, darling," Khalil told her cheerfully. "You can't hurt him now."

Elizabeth, wretched and terrified, knew she was sick. Her stomach turned, and she bent her head forward to let her dry and empty body do what it would. Unstoppably, nightmarishly, fangs forced their way down from her gums and cut her mouth. It opened of its own accord and fastened leech-like to the man's still-warm shoulder. Her hands, stretched out to push away, grabbed instead and brought him closer. Elizabeth drank despite herself, and despaired because she enjoyed it.

A sound close to her ears. Snapping. Words. Khalil's voice and hard fingers on her shoulders, pulling her away. "That's quite enough for you, my girl. Mustn't gorge yourself." A perverse and childish spirit whined in the back of her head, demanding why, if the man was dead already, she couldn't drink it all?

Other sounds: clanking chains. Her fetters were off the trash bin and back in Khalil's hands. The Ravnos jerked on them, and she stood slowly. The corpse lolled away from her feet and came to rest against the body of his bride-to-be.

Khalil shoved his prisoner down the lane and back toward the warehouse. At the corner, he looked back: The broken brick lay pulverized on the cement beside the man's smooth and unbroken head. The Setite knew nothing of taking her meals; she had opened only a tiny vein, and the sluggish flow was nearly stopped from the clotting already. No corpses at all tonight. He jingled his new jewelry in one pocket and felt the man's heavy wallet pressing on his hip. It looked enough like a robbery…. He turned his attentions to his companion. Elizabeth walked huddled in on herself. She was obviously terrified, mortified, barely holding her sanity together— Hesha's childe, in just the state he'd love to see Hesha. Khalil licked his lips and smiled. *Good.*

Wednesday, 4 August 1999, 2:12 AM
A subterranean grotto
New York City, New York

The warren was abuzz, and that irritated Calebros. *Something* had happened—near the statue that he liked so much at the Cathedral of St. John the Divine—but exactly what, no one was certain. Several nights had passed, but still Calebros could hear agitated whispers from every tunnel, speculation as baseless as idle gossip.

Gather the pieces. I will reconstruct the puzzle. That was what his sire Augustin had always said, and it was advice that Calebros had begun to impart to his own fledglings. The youngsters seemed to take it on faith.

Now he merely needed to convince himself that it was true.

4 August 1999
Re: disturbance at Cathedral of
St. John the Divine

7/31---none of our people witnessed;
statues deformed; damage to connecting
streets for several blocks---path?

Found one body; badly damaged and
burned---<u>Kindred</u>, but unrecognizable.

8/1---Cassandra sighted two Kindred
prowling around the same area; didn't
recognize either.

→ Not responding favorably
to treatment.

part two:
servant

Wednesday, 4 August 1999, 10:52 PM
Red Hook, Brooklyn
New York City, New York

Ramona knocked cautiously on the steel door of the loft. She kept watch to both sides of the catwalk and listened. Would Khalil open the door? Was he home? What if someone else had moved in on the place? And what had she said as she left the other night? She bit her knuckles and waited. Below her, was that a noise? A footstep?

"Who's there?" Khalil's voice, thank goodness.

"It's me."

Locks clanked and clicked open, and Khalil looked out through the crack left by a sliding chain. He nodded and let her in. "You're looking well," he observed. "Set of keys for you on the refrigerator. They work for everything except the big day bolt; get here before I shoot that if you want to sleep in." He glanced down at a sheaf of papers held in his hand, turned away negligently, and sat down at a cheap desk by the black windows. "Do you have any good Camarilla contacts?" he inquired, flipping through a file drawer.

"No." Ramona followed him up the step. "No, my gang tried to keep out of all that."

"Know where I can find anyone from the Camarilla?" She shook her head. "Elysium?" Ramona looked blank. "Cam turf? Cam bars?" He tapped his nails on the desktop.

I told you where to go.

"I'm just checking all available options," Khalil said aloud. Ramona nodded in answer. He spoke again, this time to her. "I'm going out tonight to find some players. People we can bargain with. Come with me." The Gangrel's eyes flicked over her shoulder to the couch. The lady in chains sat quietly listening. Khalil cleared his throat. "She'll be fine here. Safer, really. The stuffed shirts in the Cam don't care for Setites—not at all. They'll like you, though...." And on that confusing note he hustled Ramona out the door again.

"Sexton's Dirty Secret," read Ramona off the sign above the door. "What the hell does that mean?"

"It's a Camarilla club. Probably owned by one of the highbrows. Ventrue, darling. They like being coy and clever with their little problem." The Gangrel blinked at him uncomprehendingly. "Death, Ramona, death." He slicked his hair back and kept talking. "A sexton is a churchwarden. He takes care of the grounds, including the cemetery and the vault, see? The walking dead would be his dirty secret."

"Oh."

"The owner is probably British; it's a terribly Anglic word."

Very perceptive of you, the voice commented dryly. It had had to explain the exact same thing to Khalil earlier in the evening.

They neared the entrance and a bouncer, well-built for his job, eyed them thoughtfully. While still out of earshot of the line waiting to get in (Khalil hoped), he whispered to the girl, "Try and remember. If anyone asks—say, if another Gangrel comes up and gives you the secret handshake or something and questions you about me—you're not sure what clan I'm from, but I talk a little about some thing named Malkav when I'm getting sleepy, okay?"

"Why? What clan *are* you from?"

"I'm independent," Khalil said cockily. His ears rang with the voice's laughter, and his hands tightened into frustrated fists.

Khalil led the way to the back of the queue, and Ramona tailed along looking bored. Very quickly, more would-be patrons joined them, and the Gangrel's nose twitched. The whole place was in mourning, apparently. Almost everyone wore black lace, black latex, black leather, or black net—and *every* hanger-on had pale, pale skin. She caught the scent of makeup off them: pearl powder and white greasepaint, sticky mascara and fresh nail polish. Ramona set her back against the wall and kept her distance from the posers. *Freaks,* she thought.

The line buzzed. Another man had appeared at the doorway of the club. After a quick chat with the bouncer, he passed along the line in review. The newcomer was whiplash-thin, with buzz-cut black hair, and the painted people waiting looked at him with hope-filled eyes but nonchalant expressions. "You," he said, pointing to a girl wearing crushed red velvet despite the heat. "And you—" a boy, very pretty, whose eyes were smeared with black paint. "Both of you—" to Khalil and Ramona, "and you lot." A tight group of four at the back of the line tensed with unexpected victory. The chosen progressed to the door, a few of the neglected wandered away, and the rest rearranged themselves to wait a while longer.

The eight elect filed through a narrow, dirty foyer whose long walls were sheets of mirror. *Careful people,* thought Khalil. *The situation must be worse than I thought....* He smiled. *Good wars make good markets.* A girl with fluorescent white hair wrapped wristbands onto him and Ramona without asking for identification, and they shuffled along with the rest into the club.

Sexton's Dirty Secret contrived, in a building designed originally to house finance, to create the atmosphere of a decayed and moribund chapel. The first-floor ceiling had been knocked away and replaced with one that slanted from its proper place on the right to the second story on the left. This gave the amateur feel of half a cathedral roof. A balcony running along the high wall was dressed as a choirloft; the DJ resided in a glass booth atop another designed to take confessions; the bar fronts mimicked tombs; the dance floor was fenced off by chancel rails; and the booths ranged round the perimeter had seats like pews, their carved backs exaggerated into tall and imposing walls. Khalil's mouth twitched as he threaded his way past the crowds and into the dark, flashing heart of the place. Most of the people here were acting as though they were actually people, at a club, enjoying themselves as much as their tragic souls would let them. A few danced in strange and backbreaking, ridiculously serious fashions. The club seemed to be full of live ones. *Damn their Masquerade*, thought the Ravnos. *Who's kidding who?*

Khalil took a seat in one of the booths. It wasn't the position he would have occupied if he had his choice—the looming walls of the "pew" obscured anyone approaching from the sides until they were almost on top of him. On the other hand, of the tables that were left, his had the best view of (and from) the other quiet corners and private nooks. He settled in with his back to the wall and lounged ostentatiously along the entire seat. Ramona slid in across from him. She was trying to look natural, poor thing, but the crowd clearly bothered her, and the enclosed space had her on tenterhooks. Khalil took pity on his anxious partner. "Go ahead. Get up, go around the place as if you were checking it out. Obviously that's your style. So be yourself. Order something from the bar—anything but a Bloody Mary. Walk around with it. Come back here in…I don't know. Half an hour. Listen, don't talk, and pay attention if anyone says anything about sewer rats. We're looking for one, a big one. All right?"

Ramona slipped away gratefully. Khalil watched with satisfaction as the girl's animalistic looks caught attention. *She's as good as a full-page ad in the* Post. He riveted his eyes on the faces of anyone who so much as glanced her way, trying to gauge their status—living or dead, friendly or suspicious, puny or important—by the kind of approach they took with her.

You are wasting time. I have told you your next move.

Khalil licked his lips and covered them with a lazy hand. Under its concealment, he murmured softly: "Let me handle this my way. You've been out of things for a while—"

As you wish. It makes no difference to me when you make contact, so long as it is tonight—you are the one being marked by the prince's sheriff during this delay. Khalil's back muscles writhed, and he glowered across the dance floor at Ramona's head. *Never mind. Here he comes.*

"Mike?" Khalil said, as though recognizing a friend.

A short, burly man with long brown hair stopped walking by and looked into the recesses of the booth. "Yeah?" He had pale-gray, washed-out eyes and a crooked nose. "I know you?"

"No, no." Khalil sat up a bit and smiled reassuringly. "A friend of mine told me to look you up if I were ever in New York. University man, calls himself the Mongoose. 'Go and find out,' you know."

"Rick? I haven't seen Rick in ages. How's the old boy doing?" Mike planted himself squarely on the seat across from Khalil and plastered a grin across his homely face. "Did he ever finish that biography of Kipling?"

"Last time I saw him, he'd abandoned poetry. Gone on to study the background of the thing. *The Jungle Book*, the real jungles of the time, the real old city life. That's how I knew him, really. We had a common interest in the topic. I used to do a little snake-charming act in Delhi; he helped me make it more 'authentic' for the tourist trade." The Ravnos shrugged. "I'd like to set up shop again over here, but I'm having trouble finding the cobras."

"I know a lot of reptiles. I might be able to fix you up."

"Thanks. I'd appreciate that. It's just…I'm looking for one breed in particular. Very rare; recent import to the States. The handlers got it through Customs for me, and it just—disappeared."

"Stolen?" Mike's tone was sympathetic.

"Stolen, escaped, mislaid, I don't know."

"I've got some friends who are pretty good at finding things. Never tried to find a cobra before, but hey, there's a first time for everything." He frowned a little. "Just one thing, though, before I offer their help—they don't always take dollars, you know. Currency regulations, red tape, the IRS…"

Khalil nodded in complete understanding. "Not a problem. I've been traveling quite a bit recently. I haven't exchanged everything I picked up on my trip. I'm sure there's one coin or another we can agree on."

"Great." Mike tipped his near-empty beer bottle to his lips and rose to go. "Great. Hey, how can I reach you…uh…?"

"Khalil," the Ravnos said. "My offices aren't open yet…have you got a number where I could get you?"

"Sure." Mike pulled out a card and swayed slightly drunkenly. "You know, you ought to get a pager or a cell phone or something. Everybody has them here." He patted the pew and began moving on. "Give my regards to the Mongoose next time you see him, pal."

Khalil collected Ramona from conversation with the barmaid and ushered her out. "Did we get what we wanted?" she asked angrily, upset at being yanked around.

"We made contact. That's enough for one night."

Thursday, 5 August 1999, 3:54 AM
A forgotten pneumatic subway tunnel
New York City, New York

Mike Tundlight swung through a service grating and down a ladder into an old, crumbling corridor. He popped in one door to chaff a few friends gathered around a poker table. His face was no longer merely pale but maggot-white, his eyes bloodshot through the iris, his brown hair wispy and uncontrolled, his short stature and thick body clearly the result of a spine twisted in on itself. The card players, all but one of whom shared his monstrous ugliness, called cheerfully back and went on with the game. Mike poked his head into another room with a touch more deference, asking the occupant, "You busy?"

Umberto scratched an eyebrow (which was not, properly speaking, over his eye) and blinked in the light from his computer screen. "Just a second." His bony fingers flickered over the keyboard with a perfect rattling touch. "What's up?" One hand took hold of a trackball, the other waved vaguely at the dilapidated couch beside the machine.

"Just got in from Sexton's."

"The beautiful people making a late night of it? What else is new?"

"Lot of talk about the war," said Mike, settling down. "But that's not important. I'll send something on that around in the evening. But a guy did come in who might be relevant. He was Indo-Pak or something...south Asian, anyway. Had a girlfriend with him, called herself Ramona. He, or they, were looking for a snake. I think he was looking for the same snake *we're* hunting for. Certainly seems to have lost track of him at the same stage of his travels."

"Huh." Umberto took both hands off the keyboard and thought. "Interesting, if true. Cass!" he yelled down the tiled corridor. "Spare us a minute?"

A dark, pebble-skinned woman appeared on the threshold. She wore several layers of sweaters and skirts, and in her permanently clawed left fist she held a deck of cards. "Sure. It's my deal. What do you need?"

"You saw the two jokers who showed up at Saint John's the night after the commotion. Describe them for Mike." And a very short time later, the three Nosferatu confirmed that Khalil was the man from the bar, as well as the man from the cathedral. Mike and Cass thought that the girls they had seen were one and the same (though she had had an open and unusual wound when prowling about the churchyard), but were positive that she could not, under any circumstances, have been the woman in the pictures with Hesha in New York. Umberto gathered his information together and took it down the hallway. Mike Tundlight, Cassandra, and a growing crowd from the game waited, sensing something important in the offing—each of them were experts in atmosphere—and when Umberto came back in only five minutes, with new and urgent assignments for anyone who could volunteer, their expectations were more than fulfilled.

"He wants a full report on Khalil; another on the girl. If he's selling or trading information, we want to know how reliable the stuff will be. Mike, you meet with him as soon as you think wise. I'm going with you," —mild sensation in the hall as Umberto spoke of leaving his computer— "as your humble servant, just in case our Ravnos tries something."

Friday, 6 August 1999, 2:41 AM
A subterranean grotto
New York City, New York

"Good evening, sir," said Umberto respectfully into the shadows. A gnarled and twisted hand held a sheaf of typewritten reports out toward him. Red ink and faint stampings overran the pages. The technologically minded Nosferatu clipped the sheets to a folio that had its own dim light built into the cover and glanced at the manuscript notes. "Baltimore is still in conference...no news for you there. But I've got some juicy ID's on the two that came into old Gotobed's club last night...."

Large, wide-set eyes blinked encouragingly at him.

"The girl is Ramona Tanner-childe; Tanner, childe of Horrock, etc., is a Gangrel of decent reputation and moderate standing—he seems to be quite a mover, so the call is out over SchreckNET to see where he might be now. Ramona is very probably Pilar Ramona Salvador, a missing-child case from LA. Poor Hispanic family, barrio where that sort of thing happens all the time, hardly any news coverage, not investigated deeply by the police. Her parents had a memorial stone put in the family plot back in Mexico and say prayers for their lost little girl." The shadows rustled slightly. "I know. Old story.

"Khalil Ravana, on the other hand, is a two-bit Ravnos from Bihar. Good, long history there." He passed a printout into the darkness. "And he," Umberto finished triumphantly, "was last seen in a disco in Calcutta, sitting across the table from the notorious Hesha Ruhadze."

"Make the appointment."

Ramona kept her distance from Khalil as they neared the club. She wore a charcoal-gray T-shirt and leggings borrowed from the quiet lady's closet. *He* had bought a bright and intricately printed silk shirt in blue, white, and gold—very expensive, very conspicuous. If the stranger wanted an extra hand, she was ready. If he wanted to make himself a target, she would be standing somewhere else. She watched him swagger ahead, dangling his new black-leather phone bag from its wrist strap, and she rolled her eyes. At the shut and darkened door he didn't hesitate—he knocked twice, and the door opened immediately. A bartender Ramona remembered speaking to stood there in quite ordinary clothes (she had been a vision in black net the other night), welcomed them pleasantly, and led them up to the gallery.

As the Ravnos and the Gangrel mounted the steps, two other people kept pace with them on the opposite staircase. The bartender reached the top and stood aside for a moment to let everyone have a good look at each other. Mike Tundlight matched their faces with his memory of the club; Umberto with a missing children's photo and a surveillance shot. Khalil recognized Mike, saw that the other figure was swathed in cloth from head to foot, and accepted that he had a second and obviously (to his mind) lesser (because unable to hide his deformities by magic) Nosferatu to deal with. Once she was sure no fight would break out, the bartender started moving again. The gallery held five doors, all wide open. Ramona looked inside the first one as they passed it, and saw a blank—four plain plaster walls, seamless white plaster ceiling, seamless white vinyl floor. When the party met at the center door, the bartender recited, as if by rote:

"All the rooms are the same. Feel free to examine them as you will. Select one you can agree on. All the locks work only from the inside. I do not have any keys. I will not remain in the building. The management takes no responsibility for the safety of its guests, it merely ensures neutral ground in which discussions may take place. In the event of hostilities, damage to the club, or damage to the staff, the management will take measures against the offending party or parties for the sake of its own reputation." She glanced at Mike. He stepped aside for her. "We open at ten-thirty," she added as she walked away. "Mr. Gotobed told me to ask you to try and be done by then."

"Well." Mike grinned. "Pick a room? I don't think we have a preference."

Khalil slipped into the center door. Mike followed, then the cloaked person, then Ramona. She was grateful for her partner's flashy clothes once inside; they broke up the monotony—this room *was* just the same as the first, and the furniture, now that she saw it, was no help. Clear molded-plastic chairs, clear molded-plastic table. The only thing besides themselves that was not transparent or clinically white was a mirror twelve inches square hung on the back of the door. She wished she had spent the night in the ground and could at least get the place dirty. Uncomfortably, she took her place by Khalil's side.

Khalil settled in, apparently at his ease. In his mind, however, the voice kept up a steady commentary; he had hardly had a moment's silence to think since Mukherjee's cab dropped them off. *Insist on seeing what the second man has beneath his robes. He has nothing, but it will demonstrate appropriate caution on your part.*

"If you don't mind," Khalil said to Mike, gesturing at the stranger, "could your friend shuck a few layers? Just so I can see there aren't any stakes hidden under there. Mere formality, of course."

"Not a problem." Mike helped his companion stand again and stripped him of his bulky outer robe. Ramona, unprepared for the sight, gasped a little.

"Nothing up my sleeves," said Umberto reassuringly. His voice was quite ordinary, though it was difficult to tell where he kept his lips. His skin clung to his bones in some places, sagged into his skeleton in others, and very few scraps of flesh came between them. "Your own bag?" he suggested politely, and Ramona saw that his mouth ran diagonally up one cheek.

Khalil unzipped the little case. Mike picked up the phone, turned it around in his hands, and set it back. "Glad to see you taking my advice. Made this meet much easier, didn't it?"

To business. Begin by inquiring after Hesha. Trade the details of—

"Well, gentlemen. Shall we talk?" Khalil asked as the second Nosferatu wrapped his body up again. "Any progress hunting for snakes?"

"We can speak more openly here," Mike answered. "You *are* looking for Hesha Ruhadze, right?"

"Yes."

"Suppose we knew where he was. What would that be worth to you?"

Mention the Eye. They will be prepared to—

Khalil overran his master's voice. "Mike, I'm afraid I left you with the wrong impression the other night." He considered this as an opening, and found he liked the sound of it. "I know answers; you collect answers. In fact, I think you *need* answers. I need some things myself." At the back of his mind, he felt the presence pause. It wasn't sure where he was taking this. Khalil wasn't sure himself.

"What kind of things?"

"Hesha Ruhadze, first of all. I want to find him" —his master relaxed— "I want to know everything about him, and for that I'll share what I know about the inside workings of his organization." *No. Stop this at once.*

"Second, if I'm going to be here very long while you boys find things out, I want hunting grounds and a promise that I won't be interfered with by the prince's sheriff. I need some money for expenses. I want information on New York City, the Setites here, the Camarilla setup and what the Sabbat call their turf.

"Third, I want to know about a Toreador named—" He winced, choking to a halt. *Say not his name. The cure for the location, only. Do it.* "I want to—" Khalil began again. *Obey me, gnat.* Ramona stared at him. Blood trickled from his nose, and his eyes ceased to focus. "Never mind. Never mind. Those two things are all." He waved a hand weakly in negation.

Mike and Umberto exchanged quick glances. "What are you offering in return?"

"You're the ones…with…the emergency," the Ravnos managed through the continuing, vengeful pain. *I will destroy you for your insolence, boy.* "Makes it a seller's market, doesn't it? You've got a bloody thunderstorm—" he pulled himself straight in his chair— "I'm the man selling umbrellas." *Try to thwart me again and I will personally track you down and reclaim my blood; I will break your bones with my teeth and suck the marrow from them while you still live.*

Khalil stood up, and the voice raged on at him.

Mike shook his head. "I'm not sure I understand what you're talking about. You demand all these things, and you don't give me many reasons to give them to you. My friends are going to want to know what you can do for us, Khalil."

Khalil chuckled aloud. He could hold out. His ears hurt from the threats and the fury—he had trouble hearing his own voice and Mike's, and felt obscurely that one of them wasn't making sense. But the old bastard's grip was weak. He *could* hold out.

Beneath a deep and twisted scowl, Ramona glowered at the table. She opened her mouth and said sharply, "Find Hesha and we'll tell you how to heal wounds from the Eye. If you don't know what the Eye is, you don't know anything." She sprang to her feet and took her tottering companion by the arm.

"I'll take your…statement…back to my people. We'll call you."

"Good," Ramona shot back. "Make it fast." And she pulled Khalil out the door after her to the sound, if only she could have heard it, of ancient peals of laughter. Her partner put up no resistance; he kept silent, petrified by the magnitude of his humiliation, and let the Gangrel guide him.

Once in the street, she turned on him. "What the hell? Have you gone crazy? You didn't do nothing like you told me last night. The cure for Hesha, that's the plan, *you* said. What the fuck happened to you?" She pulled a wrinkled bandanna out of her hip pocket and wiped the blood from Khalil's face. The Ravnos hardly noticed—between the mocking, mind-filling sound of his master's humor, the thing had begun speaking again.

Fool. Fool, a thousand times a fool. You suffer my wrath until your heart fries with the effort, and the little girl-child of our enemy...against whom I warned you...does my bidding without the least prompting. You trebly-damned baboon's bastard. I told you she would betray you.... Its laughter kept it from finishing the sentence.

"I wanted a better bargain," muttered Khalil. "I know very valuable things, you old bastard."

Ramona let his arm go suddenly. "You calling *me* a bastard, you son of a bitch?!"

But Khalil's eyes weren't on her—they stared blankly away east, to Calcutta. *Go on, pick a fight with her. I would like to see this.* His master's agenda had nothing in it for him except, possibly, survival. And the creature had never made the slightest promise of that. Somehow, he must get out from under its power. He swore that to himself, and begged gods he didn't believe in to tell him how he'd come under the monster's sway in the first place.

With concern, Ramona pressed him, "Come on, man. What's wrong with you?" He said nothing. They walked down the sidewalk together, away from the club. Dinner crowds and early drinkers swirled around them. The girl did her best for him without understanding; she kept him from walking against the lights more than once. Blocks went by in stupefied silence.

Eventually, with walking, Khalil's head cleared—of the voice, of the pain. The streets were crowded. Mortals everywhere—walking, driving, eating, drinking, laughing, arguing. America really was the land of opportunity. So many people to be bilked out of money or goods or whatever else Khalil wanted. That thought cheered him—that thought and the fact that he had defied his master. More or less. Khalil started to have a warm feeling inside.

He stopped in his tracks. Ramona took another couple of steps before she realized.

The warm feeling, Khalil discovered, was not the rising up of newly found pride, nor was it a result of the stifling, balmy evening. It was coming from his pocket.

He thrust his hand into his pocket and felt the radiant heat of the gem—the stone that had inexplicably soaked up his blood a few nights before. Khalil took off at a jog.

"What the hell?" Ramona, who had just come back to him, followed along grumbling.

Khalil only half-heartedly tried to avoid the other pedestrians. He ignored their New York pleasantries as he made his way to the next corner. The gem was growing warmer. He started to his left to cross the street—cooler—and then to his right along the sidewalk—warmer.

He ran for several more blocks—warmer. The stone seemed to drive Khalil onward. He forced himself to pause at intersections and dodge traffic. Warmer. He wasn't sure if he'd lost Ramona or if she'd merely given up cursing at him.

The gem was incredibly hot, but the heat did not burn.

And then he saw her—across the street, hailing a cab. In the midst of the sweat-drenched crowd, one woman looked back at him coolly, as unconcerned by the heat wave as himself. Her full, painted lips were still pursed from calling the cab. Her long, black, coarse hair was swept back with beads and braided cords. She wore a costume in bright reds and purples, somewhere between a simple peasant dress and medieval court costume, and she had a number of scarves and sashes wrapped about her person. Behind the trappings, she was dark, genuinely beautiful, rather haggard, and bitterly sad.

"Khalil?" Ramona caught up with him at the curb.

He'd almost forgotten about her. She looked at him quizzically with raised brow. Following her gaze, Khalil noticed that the gem was glowing sunset red through his thin slacks.

"You just happy to see me?" Ramona asked.

"Stay here," Khalil whispered to the Gangrel. "I have to talk to someone." He strode into the street, not quite believing in the woman on the other side. He had a bad moment when a cab pulled up in front of her, but the woman waved it away and waited for him.

"Khalil?"

He nodded and stepped eagerly toward her.

"I thought that was you. What a shock," she exclaimed in their native language. She reached out and stroked his mustache with a varnished fingernail.

Khalil began to smile—and then felt a jolt of remembered panic. The last people on Earth he wanted to see were his own kind, now. But, then, he and Ghose hadn't felt the uncontrollable urge to slay one another; surely Mary would be safe as well. Khalil reached for her hand and clasped it welcomingly— to keep those nails far from his face. He became aware of Ramona watching them from across the street, and of the Ravnos woman watching Ramona.

"Hello, Ravana. It's been ages. Delhi, wasn't it?"

"Hello, Mary. Delhi it was." He took her arm; as they spoke he promenaded her around the block. "What are you doing in New York?"

She shrugged. "Travelling. Let me think…Delhi to London, London to Hong Kong—stay out of that, old man, if you would live longer—Hong Kong to California, California to here…more or less." She waved away the rest of the century with a carelessly graceful gesture. "Now tell me, where were *you* when the world ended? And don't try to tell me you were here." In another tone, she added, "*I* was here."

"India," Khalil admitted.

Mary's eyebrows rose. "*You* survived India? Where?" she demanded, only half-jokingly.

"A small town," he answered briefly, modestly.

"Oh, you can't tell the truth to save your soul, can you?" She nudged him.

"I didn't know it was at stake anymore, Mary."

They walked on for a while without speaking. "Who would have thought," she observed at last, "that Khalil Ravana would survive India? Who would have thought that I'd survive New York, for that matter!" She sighed audibly. "But here I am. 'Gypsy queen'—eldest *Romni* of the Five Boroughs." Her grip tightened on his arm, and when he looked at her, he saw a thin blood tear rolling down her cheek. Khalil offered her a bandanna (he vaguely remembered someone pressing it into his own hand a little while back), and she cleaned her face.

"There's no one else," Mary wept quietly. "I snapped out of the trance on Saturday night with Andreas's head in my hands. He was the last. I never knew I could fight like that." She wiped her eyes again. "I gave them all a beautiful funeral…I've been spending the whole week going round to their houses…." They rounded their fourth corner and started up the street they'd met on. "Who's your *gaji* friend?" Mary inquired, as the Gangrel came into view. Mary put the bloodstained end of the handkerchief in her mouth and sucked on it.

"A little outlander maggot. Nice kid; no one's told her a word about the feud, or us. Don't you go telling her," he warned. He briefly considered telling Mary about the other Ravnos newcomer to her city but decided that was a bit of information he'd keep to himself, for the time being at least. "I'm independent, that's all I've said."

"Good man. They could wipe us out in a week now, if they only knew it."

Khalil cleared his throat. "They've been hit pretty hard themselves." He beckoned to his partner, and she joined them. "Ramona Tanner-childe, this is Mary—do you have a last name today, Mary?"

"Tinker. Mary Tinker. I'm afraid I call myself Madama Alexandria to the trade. I'm a psychic now—you've caught me in my working costume— it's a very good business nowadays, and legal, even. Come by my shop sometime. I'll tell your fortunes." The Queen of New York held a hand out toward the

Gangrel and nodded politely. "I believe I've met your sire, girl…briefly. How is he now?"

"Dead," Ramona told her darkly.

Mary smiled sweetly and gathered her skirts to move on. "Aren't we all?"

Sunday, 8 August 1999, 4:26 AM
A network of tunnels and caves
New York City, New York

Cassandra Washington strode briskly along the tiled hallway of her shared home. Unlike her peers, she carried herself erect, maintaining the perfect posture she had been trained (and beaten into) in life. She rubbed her eyes wearily. Time for bed, and not too soon for her. The chief had kept them busy these last nights, and so far they had nothing to show for it. No sign of Hesha, no more luck finding their few "reliable" Ravnos contacts…no luck finding the perverse little devils, either. And the war between the Camarilla and the Sabbat for "control' of so many cities kept getting in the way of more interesting projects. She had begun to feel less like a reporter and more like a switchboard operator: latest word from Buffalo, memo from Charleston, movements in Atlanta, situation in D.C., hasty phone call from Richmond, dateline Baltimore….

Cass passed her "office" and snorted at it. She skirted the edge of the drop shaft and listened for incoming friends or foes. She turned the corner, saw that the break room was empty, and turned off its lights. Looking up again, she had a shock: At the end of the hall, an unexpected apparition staggered out of *the* doorway. Her elder's hands were bright red, smeared with black ichor, clutching at the door jamb and a untidy fistful of white paper.

"Cassandra…" he rasped.

Concerned, she ran to him, switching off the overhead lights as she came. "What is it? I'll find Umberto for you—"

"No. *You* come with me." He tugged gently on her arm. Cass let him lead her through the old closet, out the crumbling back wall, and into the small cave that the old Nosferatu had taken, long ago, as his den. The floor had been smoothed out by the elder's helpers, first by chisels, later by jackhammers, but it was most polished along the paths made by its owner's methodical feet. Cass saw old, paper-labeled wooden boxes stacked beside the door; brass-and-oak file cabinets standing next to them; elderly metal versions of the same a little farther over; and shining, modern, fire-safe hanging files beyond those. On the right, generations of rough tables and desks lined the rock wall. The newest—antique, nonetheless—came at the end of the row, and the one chair in the room stood sentry beside it.

"Look." He cleared the desktop with one careless swipe of his long arms. Reams of paper overturned and fluttered to the earth. Cass rescued a stack, set it on the next desk, and reached for the mess on the floor. "Never mind that now," said her guide. She steadied the typewriter and the lamp in their corner, but otherwise obeyed.

He laid down his papers and set them in order with his stained hands—ink-stained, she realized with a release of tension, bright red and ribbon-black from his work, not gore. His gnarled claws tapped shakily at the typescript. "Follow me through this," grated the old Nosferatu.

"On the solstice, we handed an artifact, supposedly the Eye of Hazimel, to a Setite in Atlanta. We know this happened because Rolph, who made the transfer, survived the Sabbat attack." He picked up another sheet and pointed to the words. "In the battle we lost track of the Setite agent who took it, and when he resurfaced he no longer had it. Rolph confirms this, too.

"The Setite, Vegel, worked for the Setite Hesha, called Ruhadze. He never went to Atlanta. No agent he could possibly have sent could have taken the Eye from Vegel between Rolph's reports. We presume Hesha never had it, and we have lost track of him."

Cass nodded. "Yeah."

"We have someone looking in on the Sabbat. They show no signs of possessing such a thing, and they wouldn't hesitate to use it if they did. We have many more agents in the Camarilla. If they had it, we could assume that they would have used it by now, whatever its cost, to defend their cities. We have, therefore, lost track of the Eye altogether."

"Yeah. I suppose so."

"Tonight," said the elder, collapsing gently into his old leather chair, "I received a report from our man in Baltimore. The Gangrel Justicar Xaviar arrived at the Camarilla conference this evening. The outlanders met in the mountains to fight something besides the Sabbat. By Xaviar's account, the entire party was wiped out by one Kindred warrior wielding power over flesh, earth, stone, and molten rock. This warrior had one eye larger than the other, and the emanations from that eye were deadlier than all his other powers together."

Cassandra sagged against the desk. "Holy shit."

"Xaviar thought—said he thought—that the Gangrel had fought a waking Antediluvian. If he's right, it *could* mean the end of the world. The Final Nights."

Slowly, the younger Cainite considered the implications. "But it may be just the Eye of Hazimel."

"Just," said her elder. "Merely." He rose. "Come with me. I want you to see something." They shuffled together down the ruined hall, and he leaned heavily on her shoulder.

The shelter furnished bunks for forty. Thirteen beds were occupied. Rats played on four of them. Five held corpses in various states of decomposition and recovery. In three—behind stout, electrified steel bars—there were "healthy" bodies strapped and chained to the old iron bunks. Six mad eyes stared resentfully at the newcomers, and one man's lips began to move. His jaw did not: He was as well muzzled as his prudent cell-keepers could contrive. On the thirteenth mattress (a top bunk) a tiny figure, free and unhurt, looked down happily as the two monsters walked in. "'Lo, Cassie. 'Lo, Mister C."

"Hello, Mouse. How's your patient?"

The pink-and-gray, mangy bundle of fur uncurled himself, pushed away a rat, and sat up. "Same old, same old." Mouse flicked a switch on a yellow extension cord and light flooded the berth beneath him. He twisted and scrambled until he was hanging off the end of the footboard, then twitched the army-green blanket away from his bunkmate.

"Confirmation?" murmured the elder.

Cassandra moved closer. The thing on the rotten mattress seemed to have rotted away itself. Its flesh was the texture of dissolving styrofoam—bubbling, collapsing, melting, evaporating. Its bones were visible through the stuff, and looked like gray putty. Cass felt for the light. Less of it…at an angle…there.

She could see the surface of the carcass, gleaming faintly, familiarly. She hesitated, asking, "Not one of us? I mean, it didn't look like that before…. Whatever happened?"

"It could stand up," Mouse said. "It was wearing real shoes. I saw the footprints, too. It's got puddles for feet now."

"Not a Tzimisce victim?"

"Maybe," said the boy. "But I saw the other guy walk away. He was doing the same thing to a bit of stone as he went. Never heard of a Shimmy doing that."

Cass sat on the next bed. She propped her clawed feet up next to the corpse and fiddled with the light again. At length, she nodded. "It's the same kind of thing Ramona had on her cheek."

"You're sure?"

"No."

Her elder blinked his large, sad eyes once. He held his hand out for the light. He played the bright beam up and down the arms, the legs, the squashed pumpkin-shaped head, the flattened, blasted torso.

"Can't we just pick up this Khalil and bring him in? If this is an Eye wound, he should know. Mike and I could work on him. Get him to talk. I hate those methods, but if this thing is loose in the city…"

"You can't," said her companion, "just 'bring in' a Ravnos. If he talked, he'd lie. If we thought he was lying, he'd tell the truth and confuse us. If he got loose anywhere that was our space—trouble. If he got away, or the others heard about it, we'd be swarmed by them. As for 'working' on him, they aren't…" he stopped near what had been the sternum, "…manipulable in the sense you're used to.

Every clan has a weak spot they guard, or a goal they're after, or a secret you can find out and blackmail them with. But a Ravnos makes the most of his weakness, has no plans, and couldn't care less who knows what about him. They are the only really unpredictable people, because they are the only ones who make a habit of acting in their own worst interests. Knife?" Cass clapped one into his hand, and the elder sliced gingerly into the skin of the carcass. The torporous patient lay still. "Here we are." With a quick, swiveling cut, the blade popped a little red rock out of the mess. Another twist, and up came a brassy disc the size of a quarter. The old Nosferatu's fingers scrubbed the spongy tissue off it, and traced a few glyphs graven in the metal.

"Yes," he said, and laid the disc back on the body. "Yes. You can be sure, now. Good for you, girl. Mouse, move this man out of the ward and into better quarters—secure quarters. Cass, call off the hunt for Hesha Ruhadze. We've had him here all along."

Khalil tossed his cell phone anxiously from hand to hand. Obstinately, it refused to ring. He set it down for the fortieth time, in an attempt to calm himself. *Damn the Nosferatu, damn the Gangrel,* he thought. *And damn you!* he shouted in his head.

It may be possible to save the situation. Your rebellious incompetence has put my plans at risk. There will be a reckoning for that, I assure you. For the moment, however, let me instruct you in your part should the Nosferatu call—and the voice in Khalil's mind droned dryly on. The Ravnos reached out and picked up his phone again. The light was on, the power working. He pressed a button to hear the dial tone, then shut the connection down for fear the sewer rats would call just as he tested the line. Behind him, Ramona paced and fretted. Her mood pervaded the room: tense, feral, trapped, forced into inaction. It did Khalil no good; her soft footsteps kept time to the voice in his head. He caught himself throwing and catching the phone to the rhythm. Determined to ignore his master's instructions, he concentrated on breaking the pattern. He fixed his eyes on the matte black case and forced himself to juggle that one thing quick or fast or anything but…

"Sit down, for the gods' sake!" he shouted at his partner. The padding feet stopped just behind him, and he knew her hands were in reach of his neck. A long second went by. Then the old office chair creaked as she fell into it. Khalil sat back, set the phone down, and looked around. Elizabeth, still and quiet on the couch, was watching him. He returned her gaze with his best poker-face, and vowed to calm himself. It had only been two nights. What were two nights to the dead?

Tonight, you have a chance to—

Ramona began rocking in the old chair, and the mechanism squeaked in time to the voice's chant.

Suddenly, the phone rang.

Monday, 9 August 1999, 3:27 AM
A subterranean grotto
New York City, New York

"So what do you think?" Mike asked.

"I think," said Calebros, "that we will obviously not reveal anything about Hesha." Neither Nosferatu suggested trading false information. For brokers of secrets, such was the kiss of death.

"Hunting grounds? Intercession with the prince?"

"Possible," Calebros said, as he scratched his misshapen head. "But I'm not convinced that this Khalil—even if he does possess the knowledge—is the only source. How to heal injuries caused by the Eye of Hazimel—that's the kind of detail that Hesha might well know. He's been looking for the Eye for a few centuries, I believe."

"If he ever comes out of torpor…"

Calebros nodded. "If he ever comes out of torpor."

"Are we even certain that he actually *is* in torpor? He looked…worse than that."

"Certain? Nothing is certain. Ever."

9 August 1999

re: Khalil Ravana (see biographical information)

K.R. offered knowledge of cure for wounds caused by Eye of Hazimel in exchange for: 1) hunting grounds/ concessions from the prince; 2) detailed information about Hesha Ruhadze, his holdings/operations/etc.

Credibility: K.R. could have access to that information (Hazimel reportedly was a Ravnos elder), but reports suggest him to be unstable.

Hesha might possess the same information———or he might not recover without it.

Delay and explore other avenues of information. Deal with K.R. as last resort.

Tuesday, 10 August 1999, 2:16 AM
The Nawab of Bengal
Manhattan, New York

Khalil cursed aloud. It wasn't supposed to work like this. That other Ravnos and his family were supposed to be helping *him*. Not vice versa.

An hour earlier he'd nearly shaken the neighborhood, so seismic was his reaction to his phone actually, *finally* ringing. The sewer rats were back at last with some information, he had thought. But no, it was Sarat the cab driver on the phone. The man's Bengali was rapid and nearly incomprehensible with fright.

"My friend, please, terrible things have happened! Our elder brother is gone from us, and we are lost without his protection. Please, what do we do?"

"Gone? What do you mean, *gone?*"

"They came and broke down our door and seized him—many, many demons—and beat our brother and tore at his flesh, and now he does not speak to us. Oh, he cannot be dead, he promised he would not leave us here in this foreign land! The demons screamed and danced on Elder Brother's flesh, and my cousin Prasad is near his own death, and I do not know what I must do. We are your family now, help us, please...."

Demons? Ghose in torpor? Khalil could not at the moment imagine what had taken place, but instinct made him leap at the possibilities he could hear in the mortal's abject pleadings.

Rash fool, "demons" are likely the Sabbat. You do not need these humans, not if you listen to me as you should. Nor do you need that puling idiot Ghose. Do not consider this for another moment. Send the mortal away.

But Khalil ignored the words. Having reassured Sarat, he hurried to the Nawab of Bengal. Ramona he left behind with Liz. She would only get in the way of his plan.

Khalil stepped to the door. Through its window, he could see that the restaurant itself was put away neatly, with chairs upside down on the tables and no messes in sight. Whoever had attacked the Mukherjees, they had apparently saved their wrath for the upper living areas.

They had also left the front door open, Khalil discovered. He entered and cautiously made his way through the immaculate dining area and kitchen. The back stairs were made of thick boards, so they didn't squeak or complain, but they were shallow and narrow, wedged into a tiny portion of the structure. *Made for Americans before they got so fat*, thought Khalil. *Perfect for a skinny gutter boy like me*. He quietly mounted the stairs and worked his way up.

After two short flights, he passed a landing and went higher. Two more flights and the stairs terminated. Here at last was evidence of an assault—the door at the top was savagely splintered, and had been ripped bodily from its hinges. Although the wrecked slab of wood had been propped up to block the doorway once more, Khalil could hear a commotion beyond. He knocked once, gently, and the gabbling voices inside hushed instantly. Sarat's terrified face peered around the door through a gap at about knee height. "My friend, is it you?"

Khalil smiled pityingly. "Of course it is me. Demons don't knock, now do they?"

With some grunting and scraping, the door was shifted from the inside, and Khalil got his first view of the damage. It was certainly impressive. The cheap wooden furniture of the apartment had been matchsticked. Blood was splattered across the far wall like a monochrome Jackson Pollock. A woman peered, dark eyes wide, from a back bedroom, vainly trying to keep behind her the young boy who had first let Khalil into the restaurant. Another woman crouched on the floor, kneeling heedlessly in a pool of blood that spread across the bare, polished floorboards. Wailing and beseeching, she was striving to bandage a dreadful gash that ripped Prasad Mukherjee's abdomen raggedly from groin to sternum. The torn sheet she held was already soaked through with red. A piece of what looked to be the same sheet was wound around Sarat's thigh, and that, too, was splotched with blood.

Blood…Khalil snuffed the air with unexpected hunger. Mortal blood, of course, from the wounds inflicted on Sarat and his cousin. But even better, *old* blood, Ghose's blood, beckoned to him, singing along his nerves. Sternly, he brought himself under control. He must not frighten these people. Not yet, at any rate. He forced himself to speak gently.

"Sarat, my friend, but this is terrible that you should be hurt! Where is Ghose?"

"In there. Oh, Khalil, he said to us often that he could never die, but I fear what the demons have done to him. Quick, please help…" Sarat trailed off, his face pale with anxiety and fear, gesturing toward another door. With two swift steps, Khalil reached the door and pulled it open.

The general carnage had not reached this room. Ghose lay curled up on a woven rug which had apparently been used by Sarat or one of the women to drag the body in here. It would not have been very difficult even for the boy, in truth—that smashed and shriveled husk could not have weighed more than a large basket of laundry. Khalil bent over his clansman and prodded him gingerly, but he knew already what he would find.

"He is not dead, friend Khalil? No breath, no heart, he is cold, but you know how those lie—he said he was immortal and needed not such things. But he does not speak or move, and I am terribly afraid for us all."

The wheels of the Ravnos's mind spun as he crafted what to say. Obviously Ghose had not enlightened his family as to some of the peculiarities of vampiric existence—not to mention exaggerating its durability. "No, Sarat, your elder brother is not dead. But grave harm has been done to him, and the demons tried him sorely, body and spirit. He…sleeps. Now you and your family must protect him as he has protected you for so long, until he can regain his warrior's soul. Tell me, where did Ghose rest during the daylight hours? We must hide him away from the demons while he is weakened."

Sarat slid down the wall and slumped to the floor in exhaustion and relief. "There is a trapdoor underneath the bed," he said. "Down there."

Khalil scooted the foot of the cast-iron bedstead to one side. Sure enough, there was a trapdoor that opened onto a tidy little coffin-shaped space between the floors. Misliking the vacant glare of the torpored vampire's eyes, he folded the rug over the shrunken carcass before shifting the entire bundle into the hole and restoring the appearance of the room. Good enough for the moment. "There. He will be fine for a while, you must not worry. I will watch over him and your family both. Come, I should tend to you and your cousin. Neither of *you* are immortal, after all."

Here came a tricky bit. He was relying on Ghose's having kept the Mukherjees in ignorance of other things besides the nature of torpor. If he could convince Sarat and Prasad to take some of his own blood, it would certainly heal their wounds—without it, Prasad at least looked likely to die. No need to explain the other little side effects of ghouling to them right now.

Khalil raised the trembling mortal by the arm, smiling reassuringly, and led him limping back to the front room. Yes, they'd all have a new elder brother now.

Khalil lay listlessly in an old armchair, eyes closed against the droning, petulant complaints of his master. Sometimes they stopped...the young Ravnos opened his eyes with a little more hope...and then the tongue, sharpened by thousands of years of inactivity, began whittling on him again.

Ramona was gone; she had stormed out early Tuesday, unable to stay still any longer. She had tried to drag her partner along and take him out of the dark, queer mood that had come over him—but she hadn't tried very hard. She hadn't come back yet, either. *Maybe she's dead*, Khalil thought, without caring very much. *Maybe Mary caught her and ate her. Maybe Mary will catch and eat me*. It seemed like a fine idea, on the whole. Mary had power, now. Real power. She didn't have an evil old bastard looking over her shoulder all the time and shouting in her head. She probably had enough strong blood in her that the old demon *couldn't* crawl into her mind. Gods, what he would give for that freedom again....

A faint papery noise caught his attention. His lackluster eyes drifted to where his prisoner sat calmly on the sofa, poring over her books and papers. She turned a page—that was the sound. Khalil slumped back into his misery. Through sheer inertia, he kept watching her, and a new train of thought began, slowly, to move.

Hesha Ruhadze, he mused, *is a very powerful snake. I was dirt under his feet in Calcutta. I was nearly nothing to* him, like I'm fucking nothing to the old bastard. And what's the real difference between us? I'm a smart guy. I've been around. But he's an elder, or the closest thing to it, and I've got eight or nine ancestors between me and Ravana, let alone the King of Demons or Caine or whothehell.

Hesha will always have the upper hand because his blood is thicker than mine. Khalil stood up, and his dull gaze remained fixed on Elizabeth. Elizabeth…one generation younger than Hesha. Devil knew how many generations older than Khalil, no matter how few nights she had actually seen. Slowly he crept down the room toward her, unconsciously opening his mouth, licking his lips, sliding his body against the sofa as he went. He hopped up, catlike, and took a cross-legged perch on the narrow arm of the couch.

The Ravnos stared down at the Setite like a vulture. He considered her for the first time as a stepping stone, rather than a bargaining chip. He liked the idea. He thought of finding Hesha with his own teeth still stained from the Setite's childe. He realized suddenly that his mouth was open, nearly drooling. He snapped it shut.

You will not take her blood, rebellious whelp. I forbid you.

Go away! You may be an elder, but you are still stuck in the mud of Calcutta—I will not let you make me your slave any longer! I am a free Rom, and do as I please!

After a moment, Elizabeth turned her head and regarded him coolly. Khalil bit his tongue, bothered by the fact that she could ignore him even while he thought about destroying her…that she was calm while he hungered after her blood. She didn't fear him—not really. His hands made fists. The woman's eyes dropped, took notice of his tightened knuckles, then flicked back to his face. Khalil's pointed fingernails popped into the upholstery. She raised an eyebrow.

"Damn you, bitch. Say something," he hissed.

Elizabeth's face went blank.

"Why don't you say anything to me? Plead for your freedom. Ask me to let you go. Ask me what I plan to do with you."

And she said nothing.

He struck her.

"Say something!"

He hit her again.

"Beg me for mercy. Beg."

Khalil hit her hard enough to break a mortal jaw. The sparks rose in her eyes, but she held her head high, and was mute.

He bent his fingers back and forced his claws—inch-long, dirty, dark claws—out of their sheaths six inches from her eyes. He set one hand at her throat, the other on her face. "*Beg* for mercy."

Elizabeth looked up at him without emotion. "Do you have any?"

You have neither mercy nor wisdom, slave.

And Elizabeth's eyes finally widened, as Khalil began to thrash in pain, hurling himself away from the couch and the sudden, roaring fire in his mind.

There were several hours of quiet after that, before the next explosion occurred.

Khalil paced, rubbing his aching head, glaring at his prisoner, sullenly trying to ignore the voice—gods, he wished he were mad, so there might be *voices* and some variety—heard the thing in Calcutta roar:

LISTEN TO ME!

Khalil felt his guts leap up around his own heart to strangle it. He screamed. He felt the Setite watching him in this fresh humiliation, and didn't care—he ran for the wall, trapped like a rat, and beat his skull against it.

"*No more!*" Khalil yelled and scraped his hands on the rough bricks. The real pain in his palms, his head, his knuckles—drove out, barely, the torture in his belly (*Not real,* he swore desperately, *not real, notrealnotrealnotreal!*). In his fury and fear, the mantra slipped out his mouth and into the room.

"What isn't real?" Elizabeth asked sharply.

This *is* real. Khalil screamed and staggered to the kitchen island. Clutching at the countertop, he stared at his own fists, cutting deep furrows in the formica. His eyes snapped up to meet his prisoner's. She was standing, reaching out to him as far as the chains would let her. Sympathy—from her? In a flash, he felt he understood. She was afraid. She had been afraid all along. She concealed the fear from him the way he hid his master's domination from her…and what good did it do either of them? Her weak, soft heart betrayed her. His weak will betrayed him. *I am real,* shrieked the presence in his head, and Khalil allowed the storm of that voice to howl forth into the room, for his ears, for the Setite's ears, for the rats and mice and roaches. "I WILL DESTROY YOU IF YOU CONTINUE TO DISOBEY ME!"

"Good God," whispered Elizabeth. "Who—"

"SULLEN WRETCH!"

That no windows broke seemed a miracle. The booming noise went on making words, but nothing vibrated to their timbre.

"HOW DARE YOU?" Khalil fell to the floor, the hateful words spewing from his mouth, seeming as though they must wrench his body apart with their violence. "SHE MUST NOT HEAR ME! THE SNAKES MUST NOT KNOW OF ME—YOU WILL HAVE US ALL IN THE FIRE! I FEEL YOUR MIND, BASTARD SPAWN, I FEEL YOU FIGHTING ME." With slow, heavy, painful movements, Khalil crept toward Elizabeth. Though she could not comprehend what was happening, still she helped him onto the couch and grasped his shoulders in an attempt to still his contortions. "IS THIS YOUR IDEA OF COURAGE—YOUR IDEA OF DEFIANCE? HOW LOW YOU ARE," the voice rolled on, "YOU DOG, YOU FLEA, YOU WORM!" And the gypsy writhed and whimpered like a wounded animal. The cruel voice changed to a language Liz did not know.

"Khalil? Khalil!" The Setite clapped her hands over the *shilmulo*'s ears, but he shook her off. She tried, without any real idea in mind, to run to her workshop—the leg irons jerked her back. Falling, her shoulder hit the glass-topped table and knocked it over. Papers and books tumbled around her. The remote control must have crashed to the floor as well—suddenly, soft music filled in around them. She groped to turn the sound off, but stopped at the change in her jailer. His eyes had opened, just a little. She turned up the volume, and Khalil nodded, desperately. He sprang up and yanked the controller out of her hand. Violins and vocals flooded the room. The strange language was (very nearly) covered by the sound.

"Something to see," demanded Khalil, hacking and gasping.

Elizabeth caught up a deck of cards from the scattered amusements Ramona had provided her. She fumbled the rubber band off onto her wrist and turned over the top card—

"Knave of diamonds," Khalil shouted.

"Four of spades," Liz yelled back. The second card—

"Knave of diamonds!"

"Ten of clubs."

"Knave of diamonds."

"Queen of spades."

It went on and on. Elizabeth shuffled and cut again and again, and Khalil went on seeing the wrong card fifty-three times out of fifty-four. The music and (when they thought of it) the television blared out around them, but for the longest time it seemed to make no difference. Khalil crumpled at the end of one run, wracked with phantom pains, but Elizabeth urged him on. The effort to see the real card behind the false one…that took more of his mind off the punishments of his master…straining to hear or lip-read from Elizabeth…another layer between his senses and the lie. He worked like the devil to ignore the pain inside (*Not real*, he reminded himself over and over) and the voice (real, but less real, when he truly concentrated, than the news anchor, or the singer, or the Setite's quick answers). At last he had no thought left over for anything but the glossy red and black pips in front of him.

"Knave of diamonds."

"No."

"Knave of…" It *was* a court card—it was a…king— "King of clubs?" he mouthed at Elizabeth. The next card was stubbornly the jeweled jack again, but he knew now that he could turn the trick. In another hour, he had his own eyes under control. He turned off the television, and found that the rant had subsided some time before. He pressed the switch for the stereo, and realized his body only hurt him where the wall and the bricks had left their marks.

"Now, you old tyrant," he said to the empty air. *Are you entirely finished?*

"Yes. And so are you."

"Death to tyrants," murmured Elizabeth, curled up once more on her couch, watching the one-sided conversation.

What was the purpose of this little game?

"I am *not* your slave. Treat me with some respect, and I might keep working for you. As a free Rom. If you give *me* what *I* want while I get you what you want."

What have you ever done to earn my respect, you vain little dung beetle? said the voice. *I have lost patience with your obduracy. Perhaps I should leave you to your own pitiful devices.*

Khalil blinked. He licked his lips. He walked over to the library and ran his hand along the book spines.

"There's a copy of the Declaration of Independence in the dictionary," Elizabeth suggested brightly. "Emancipation Proclamation, too."

The Ravnos shot a suspicious glance at her. She'd helped him. And now she had something to hold over him. She might be sweet enough tonight, but she was a Setite and they used everything, eventually. Liz wouldn't be able to stop herself from twisting the secret round him—and she was Hesha's childe and thrall. She *would* tell him. Now there was no way he could use her to track Hesha, allow the two of them to come together, unless he was sure of killing one "accidentally" as they met. Should he go ahead and drink her blood now? No, she could be useful just in case the elder asshole decided not to lie down for it again. Who knew how strong his blood would have to be to drive out the monster? Besides, the voice in his head probably *wanted* him to kill her now, now that she knew of his presence. He didn't want to give it the satisfaction. *Damn*.

And the Nosferatu hadn't called back. That door was closed. He found what he was looking for and snatched it up: a phone book. *I'll find that snake my own way.* He flipped through the Yellow Pages, hunting for fortune-tellers. Mary would be able to give him the dirt on every turf war and snitch in the city. If she had the Sight (never likely but always possible for a *shilmulo*) she might put her finger on Hesha from where she sat.

The book referred him to "Psychics and Mediums," and he let it drop to the floor as he took up the M-Z. He found Madama Alexandria in a quarter-page display ad, offering everything from "Astrology" to "Yi Ching Readings." Her address, her number, her website were all done up in black on a sky-blue background, and the list of services ran three columns on green below. Between them was printed a bright red sixteen-spoked wheel. Khalil chuckled. Mary had dodged the anti-gypsy fortune-telling laws throughout the British Empire for decades. Now she could bring in the *gaje* with an ad designed on the Rom flag. He'd no idea she'd become such an internationalist....

Khalil ripped out the page and set the volume back on its shelf. He crouched to pick up A-L, put it up. He saw that the other book had flopped open amid the nightclubs: "Gala Knights Exotic Dance Club" and "Gary's Grill" and "Gehenna."

Gehenna. Khalil looked again. In huge but emaciated capital letters: the end of the world, the rising of the Antediluvians, the name of a bar. *Amusing.* Khalil read more. "Leave the Herd Behind." "No Cams or Videotaping Permitted." The Ravnos blinked; that was an odd way to put that, and an odd thing to waste space on in the phone book. "Live Adult Entertainment" and "Free Buffet with Cover" were set so close together and so raggedly that it was hard to say where one stopped and the other started; the two lines could nearly be read "Live Adult Free Buffet" and "Entertainment with Cover." "Open Sunset to Sunrise 7 Nites a Week." Khalil gaped. Surely, no one could be this blatant…. "Club 666—Party with DJ The Beast Every Friday." He looked at the number under the ad. 718-722-2288. He picked up his portable phone, frowning, and worked the word out. 718-SABBATT.

"Holy shit," said Khalil, and began laughing out loud. "Holy…" It was hilarious. It was so ungodly obvious. It was so stupid; it was brilliant…the Sabbat, slapping the Camarilla prince in the face with their presence, setting up a contact point without all the tiresome Elysia and rules and…he'd go tonight, to see if it were true. It couldn't be true. But it had—

The bolts on the door began grinding open. Khalil's whoops and cackles died abruptly.

Ramona slipped in, filthy with dirt and dust. She started doing up the locks again, throwing a glance toward her partner. "Any news?" she asked, in a voice that expected none.

"Yes," Khalil yelped wildly. "No!" He grinned from ear to ear. "No, the Nosferatu have not called to set up another meet; yes, I have news. We're going out. We're going to see the competition and start a little game."

Gehenna was alarmingly easy to enter. Khalil, as confidently as possible, led Ramona up a short flight of steps to a loading dock, past a tight knot of smokers, and into a crushing crowd. No one challenged them. They filtered through the dancers and the lurkers and the drunks and came to rest in the calmer eddy caused by a six-foot-high amplifier.

"Why d'we always got to meet people in fucking bars?" Ramona shrieked into his ear.

"What else is open all night—" the Gangrel shook her head, and Khalil bellowed it again, louder, "and full of freaks anyway? Who the hell's going to notice a few corpses in this place?" And he looked around at "this place."

Khalil's feet felt the music through the concrete floor; his ears suffered. The décor ran to metal—corrugated aluminum roofing sheets, inch-thick distressed steel tables, and wrought-iron things that looked more like medieval torture devices than chairs. All of it drove the sound back into the room. The echoes made the music impossible to follow; only the beat survived the acoustics. He looked toward the ceiling, and found other levels of flooring blocking his view. He pulled Ramona toward a spiral staircase and fought the swarm to go up.

Most of the patrons wore black—a different black, he realized, than the kind that waited outside Sexton's Dirty Secret. That was mourning black, raven black, Hamlet black, crêpe black—deliberate and romantic, or desperate and nihilistic. These people dressed in burnt black, iron black, tar black, coal black, dead black—just black.

The second level—one of them—lofts and platforms seemed welded and bolted to the old building's steel framework almost at random—was a trifle quieter. From here they could look down on the mass of writhing bodies in the pit, moshing...or fighting.... Khalil swore under his breath as he caught sight of blood and teeth in the dance below. A body fell under the crowd, and half a dozen people went down after it. They *might* have been friends of the broken boy, trying to rescue him. A girl, undeniably mortal and screaming at the top of her lungs in real panic, tried to run for the door. Another woman blocked her way. Other guests surged in and Khalil lost sight of the little drama. Obviously, anyone who did notice things here was taken care of before they left. The *shilmulo*, hardened as he was, shivered. He stepped away from the railing and unconsciously moved closer to Ramona. Instinctively shoulder to shoulder, Ravnos and Gangrel continued up the stairs.

On the third level, Khalil caught sight of a few black-curtained, enclosed rooms. After a moment's hesitation he made for the largest. The inner door was guarded, not by a large and burly bouncer, but by a short, thin, teenaged girl. Her dead glance flickered once over Khalil and twice over Ramona, then focused again on the distance. "Enter."

"Thanks, babe." Khalil forced himself to sound more confident than he felt.

Inside the glass walls and black canvas drapes it was whisper-quiet. Small groups of men, women, and children sat around on couches, at tables, and in booths.

Every eye in the room turned on the newcomers. Every eye in the room looked away—not all at once, not individually as interest waned—as each little band dropped back to its own business as a whole entity.

Khalil felt ice prickle down the back of his neck and moved forward, smiling a little cruelly to cover his repulsion. Ramona nearly trod on his heels, she was so close, and he found he didn't mind at all. She was almost comforting.

The room hummed back into life. People stood, sat, moved, drifted into other conversations. A table by the wall filled in; stools from a counter disappeared to seat larger parties. By apparent chance, a comfortable couple of loveseats opened up near the center. The *shilmulo* checked the layout and swore under his breath. That was the only place left to sit; the Sabbat had forced a card on him as neatly as any conjuror.

Ramona and Khalil walked softly to the two small couches. They sat apart automatically, giving up the physical proximity of their allegiance for the ability to see in both directions. This left an empty spot beside each of them; the Ravnos watched his companion arrange herself so that there really was no possibility of anyone sitting next to her. He placed his own bag down and lounged a bit. That would do for his own vacancy.

And now what? He wondered. This venture seemed less like a bright one every moment. The scene on his right kept shifting, and he found it difficult to track faces and movements; another surprise could come out of that deck at any moment. On his left, there was a sprawling mess of people sitting around a table. He labeled them in his mind...one uncaring shark, one slinking cat, one stoic turtle, one chattering monkey, one strutting cock, and one pathetic little dog. Their body language alone was enough to unnerve the *shilmulo*. The animals touched each other too much; hands, legs, words, looks, and mouths intertwined about the booth. The dog and cat stroked the shark and he settled down farther amongst them. The rooster preened and let the monkey put her fingers on his face and through his hair. Khalil found himself staring, and the young rooster, birdlike, fixed a beady eye back upon him.

"What the fuck do you want?" demanded the man from where he sat. The monkey's hands flicked back sharply. Suddenly the whole band was watching Khalil.

The Ravnos kept his gaze on the proud one; fighting cocks, he reminded himself, were still chicken...the louder the crow, the weaker the punch...just don't look at the shark....

"Not you," sneered Khalil. He sized the man up, visibly, and watched him take offense, take another look, and take a step back from the fight. The Ravnos smiled and licked his lips. "Definitely not you," he said. "I need to talk to someone...important."

The rooster lunged forward. The dog shook himself and followed to keep from being left behind. The shark was ready...but settled lazily back. The cat touched the monkey with her toe, and the monkey took the fighting pair by the shoulders and whispered to them. The entire table looked across the way, past Khalil, and blinked in respectful satisfaction.

The perfect stereotype of a colonial aristocrat peered down his long nose at the intruders, and the gypsy boy in Khalil instantly hackled. "Well?" the narrow-faced man asked in an infinitely tired voice. "What is it that you *do* you want? You may speak to me."

"You the top man here?" Khalil shot out, in deliberate disbelief.

"I am," answered the aristocrat, guardedly. He studied them as though they were pinned insects in a museum exhibit.

Khalil grinned widely. "Do you mind if I just check that?" He pulled a small, round plastic mirror out of his bag and whipped it under the man's hand. The thin, gray skin turned a bit purple with rage…but it was also reflected in the mirror. Khalil shook his head and tsk'ed. "No. Don't think so."

A woman appeared out of the crowd beside him and laughed like wind-chimes. She wore a platinum-colored jumpsuit over a slender, pale body. Her bones were beautiful; her hair and eyes were jet-black and striking. "Sit down, Jean-Paul," she suggested pleasantly. "How is this man to know how highly we hold you in our counsels?" She plucked the mirror from Khalil's hand, and her shining white nails had no reflection. "Relax, all of you," she insisted, smiling at the crowd around her, the animals, Jean-Paul, and the two intruders—now unmistakably her guests.

"Now," said the silvery woman, edging her way onto Khalil's couch. "I'm Yve. This is Jean-Paul." Jean-Paul took up a standing post at one end of Ramona's seat. "You look like a man with a purpose. What did you come here for?"

"I have a few things worth trading; I have a few things I want. I'd like to make a deal."

"I see." Yve crossed her long legs and regarded him curiously. "What kind of 'things' do you bring to my table?"

"I have knowledge of," Khalil paused significantly, "the Eye of Hazimel, that object of dreadful fame. I can tell you how to heal the wounds it causes."

Yve's shadow-black eyes widened slightly, but her voice remained nonchalant. "What makes you think we don't already know all we need to know about this Eye? Tell me more, if you please."

"I can offer a means of tracking the Eye." *It's not transferable*, he thought, *but this darling doesn't need to know that.* "Information on how to use it, when you have it, and how to shut it down when you don't need it anymore." He went on, carried away by the attentive expression of his companion. "Missing pieces from the legends about it. The true story of its origin. The tale of what it has done since coming to America." Khalil smugly folded his arms. If push came to shove, he could even deliver on a little of what he promised.

"Why, if you have all that, don't you..." Yve searched for words, "track down the infamous Eye yourself?" She seemed genuinely interested, moving closer to him.

Khalil grinned. Quite a compliment, being asked that seriously by one who knew. "Healthy respect for my own skin," he answered with a casual shrug. "Besides, you folks are the ones with a beef against the old-timers, if you know what I mean. Some night you're going to go after them. The Eye, assuming you have somebody tougher than J.P. to hold on to it..." Khalil glanced skeptically at the not-amused Jean-Paul, "could be a powerful weapon. And where there's one eye, there's bound to be another. Knowing how to heal the wounds could come in handy." Khalil stroked his mustache proudly. "Also—"

"There is more?"

"I get around, Yve. I see things."

"So what else have you seen?" Her shoulder grazed his.

"What can I expect in return?" He gazed down at her.

"What do you want?" And Yve's flirting, long-lashed eyes promised a great deal.

"Money, to begin with."

"Well, that's cheap enough." She winked. "Money for our new friend, Jean-Paul."

The aristocrat reached into a pocket of his long black coat and fetched forth a thick, old-fashioned wallet. He glanced inside and abstracted the entire contents—nearly an inch of hundred-dollar bills—and set them gracefully on the table before Khalil.

He took them without counting, and kept his eyes on his hostess. "Camarilla blood."

"Oh, I like that. For magic or for…"

"For the other. American princes spawn childer like rabbits, don't they?"

"Yes, indeed. Particularly in New York. We could mark down a pretty young cony for you quite easily. Michaela simply can't keep her hands off the old money here, and so few of them can fight. Catching one once we've named her will be your problem, of course." She laughed again in her bell-like way. "That's almost a favor *to* us, not *from* us, my dear Khalil. Ask for something difficult."

"Security while I'm staying in New York."

Her eyebrows lifted. "That *is* harder to arrange. I don't care for it myself…." She paused thoughtfully. "We might be able to fix something up. Escorts through our territory, a fairly safe haven for your days.

It would be far less complicated, of course, if you were one of us." Her inflection made a question and an invitation out of the statement. Before Khalil could reply, she shook her head, dismissing the matter. "Just think about it. There are…considerable benefits, you know."

Ramona cleared her throat loudly and shattered the mood. Khalil caught a glare from her, and brought himself back to business. Not quite what the Gangrel was waiting for, but these were the people to get it for him.

"I want Hesha Ruhadze."

Yve's eyebrow lifted again. Jean-Paul merely seemed lost. "Ruhadze?" he repeated carefully. "Ah." He nodded. "Hesha abn Yusuf."

It was Khalil's turn to look blank. Yve glanced from one man to the other and translated. "Black, bald, arrogant Setite. He toured Europe a great deal last century. How do you want him?"

"Battered, burnt, staked, and left for the sun."

"Head on a silver platter?"

"If that's easier for you."

"Fierce, aren't we?"

Khalil thought of Hesha's black hand staking him down as he was about to take his prey, of Hesha's cultured voice lecturing him, of the humiliating wait in Chicago for men that never came, the fact that had Hesha not hunted the Eye to Calcutta, the voice would not have called Khalil into service. The snake should not be allowed to live.

"Call it that," he uttered shortly. He shot a warning glance at Ramona, who showed signs of speaking. "Can you do it?"

"I would need to consult with my partners; this Setite has a certain...reputation. And there is a very strong temple here—" She shrugged. "We can kill anyone. It's a matter, more, of whether what you offer is worth the risk of allying the snakes with the Camarilla. Would you," she said, rising, "give us just a moment?"

Ramona shifted nervously, glaring a warning at Khalil, and he felt a little fear of his own creep up beside him. Still hearty with confidence, he held up an arresting hand.

"I can do better than that. Here, take my number—call me back when you know what we can do for each other, and when." He stood up. "My friend here has another appointment tonight, and I'd hate to have her miss it."

Yve took his handwritten card and held her guest's glance a moment. She seemed disappointed, and the Ravnos was uncertain whether to be flattered or frightened. "We'll call. I'll call. Either way we decide. I do think we'll be able to help you."

Khalil scouted the way out. It was clear, and Ramona was already making for the door. *No goodbyes*, he thought, and followed her example.

Outside, on the walk home, Khalil's partner grabbed him by the sleeve and searched his face. Her own darkened. "You want them to snuff Hesha. You told *me* we were just goin' to find this guy. And you told Liz you're gonna bring her back to her boyfriend. What the hell's goin' on?"

Khalil had known this was coming; he'd had the whole way down from the Sabbat's nest to come up with an answer Ramona would accept. He detached her claws from his clothes and replied patiently.

"Hesha bound Liz to him with his blood. She only thinks she loves him. If we kill him, we free her, all right? What do you know about blood bonds, hmm? Don't you know that she's nothing but a *slave* to him? He was the one who chained her up and left her for the sun—and she still couldn't help crawling back to kiss his feet if we let her go now. Do you think I *like* keeping her locked up like that?" A little thrill ran through him—actually, he rather did....

"I'm not going to use her to track Hesha, not knowing what he did to her. But you can't let her know what we're doing for her, or the blood bond would probably drive her insane trying to stop us. And we can't unlock her, or she'll run right to him."

Ramona said nothing, but the tension lifted. Khalil licked his lips and smirked slightly into the darkness.

Jean-Paul, livid, turned on his pack-mate. "He's a Ravnos, isn't he?"

"Oh, Jean...how can you possibly tell?"

"I *know*. Damn gypsy mongrel."

"You're right, of course. But how reactionary of you."

He quivered with rage. "Why didn't you give the word? Stake him, question him...turn him over to the—" he made a flat, palm-up gesture as meaningful as a finger across the throat.

"Jean-Paul, you know better. Touch a Ravnos without precautions and every gypsy leech on the continent will camp on your doorstep and haunt you."

"In case you haven't noticed, there aren't too many of them around these nights. One of our packs was boasting about pulping some old gypsy in his haven the other night." Jean-Paul raised his open palms. "I don't see any repercussions."

"What do you think *this* might be?"

"I just can't imagine a trap, with that loser involved. Nobody that dresses that badly could be dangerous."

"Still…"

"But why in hell did you bargain with that trash? Yve, it demeans you even to speak with him." His long, pale hands reached out, not quite caressing her shoulder.

The Lasombra watched her companion run down. "And you a blueblood, too. Where were you when the *intrigants* were busy in your chateau? Jean-Paul, haven't you ever heard of giving a man more rope? Letting the accused convict himself? If you let a man under pressure talk long enough he *will* tell you more about himself than he intends to. Quiet yourself."

She left him for a moment to have words with the youngsters at the booth beside them, the ones who had had first contact with her new problem. They listened eagerly and slipped out of the quiet room together. Then she returned, and after a pause called to him.

"Jean."

"Yes?" Sullenly.

"Speak to the archbishop for me. Tell him about our visitor—tell him what Khalil said about the Eye of Hazimel, and ask him if there is such a thing." Jean-Paul stared at her in disbelief, then stalked away to do her bidding.

And Yve, sitting alone, stared thoughtfully into the mirror Khalil had left behind him.

Friday, 13 August 1999, 8:02 PM
Red Hook, Brooklyn
New York City, New York

Khalil lay, still drowsy, on Elizabeth's bed. He held his wallet in both hands, counting the crisp, fresh American dollars by touch. A shrill tone filled his ears—he reached for the cell phone and grasped for consciousness.

"Hello," he mumbled. A dull tone—the dial tone—answered him back. The shrill note sang again. Another phone? Who had another phone? Ramona hadn't slept here…Ramona didn't keep a phone…. A fourth ring, a click, and then the message of the answering machine droned until the beep.

"Lizzie? Are you there? This is Amy—Amy Rutherford. Antonio tried to make a delivery to the apartment this morning, and he couldn't get in; he says there seemed to be another bolt on the door? And that the windows have been painted black. Aunt Agnes doesn't know yet, but she will soon, and I need something to tell her and…Mother. Lizzie? Pick up? Are you in trouble? Do you need help? Call me!" Frustrated silence filled the gap. "Anyone! Where is Elizabeth Dimitros? Why have you painted the windows? Why is the door bolted? You are trespassing on private property! Pick up the phone or I *will* call the police." Khalil walked bleary-eyed out of the curtained room and saw Elizabeth, chained by the wrong end of the sofa, desperately straining against the shackles to reach the phone. The voice went on, more softly:

"Liz. Hesha's service doesn't answer; I can't get past his secretary's secretary. What's going on? Did the terrorists find you both? Are you all right? Some-one please answer this message and—" The tape cut her off in midsentence.

"Friend of yours, Lizzie?"

The Setite swung a guarded glance his way. If she resented him, if she were worried, it didn't show on the surface. He put on an inquisitive, charming, damnable expression to fence with. Khalil felt very arch, very superior this evening. It had something to do with the wad of currency in his hip pocket. He'd never had an opportunity to really test the limits of his greed before. How nice finally to find something boundless for which he had talent. This phone call—it gave him ideas, as well.

He pressed PLAY and listened to the pathetic mortal voice plead again. "Rutherford—Rutherford House is where you work, isn't it? Before you died, of course." He stepped up to her studio and poked at the antiques laid out on the workbench. "Is this real silver?" he asked, holding up a tray. "Looks valuable."

"To a collector…" the Setite admitted carefully.

Khalil crossed to the computer desk and file draw-ers. He plopped down in front of the stacks and rummaged through the mess he'd made of them since moving in. There had been a folder marked *Insurance*…there it was. He opened it and traced a dirty-nailed finger down a list of appraisals and pre-miums. "Looks like a lot of money goes through Ye Olde House of Rutherford. This Amy. She's a friend of yours?"

"She's…just my boss."

"Sounds awfully fond of you."

"Probably more concerned about the apartment,"

Liz parried.

"And that's why your desk is full of cards and letters signed, 'Love, Amy'."

Elizabeth said nothing.

"Well, you'll get to see her soon enough. We're going to pay the Rutherfords a visit, you and I. One night before long."

The Setite looked up, startled. "Why?"

"When we're there, you're going to point things out to me. Expensive things."

"I won't help you."

"Oh, yes you will. I'm a terrorist. Amy said so. Terrorists kill people, if people don't do what they want...and you *know* I kill people." He threw down the files and sprang over to where she had to sit. "So you'll do what I say, and you'll be goddamn nice about it. You'll help me get in and get out. You'll tell me all about the security systems, and you'll remember every single fucking detail. You'll use that forked tongue of yours to tell a plausible story to your friend, or you won't have a friend anymore." He let it sink in. "And you won't try anything sneaky and underhanded with me, either before or after. Dear Amy's home address is in your desk, too."

Relaxing a little, satisfied with the effect, Khalil coiled into the wide easy chair that faced Elizabeth's seat. He let some time go by thinking about the numbers in the insurance folder, the little tricks and cheap illusions he could have ready, and the problems a really sweet haul would cause. His jetty eyes drifted back to the childe Setite, his trump card, and narrowed.

"You're looking peaked, girl. I suppose we'd better hunt tonight, or you'll be no good to me." He picked open the fetter and unwound her chain from the support column. She made no move. "Come along," he urged her, and pulled a bit.

Elizabeth sat where she was. Her hair had fallen forward, covering her expression. Khalil prepared to strike her for rebelling; he thought of the voice and hesitated; he looked at the set of her shoulders, and saw despair there, not resistance.

"Would you be happier if I left you to starve?" he barked, trying to make a joke of it—trying to clench his hand back into the fist he'd had ready.

She asked quietly and without interest: "Would I die?"

What a complete infant—she knows less than nothing, Khalil thought contemptuously. "No," he retorted. "You'd have about a week of agonizing hunger and pain, then you'd shrivel and curl up, until you smelt blood. Then you'd go after it, darling, and it wouldn't matter who or what it was, you'd drink them dry and look around for seconds." He tilted up his chin, playing up mental calculation. "You *might* get yourself under control before you'd murdered more than…say…two people. Adults, that is. Really, though, I've found that children are more likely to come poking in caves and old buildings and things—"

"I'll go." Elizabeth spoke through clenched teeth, images of young lovers lying savaged in a dark alley flickering in her eyes. "I'll go."

"Ramona," Khalil said, as they pounded the pavement, hunting together.

"Yeah?" The Gangrel kept her eyes on the street; she was hungry.

"Find me a fence. A classy fence."

"What d'hell you mean, 'classy'?"

The Ravnos lowered his voice. "I'm planning something big." Ahead of them, a lady was walking toward…was it a bar?…by herself. "I can't keep going to the same vulgar little hock shop. I need a man who can move *quality* items." He bent their path to take them closer to the watering hole. Ramona stopped dead, flaring up in a now-familiar way—*what the hell have I said this time?* Khalil asked himself.

"Why d'you think I'd know anything about that shit? I come from a good family, you son of a bitch. I'm no thief—I don't go stealing shit unless I really fucking need it—"

"But you know New York better than I do," he flattered her. They were outside the door of the bar, and he could see from here that his lady was sitting self-consciously by herself. "I've found my mark. Go get yours and meet me back at the post office by midnight, or I'll go off to the meet by myself."

Their cab rolled up in front of a small, ornately decorated restaurant in Manhattan. Sarat Mukherjee put the car in park, turned off the engine, got out and held the car door open for Khalil—a courtesy Ramona had never seen from him before. When the

Indian didn't get back in the taxi, she stared at him strangely. To Khalil, she whispered, "Is he coming in with us?" The man scampered toward the establishment with enthusiasm and a promise that it was all ready, just one minute, please.

"Sure. Why the hell not, it's his cousin's place."

"You set this up on your friends' turf? I can't believe you, man. Putting them in that kind of danger—"

"What danger, sweetheart?"

She mouthed the word over the top of the cab. "Sabbat."

"They're already in danger, darling. They're alive. They know me." He smiled wickedly and passed through the arched entryway.

The Gangrel followed him guiltily. A hostess in sari came up and greeted her. A little boy turning chairs upside-down onto tables for the night gave her a shining, curious grin. Sarat, Khalil, a man in a suit, and a man wearing aproned white were all talking together near the center of the room. Ramona couldn't follow the language—couldn't even guess which one it might be—and sat down heavily at the table closest the door. The little boy came over to her and wiped the table clean, still beaming, showing off his mismatched front teeth (two grown-up, one baby, and one gummy gap where only the thinnest line of new enamel poked through). She thought of a biker—a Sabbat enforcer she'd last seen with his jaw sliding half off his face—and she thought of Gehenna, of the skinny chick on guard, of the guy Khalil had had words with, of Yve and of that stick, Jean-Paul—and sprang up again.

"Khalil, we gotta talk." All four men turned to look at her.

"That's what I came to do, sweetheart." He checked his watch. "That's what I *was* doing. The Sabbat's emissaries will be here any minute, and the Mukherjees and I need to finish arrangements." He shot out another quick phrase in that tricky language, and the cook, the hostess, and the little boy started dragging furniture around.

"Khalil! You get them the hell out of here before your goddamn 'emissaries' arrive."

Her companion turned slowly to face her. "Scruples, dear heart?" He glanced about—there was one table and two chairs left in the middle of the floor; two large, round tables, one on either side of the door, surrounded by six chairs each. "They were going to sit with you while I talk to the bigwig. If they leave, the bigwig will know for sure that you and I are all there is to *us*. Do you really want to sit alone across from one of those gangs we met the other night?"

Ramona clenched her fists in an agony of fear and self-control. With a major effort, she managed: "Send them home."

Khalil came closer to her, laughing. "They live here. Sarat and his family on the third floor, the restaurant owner on the second. I'll get the boy out of sight, if that's what's bothering you."

Ramona spat out a few choice expressions she'd learned in the LA barrio growing up.

"So long as that means 'yes'. Now have a seat, sweetheart." Another word to the man in the suit, and the lights dimmed. The Mukherjee family—adults only—took their places by Ramona, and Khalil settled down in one of the chairs at the center table.

Presently, the door opened and the bells hung from it chimed faintly.

Khalil watched, as coolly as possible, as the shark and the cat slithered into the room. They checked the setup and beckoned to a little face at the entrance. The monkey came through, and the dog held the door for the rest of the party: The turtle and the rooster took up posts nearby, and Jean-Paul walked calmly in behind them.

His icy glance took in Ramona, Khalil's props, the empty table for six, and the seat left open for him. He sniffed the air with obvious distaste. With a snap of his fingers he sent the gang to their place. After a careful scrutiny of his own chair, he sat down himself and began speaking without greeting or prelude.

"Regarding Hesha. We are willing to take that commission, but the man has dropped out of sight. There is even a suspicion that the reason we cannot trace him is that—there simply isn't such a person anymore?"

Khalil frowned slightly. "I don't believe it. I would know."

Jean-Paul's face registered well-bred surprise. "Really."

You would only know if I told you, you squealing runt. And you would beg before I told you.

Khalil ignored the interjection; this was his deal.

You are more than welcome to your "deal," boy. Just wait and see.

The Sabbat lifted an eyebrow, and continued. "If we find him, of course, we will fulfill our bargain…but to protect ourselves from fruitless work, I have to ask whether, if the man has met his second and final demise, you will honor whatever price we set?"

"So long as you prove it."

"Quite so."

Jean-Paul took out a small leather-bound notebook and a gold pencil. "Is there anything you can tell us about Ruhadze's recent activities that might help our search?"

"You want information from me?"

"This Setite's enemies, friends, associates, habits, haunts…whatever could be of assistance."

The Ravnos's expression soured. "Put something definite on the table for that. You may not catch him, and then where would I be, giving you all this for free? This is the goods on a high-ranking snake, you know. From the inside."

The aristocrat's mouth twitched. He tore a leaf from his little book and wrote down a name, a description, and a location. Jean-Paul slid the paper across the table and remarked pleasantly, "That is the prince's latest baby girl. She misses Mommy and Daddy, poor thing. She sleeps at Michaela's haven, of course, but goes most nights to visit her old home after the lights go out. Take her in that place and you may get away with it. Is that enough for you?"

Khalil read, smiled, and nodded. He folded up the scrap and stuck it in his bag. And then, carefully, ignoring the ill-tempered rumblings of the voice in his head, he spilled everything he knew about Hesha Ruhadze. The Sabbat (*Renegade Ventrue*, Khalil decided. *This fop can't be anything else.*) took it all down. He asked the occasional question; the Ravnos answered almost all of them truthfully. He skirted, gingerly, anything and everything to do with Elizabeth and Hesha's interest there—he didn't care for the chance that the animals might pay a visit to the apartment he had made his own refuge.

"Excellent," said Jean-Paul. "Now. As to the Eye. We are not ready to discuss payment for the bulk of your offer; it's hard to judge the extent of the debt we would incur, as I'm sure you can imagine."

Khalil grinned. What price the Eye of an Antediluvian vampire? Or a Methuselah, depending on which story you believed.

I shall give you warning one last time. You are young and foolish, thinking to meddle with the affairs of your elders. Bargain with these things without my sanction, and you will regret it.

"There are...certain gaps in our knowledge. You know how difficult it can be to sort truth from fancy with these fabulous objects. We were hoping that you could tell us something more of the Eye. I need a little less legend and a little more fact to whet my associates' appetite. I'm not sure *they* realize the full importance of the thing." Jean-Paul sighed and smirked slightly; he gave the impression of a man taking the Eye seriously, despite old-maidish doubts from above.

He didn't fool Khalil. The Ravnos's eyes blinked once, startled, but other than that he gave no outward sign of his near-paralyzing fear. *They don't know what the Eye is after all. This can't be happening to me. I don't believe it.*

"Fact, legend, a tricky distinction, eh? I can tell you what my own people speak of among themselves...." He launched into the legend that was supposed to have made the Eye of Hazimel *the* Evil Eye in mortal folklore. And while he spoke, he thought hard about the misstep he'd made. He'd assumed the Sabbat knew the thing existed, that they were aware of what it was doing and the havoc the monster who possessed it had wrought. And they didn't, or surely this whey-faced French creature wouldn't be poncing around the issue like this.

Khalil rambled on, telling how Hazimel had sent his own Eye out from his tomb. *Everything they know about it, I told them myself.* Why would they believe the danger when he told them truth about it? Why should they give him anything he'd asked for, if they gave his information no credence? Or worse, perhaps, they *would* give him what he'd asked for, but reject his payment. Information was all he had. He flinched to think what else these creatures might consider coin in kind. If the Sabbat didn't appreciate his real value in relation to the Eye…his solid bargaining position was cut right out from under him by the ignorance of the enemy. His safety lay in his value—and his value, apart from the Eye, was in his clan (which was gone), his inside information on Hesha (which he had just given away), and his blood, which was a commodity he would rather keep to himself.

Deep in the corners of his consciousness, he could hear hateful, mocking laughter rolling across barren distances.

Shut up, you poisonous old monster!

Jean-Paul finished writing, looked at the page, and slipped the pencil back into its sleeve. "I believe that will do very well for now." He stood. "You will hear from us as soon as there is any progress with Hesha or with the…Evil Eye. May I say, it has been a pleasure working with you. I must confess, I had some worries, dealing with a Gypsy…Rom, you call yourselves?"

Khalil rose. "Some of us."

"Times change, don't they. A Ravnos and a Gangrel working together...a man like yourself coming to my organization for aid.... Having any trouble finding your own clansmen in New York?"

"No," the Ravnos answered abruptly.

"Strange," the Ventrue mused, gathering his guards with a gesture. "Most strange. Good night, Monsieur Khalil."

Later, after Sarat's taxi had deposited them on the street outside the warehouse, Ramona gave her partner the once-over. Swarthy, shiftless, thieving...

"*Gitano*," she said aloud.

Khalil stopped fumbling for his keys and regarded her resentfully.

"Why can't you find your own fuckin' fence, *gitano*? I thought you people had that down to a fine art."

"'You people'?" He grinned mirthlessly. "I hate to ruin your sense of romance, sweetheart, but 'my people' are just as honest as any other dago or spic or nigger."

Flame rose in the girl's eyes.

"Mongrel blood, too, aren't you, darling? Know your own father?"

He saw the shot hit home, and her claws prick out a bit. He resumed, in a less taunting tone, to give her her answer. "Except by the most fabulous stroke of luck, I'm not going to find a *crooked* dealer from one of the tribes I'm in with, even in one of the world's largest cities. And if he or she were the real thing, they'd spot us for *shilmulo* the moment we walked in the door. 'My people' see little things like that. 'My people' have a reputation for it, too." He paused. "And just because I am a thief, doesn't mean my family or my tribe were thieves—they were tinsmiths. Poor and spat-on tinsmiths."

"Sorry," Ramona mumbled.

"Just 'cause a *shilmulo* can't help himself shining up the truth a bit, or taking something no one was using—"

"I *said* I was sorry."

Enough about family weaknesses, jackdaw. Perhaps you would not be in this mess if you had not been too busy crowing on your dungheap to listen to your elders. Open the door and shut up.

Sunday, 15 August 1999, 2:41 AM
A network of tunnels and caves
New York City, New York

The sun sank under the curve of the earth; the gods of day followed it and left the gods of night, their worshippers, and their slaves free to do what they would.

The Setite who called himself Hesha Ruhadze woke, and knew the unbearable face of Ra had gone on to other lands. He was stiff. In pain. He had been sleeping…how long? Limbs and mouth and eyes refused to obey him; he was as immobile and as helpless as the truly dead. Vague shadows floated up from his memory, and he remembered the Toreador, the statues, and the Eye in the churchyard. Could he have survived that? Or the dawns since? This must be Duat, the afterlife, and his pain the punishment for failing in his duty to Ma'at and Set and the honor of Henem….

He felt something press on his face. His teeth were forced apart (strange to feel, when he himself was not resisting) and a trickle of blood (his heart leapt) dripped into his mouth. Desperate hunger drove every consideration from his mind—the flow stopped, and he sucked on the aftertaste. Fresh, warm, weak, and unpleasant. Another stream of life ran down his throat…enough to bring him to full awareness. Rats. He was drinking rats. A third struggling rodent was held to his teeth and he obediently, gratefully, resentfully, disposed of that as well.

Slight sounds of movement began to reach him through the darkness (or blindness) around him. And conversation:

"Bring me some more…."

"Call the Monster in…. If he starts moving, I'm running, not holding him down!"

"Somebody run and tell *him*."

There were more rats brought, and then silence. Hesha was left alone inside his corpse, and he bent his mind to the slow, difficult repair of bone and flesh.

Elizabeth Dimitros held her fistful of keys in her hand and hesitated. Physically, she was unshackled. Mentally—Khalil had taken delight in pointing out that every man, woman, and child they passed in the street was his hostage, and their lives depended on her good behavior. Now she stood at the back door of the antique store, of the Rutherfords' business, just as she had a thousand times before. If it were morning…

Amy Rutherford was her best friend, despite the difference in their ages. Even the tyrannical Miss Agnes or the autocratic Mrs. Rutherford would have been a welcome sight, a flashback to normality. What she would give to be mothered by Amy or bullied by Agnes or ignored by Hermione Rutherford…

There would be no more mornings for Elizabeth. She prayed fervently that none of the staff would be in; that the senior Rutherfords were in London; that Amy had gone home; and she turned the key in the lock.

Khalil pushed past her, saw the alarm box, and pointed her toward it. Lord, if only she knew whether the store were occupied. She could trigger the silent alarm from here…she could lock him in and hide herself…the police would come…*and they'd be slaughtered*, she finished the thought. Liz punched in the code, and her captor looked a question.

"Storage to your left. Mostly furniture and paintings. Offices, restoration rooms, and access to the showroom up the stairs ahead of us."

"You go first."

Elizabeth mounted the steps slowly, trying still

to think of a way around Khalil. If the offices weren't lit, the staff and the partners would surely have gone home for the night. She opened the door at the top, and the lights *were* on. *Damn.* She turned the corner and there, just walking out of her office to see what the noise might be, was Mrs. Rutherford—substantial, pampered, face-lifted, and looking like a genteel reptile within an elegant shell.

"Miss Dimitros." Hermione's dry tones held unpleasant surprise. "I trust you have come to explain your vandalism of the apartment we have been so generous as to entrust you with?"

Liz flinched, and for a fleeting second she was almost glad to think of the monster standing behind her. *God forgive me, and let her be frightened, not killed....*

"Miss Dimitros isn't here to explain anything, you old tart." Khalil shoved his prisoner forward roughly and brandished a large and impressively ugly knife at *the* Mrs. Rutherford. "Get moving. Downstairs."

"Hermione? What is going on out there?" Liz recognized Miss Agnes's high-pitched, cultured voice. *Two of them—please, let Amy have gone—* she prayed, though she knew Agnes and Hermione would never send their junior home while they worked themselves.

"You, too, grandma." Khalil waved the knife and herded the old ladies down the corridor. "Liz...which way to the good stuff?" He held the blade to Miss Agnes's pearl-clasped neck and demanded, "Answer me!"

"Turn right, go downstairs to the showroom."

"Anything I ought to know about?"

"Three panic buttons. In the consultation desk, on the light-switch panel, and behind the door jamb."

"Elizabeth!" Mrs. Rutherford's voice; Liz could not look at her…only follow the *shilmulo*, the knife, and her former fears down the steps.

"Lizzie?!" Amy called up in disbelief.

"Quiet, Amaryllis. We have a problem," Mrs. Rutherford said calmly.

"Amaryllis? Amy? Got your message." Khalil grinned at her, and recognized her as the original of a photograph in the warehouse loft. "Hey, Liz, why didn't you tell me she's the woman on the end table?"

Khalil herded them all into the center of the room, well away from the walls and desk and phones. "There you go. Sit down on the floor, nice and easy, ladies. Hands where I can see 'em. Cuff them," he ordered the Setite, "hands and feet." Liz reached slowly for the duffel bag he had made her carry, and pulled, reluctantly, four sets of handcuffs from the depths of it. "Hurry, girl, or I may have to carve one of them instead." She quickened her pace.

Agnes first…lessons from the old woman on manners ran through her head…*always greet the eldest lady of a party first, Elizabeth, to show proper respect*…. Miss Agnes looked at her former employee with a petrifying stare. "Why are you doing this?" she hissed under her breath.

"You sold me to Hesha Ruhadze. Hesha left me…for him to take."

"What's that?" Hermione, dignified and determined to deal with this crisis as though it were a mere stock-market crash or warehouse fire, held her hands out regally. Liz bound them, then knelt to put the steel around the senior partner's silk-clad ankles. "You *sold* her, Agnes?"

"She did," Amy said quietly.

"That is *not* what happened, impertinent girl. Mr. Ruhadze needed a restoration expert; and I agreed to lend Miss Dimitros to him. It was a measure I took for her own safety. Ruhadze assured me there were terrorists marking her down as a target because of an antiquity she—"

"Enough! Quit your chattering. Lizzie—these are too loose. I warned you not to play tricks on me. Go stand in the corner." Khalil picked a roll of duct tape out of his bag, bent over the Rutherfords, and strapped Agnes's thin, rage-livid mouth shut. "Not a word out of you, unless you're asked," he warned Mrs. Rutherford. "Or I'll tape her nose up, too." He laughed, and started stripping them of necklaces, earrings, watches, rings....

"Let them keep their wedding rings," Elizabeth pleaded.

"Sentimental," he accused her, taking them anyway. "Shut the fuck up." He looked around. "Cameras. Why didn't you tell me? Go turn them off."

"I can't. I don't have the keys to the security room."

"Who does?"

No one spoke. Khalil turned in a blur of speed and slashed out with the knife.

Elizabeth stumbled backwards, spun, and fell. She looked at her arm in shock. A long slice curved across the fleshy part of her upper arm. It was like looking at an anatomical diagram in a book—muscle, nerve, tendon, bone, all laid bare. There was a very little, sluggish, blood. The wound grew smaller as she watched it, closing up before her eyes. She got her feet under her. There had been a scream. Her own?

Amy's, she realized. Liz stood up, a little weakly. Miss Agnes was sitting stiff as a poker. Mrs. Rutherford was pale, shaken, telling Khalil where he could find her own set of keys and the security room. She held her sobbing daughter-in-law the best she could with fettered hands, and Amy wept and trembled on her husband's mother's shoulder. The Ravnos threatened them once more and ran up the stairs to the offices.

Hermione Rutherford was the first to notice Elizabeth's rise. "Miss Dimitros? Are you...all right? What—"

"Lizzie!"

"Amy—" The Setite reached out to take her old friend's hand.

"He cut you!"

"He did." Liz realized, suddenly, that she was hungry, and pulled away. "I'm all right now." None of them understood; what could she tell them? "Just a little weak. No—don't come any closer. It's not safe."

"What's happened to you?"

"Where *is* Hesha Ruhadze?"

Looking nervously at the stairs, Liz spoke as quickly as she could.

"Don't contact Hesha. He's as rotten as this one. Keep away from the apartment, Khalil's made it his base. He's here to steal as much as he can; make the most of the insurance, but don't send anyone after him. They'll die."

"What about you?"

"You can't help me. Just don't make him angry." She paused, listening for the *shilmulo*'s return, and a thought came to her. "There is one thing. Call Professor Kettridge and tell him what's happened. There might be something he can do for me—"

Khalil clattered happily down the stairs, and the Setite leapt away from the other women. His bag, Liz noticed, was heavier now, probably with the Rutherfords' wallets. He hung the duffel off one shoulder, hooked a crowbar on the other, and proceeded to clean out the room.

The Ravnos's tastes were magpie-basic. He skipped over a million-dollar display of china to grab a watch worth only ten grand. Anything bearing gems, gilt, silver, gold—that he took, and the dull-looking reality he let sit. A glass case—the crowbar swung at it—and he turned and bragged to his guide.

"This is easy. Why the hell did I bring you?" He swept the contents of the cabinet into the bag and reached down a little statue from the top shelf. "That's gold, darling, that's solid fuckin' gold. Don't have to be a bloody expert to know that," he sneered. "Good gods, what a haul."

He finished the room in five minutes, spent another five picking through the table displays, and finally smashed into the little window boxes for the jewelry inside.

"That's set off the silent alarm. You'd better go now," Mrs. Rutherford spoke with glacial disdain.

"Shit. Why the fuck didn't you warn me, Lizzie?"

"You didn't give me time." Elizabeth glanced at the Rutherfords, and crossed her fingers. *And I didn't think of that trick....*

The Ravnos looked savagely from one to the other. Then he flipped open his phone and called the cab around. "Sarat—front doors, this instant," he yelled in Bengali.

"Come along, sweetheart, and give us a hand." Liz opened the locks for him and held the doors open while he dragged the heavy duffel along the floor. He tossed the crowbar away and stuck the knife in the sack. The taxi screeched to a halt halfway up the sidewalk. Khalil was busy with the bag; she could close both sets of doors between them and go back to the Rutherfords—

"1774 Church Hill Lane…" the *shilmulo* began, tauntingly. It was Amy's address, and it got Elizabeth into the car.

Wednesday, 18 August 1999, 10:37 PM
Red Hook, Brooklyn
New York City, New York

"Nobody looks up." Khalil sat alone. His feet dangled over the edge from his perch atop the warehouse that contained Liz's—now *his*—apartment. Every few minutes, a car drove by below.

"And *everybody's* got a car. Everybody who's somebody." He mulled that over for a minute, until the next car passed. "*I* need a car," he decided. It seemed a basic truth. In a way, it was simpler just to have Sarat drive—the cabby knew his way around the city. But that was something Khalil could learn easily enough, if he bothered to put his mind to it.

On the street below, a black stretch limo cruised past—and Khalil began to salivate.

"Sarat could drive one of those."

You should hoard your wealth, boy. Not waste it on trinkets.

"So you're back again, are you? Who asked you? Besides, did I say anything about *buying* one? Everybody in America can hot-wire a car." Khalil had seen enough late-night TV to know that.

He reached into his jacket pocket and pulled out the wad of hundred-dollar bills that was never far from his side. "And who are you to tell me to hold onto things? You can't even keep up with your own damned eyeball." Illustrating his disdain for the voice's advice, Khalil peeled off one of the bills and dropped it over the edge of the building. The first moment of exhilaration—as some fat, bald guy named Franklin drifted away—gave way almost immediately to a flash of panic. Khalil forced himself not to lunge after the bill.

"Plenty more where that came from. I'll do whatever I want with my hard-earned cash."

Hard-earned—?

"You know," Khalil said through clenched teeth, "it sure has been *nice* not having you bossing me around the last few nights."

You would be nothing without me.

"I was nothing *with* you. Now I'm *something* on my own!"

Are you?

"Yes, fuck you."

You have some money, which you will spend. You have a haven, which will be taken from you eventually—

"Those old ladies were too scared to do anything but soil their panties. The cops would've been here last night if anybody'd called them. And I plan to get more money."

You have a chained snake, who will bite you at the first opportunity. You have an ignorant outlander—an outlander! the bane of our clan—and a cab-driver ghoul....

"What did I have before? I had *you* telling me what to do. Now *I'm* calling the shots. So you can just piss off, Mr. Whistle-Through-His-Eye-Socket."

You would speak so to your elders? You certainly called the shots with the Sabbat, did you not? I shall laugh when they come for you. Your weak blood is not worth preserving.

"Well, let's just say that I'm not planning on heading back to Calcutta for you to spank me with a ruler."

There was a silence. Khalil looked around. He self-consciously slid back from the edge of the roof.

Breaking the old one's hold had not been easy—or pleasant. Just the memory of the pain threatened to nauseate the *shilmulo*. He wasn't at all sure that his former master couldn't "urge" him off the roof, and although the fall wouldn't do him in, it would damn well hurt. And he had no desire to spend nights and blood recuperating.

But perhaps you are not as completely rash as I suspect.

Khalil didn't trust the conciliatory tone of the voice.

Perhaps you might still serve me—in a more limited capacity. And I, of course, would reward you.

Khalil hesitated. "Now, when you say *reward*…are you talking about *your* idea of reward, or *my* idea of reward?"

I could remove the attention of the Sabbat from you, to begin with. I could give you knowledge, power…you know what an elder can do..

"Hm. That sounds like my idea of reward. So you're not going to get cute and *say* reward, and then nail me to the wall, or something like that…?"

You have my word.

"Yeah, right. That's a great comfort." Khalil hesitated again. He felt that he was backsliding, throwing away all the progress that he'd made—but there was no guarantee that the voice couldn't somehow *make* him do what it wanted. At least this way, he'd have some say—and compensation.

Although he was reluctant to concede that his brilliant plan to deal with the Sabbat hadn't been so brilliant after all.

"Okay, look…I've got one more condition."

Speak it.

"I don't *ever* want to hear you call me 'worm,' or 'dog,' or 'boy,' or any of that stuff again. My name is Khalil."

Silence.

"I'm not kidding. I walk away…."

Khalil.

Khalil liked the sound of that. He stretched slowly, luxuriously, and popped his knuckles. He had every right to be satisfied—he'd exacted concessions from an elder, and his other assets were not inconsiderable, no matter what the voice said.

"You know," Khalil said, thinking of those assets, "I don't plan on staying here forever."

Of course you don't.

"And Ramona doesn't know enough to do me real harm."

Not yet, she doesn't.

"And *you're* the one who wanted me to hold onto the snake. Personally, I could go for that high-octane Setite blood."

Yes, very sensible to be rid of the girl. Now, listen. This is what you do next—

"I *think* what you mean to say," Khalil said with a finger in the air, "is that you have a *suggestion* about what I should do next."

There was a pause, and a flash of distant anger like heat lightning.

As you say…Khalil. You must do nothing from this point to enrage the Camarilla—

"But there's this Ventrue chick, the name the Sabbat frog gave me—"

Nothing to anger the Camarilla, especially the Nosferatu. They are how you will find Hesha. I know what has happened to him, but still not where he is at present. Offer them the knowledge to heal wounds caused by the Eye, in exchange for his location.

"I don't know that I *want* to find him anymore."

Not even for his blood?

That caught Khalil's attention—but he also knew that there were lots of reasons why Hesha had survived long enough to become old and powerful. "I've got the next best thing to Hesha's blood chained up downstairs. I don't see any need to tangle with her sire."

There is no need. Hesha will take the Eye from this Leopold, and then Hesha will be under my power. I will deliver him to you.

"Doesn't seem like Leopold is exactly under your power."

His mind and his blood are too weak. He slips through my grasp like water. Hesha will be a more able servant.

"So I can't piss off Hesha either."

Not yet.

"So I can't have his little sweetheart."

All in good time.

Khalil didn't like it. He'd kept Liz around as a taunting reminder to his distant master that he'd been able to break the old one's hold, but now that they seemed to be back where they had begun… "Instant gratification is more my style."

Perhaps the Nosferatu would not be upset by one fewer Ventrue whelp.

Khalil clapped his hands together. "Now you're talking!"

It was among the most nauseating views Khalil had ever encountered—he who had waded through shit waist-deep in the housing districts of Calcutta. Really waded through shit waist-deep whenever he stepped that far into the Ganges. Seen blood and mucus and every other bodily fluid spewed and sprayed in situations from decapitation to orgasm to vampiric feeding frenzy.

But this bland, lifeless room was among the worst. The clinical perfection of the arrangements of flowers, the icy-smooth bedcovers, the dustless windowsills…it all added up to an environment so alien to the *shilmulo* that he shivered and frankly could barely stand the wait.

Wait he did, however. This Bauer House was the address the Sabbat had provided for his delectation. And the one his ethereal master had been forced to allow him to visit. Whatever came next in his dealings with Jean-Paul, he *would* take his blood-prize now, while he could. He was, after all, a clever Rom, used to living by his wits. Somehow, this gypsy boy would get what he wanted. Somehow, he would outmaneuver both the Sabbat and his so-called master.

Khalil chuckled silently when there was no retort sent streaming through the atmosphere from India. He really *had* fought the old goat to at least a temporary draw, despite this latest awkwardness.

These thoughts managed to keep Khalil's mind off the distasteful surroundings for a few moments. Around him was everything for which the United

States was hated and ridiculed in the poorer nations of the world. Not because everything in here was wastefully expensive and tacky. Not because one of the walls was adorned with glamorized photos of Hollywood celebrities and sports heroes. But because the occupant of the room, and hence the occupants of the house—for they'd taught the bitch who had lived here—were so far removed from the realities of the everyday. The concrete truths, like blood and filth and terror.

That's what the world was like, everywhere but in this bedroom, the Ravnos thought.

He sat down roughly on the bed, purposefully wrinkling the covers. Then he cursed, stood and straightened the bed. He wanted to get her from behind. Get her when she didn't know what was coming. He wanted to do this because she was certain to be an overconfident bitch who thought she knew everything that was important, and mostly that meant knowing what she should do next, because the world had clearly been designed with her exclusively in mind. Hell, the payday of her mortal years was when she was chosen among the billions to be made immortal. Clearly, life on Earth revolved around her!

Khalil clenched his fists in anger. Then he laughed it off. Maybe there was a reason other than blood that he wanted—needed—to do this. But he laughed that off too, because thinking about the reasons behind things wasn't what he did. After all, everything was about instincts.

He patted the bed a final time and walked toward the large closet he'd inspected earlier. He walked past the walls of magazine photos and glossy candids pasted to the wall. Khalil had been confused at first, because among the pictures of singers and actors and sportsman on the wall, was an attractive young woman who was doing all those activities among the celebrities. Khalil admitted that this woman looked pretty fine, with the soft, sun-bleached blonde peach fuzz on her arms and legs, her long hair pulled back or hanging, her blue eyes triumphant in a field of countless other bright colors. He finally realized that woman was his mark tonight, Tabitha Bauer. She was a stereotypical California blonde, despite living in New York City.

He stepped into the closet and pulled the door nearly shut. Entry to the house itself had been just as simple. He had waited until the girl's folks were returning from whatever gala event they'd dragged themselves to in the wake of their little girl's disappearance a month ago. In the span of the twenty-odd seconds it had taken for them to disarm the alarm, enter the house and re-arm the detection devices, the slippery *shilmulo* entered as well.

A rustling at the door to the bedroom silenced Khalil's thoughts. Instincts prepared to take over again.

It was Tabitha. Visiting her old room just like Jean-Paul had indicated. He watched tensely as she stepped into the room and quietly closed the door. Clicking on a small table lamp, the girl turned and opened a drawer in a long dresser against the wall. From it she pulled a flowery nightshirt. Laying it on the pillow, Tabitha began to disrobe. Her long, slender legs emerged from the confines of silky pants. She brushed the covers smoother as she placed those slacks on the bed, and she smoothed the sleeve of her violet blouse when she folded it on top of the pants.

Khalil watched, and thought that this was another reason the world hated Americans. They really did have the best-looking women. He could almost smell the sunshine drifting off her skin, and she retained a sheen of tan despite her weeks among the undead and away from the sun itself.

As she unhooked her bra, Tabitha shook her hair out. It was so long that it fell well down her back and far enough across her chest to veil her rounded breasts and supple stomach.

When she leaned forward to pull off her underwear, Khalil emerged.

Tabitha jumped at the sound of the closet door, but turned slowly toward her assailant, narrowing her eyes at his cocky smile. "Be careful, stranger. You don't know what you're getting into here."

Tabitha clearly didn't realize he was a vampire. Khalil pounced, one-handing the young Ventrue onto the floor between the dresser and the bed. The girl cried out in surprise, struggling against his unnatural strength and speed, but he muffled her voice with the nightshirt. He pushed her roughly down on her back and made a seat of her smooth and writhing stomach.

She was muttering and pleading and cursing, but Khalil couldn't make out any words, nor did he want to. While she tried to buck him off her, Khalil briefly suckled each breast and then plunged his anxious fangs into the large artery in her left armpit exposed as her arm was stretched upward.

Unbelievable sweetness drowned his mouth and drenched his senses. He pulled back after two big gulps, the girl still thrashing but now also shivering and he in complete control.

He said, "Thanks for shaving there, sweetheart. Another nice American habit."

And then he was at it once again, his tongue probing the walls of the artery. As the ambrosia of her life force swept into him, Khalil tingled from head to toe. He regretted that her struggles lost energy as he became stronger, because he liked the semblance of fight.

But more than he'd ever regretted anything before, he lamented the flow of her blood slowing. The gushes became a trickle and what had swept into his mouth now required sucking to extract.

Tabitha was virtually motionless by then, so as he dragged on her flesh like a second-hand cigarette, he flipped the nightshirt off her face. She had just enough energy left to look at her murderer.

"Just sucks, doesn't it," Khalil said with a growl, as he returned to the attack and extracted the very last drop from her. And it was the brightest, tastiest drop of the liters he'd swallowed. It was the essence of sunshine, and Khalil felt that tingle in his body become a warmth and he knew the favors bestowed by devouring a Kindred with older blood. Diablerie.

He reveled in this sensation as it passed ever so slowly. And when he recovered, all that was left of the All-American girl was a delicate outline of ashes as soft and silky as her hair had been.

Khalil stood, but then paused, crouching with his head low to the floor. He inhaled and blew a big breath that scattered the dust across the breadth of the room. The meticulous mother would never know exactly why the room was so dusty that Thursday morning in August.

part three:
pawn

Hesha, from his sickbed, half-saw, half-smelt
a figure in the dark room's open door. He considered the shape and the odor. It was not the small
one, smelling of mange, who brought the rats each
night; not the busy, cheerful man who came to joke
with the boy; not the tall one with the laptop who
sat and typed through his visits; not the woman
who inspected his carcass each evening and
brought needle and silk to help mend him. Not
these, not any other he knew, and he felt, by now,
he knew the whole warren's worth by scent, voice,
or build. Therefore, this was a new person—very
possibly "him," the chief the others mentioned
from time to time.

The squat, rather crooked person turned up the
lights, very slightly. It was a much older Cainite than
the others: an elder Nosferatu, clinging to leper's dress
of hood, cloak, mummy-like wrappings. The young
ones took more to overcoats and sweatshirts. It had
been hats and trenchcoats, forty years ago. How old
would this one be?

It shuffled closer. Hesha caught a glimpse of
misshapen face and the impression of large, black
eyes that neither matched each other nor occupied their proper places in the very round skull's
sockets. The jetty orbs pored over Hesha's face.
Gnarled, clawed fingers reached out and took off
the blanket. There were dark red and brown stains
on it in the shape of the Setite's body. Some of the
wounds, Hesha could feel, would not knit. They

leaked what blood was sent to them, and it was caked now on the cloth. Gently, with the backs of the terrible claws, the elder probed the ragged wounds, and seemed dissatisfied.

It sat down, rustling in its robes, in the chair by the foot of the Setite's bed. It looked toward (not threateningly *at*) its patient's face.

"They tell me you've regained consciousness." A hoarse voice, probably male.

Carefully, Hesha tried speaking. A rasping, painful "Yes" emerged. He would not have recognized it as himself. He said nothing more, though the silence dragged on.

"Cautious. No 'Where am I?' from you; that's the classic first question, I understand."

The Setite said nothing.

"Would you care to introduce yourself?" After a brief wait, the Nosferatu went on. "Well, then, Hesha, Hunter-of-the-Sun, Prophet of Henem."

"Who…gave you that name?" the Setite croaked angrily. "Don't profane it by—"

"Prophet of Typhon, if you prefer."

"I do…and I like—Ruhadze far better," Hesha whispered.

"As you like. You may call me Calebros; all of my young friends here know me by that name."

"I am honored," managed Hesha.

"You have heard of me?" The Nosferatu seemed almost alarmed.

"No," replied the Setite, meaningfully. His host chuckled.

"I see you understand us."

"I thought…I…did."

"What doubts do you have now? You *were* an ally to us."

"Atlanta—" Hesha gasped. Talking hurt from the chest upwards, and there seemed to be trouble with his lungs. "The Toreador's party...you invited me...to," he waited and struggled to pull more air in. "Sabbat ambush. Vegel killed...by Sabbat, or by you...trap either way...raises...suspicions, yes?"

"I see," Calebros replied tonelessly. "And did these suspicions give rise to any retribution on your part?"

"...Beg...your pardon?"

"Retribution," Calebros repeated. "Not against us. I suspect you're too canny for anything so direct, and frankly, you need our assistance every so often, it seems."

Hesha couldn't speak—his mouth and throat were flaky, like scorched paper—but Calebros could read the bewilderment on his patient's face.

"I'd always heard you had a mind for details," the Nosferatu said, reaching into a fold of his cloak and producing what appeared to be a thin paper roll, the receipt tape from a cash register or adding machine. "Let me refresh your memory." Calebros began to unroll the tape as if it were a treasured scroll, and to read aloud from the tiny, cramped scrawl of handwriting on the reverse side of the purple numbers:

"Atlanta. Your associate, Mr. Vegel was present. A certain warlock regent evidently disappeared. There seemed to be Assamite involvement. This is difficult to confirm since the Sabbat blew up the chantry shortly thereafter, and the Tremere high command doesn't exactly return our calls—not when their internal affairs are involved."

The Nosferatu unrolled the tape a bit farther. He read almost disinterestedly, as if relating items from a grocery list. "Calcutta. A warlock you contacted was fatally attacked on his way to meet you. The assassin was an Assamite. We have confirmed this. Also in Calcutta, the Rani Surama, after a visit with you, came due for some rather severe punishment from her sire, Prince Abernethie. Surama is reported to be no longer among the living or the unliving."

Calebros pulled more tape from the roll. "Perhaps Surama's demise is less significant, considering that, during your stay in Calcutta, every Kindred in the entire Bengal region was mysteriously wiped out...with the exception of yourself and an associate.

"Closer to home, it appears that two Tremere, a regent and a council representative, had their service prematurely abbreviated in New York and Baltimore, respectively—two of your centers of operations. Assamite involvement strongly suspected in both cases again.

"You can imagine my hesitancy to meet with you," Calebros said. "A tête-à-tête with Hesha Ruhadze does not seem to be a boon to longevity."

Hesha painfully cleared his throat and politely turned away from his host to spit bloody phlegm and charred throat tissue in the other direction. "Three survivors...Bengal."

Calebros double-checked his notes, then looked quizzically back at Hesha.

"Three survivors," Hesha repeated, his voice gaining a little strength. "Nosferatu bookseller. I spoke to him before and after...whatever happened. Promised he'd contact Bombay for me—about Atlanta."

"We've heard nothing of that," Calebros said.

Hesha rested his voice. He was no more in a position to explain lapses in Nosferatu communication than he was to understand the great upheaval that had struck Calcutta during his sojourn there. Nor did he have an explanation for the coincidental Assamite activities that seemed to follow him and his personnel like a shadow. Could the children of Haqim be tracing the Eye as well? That was an unwelcome thought. The less contact with Assamites the better.

Wearily, Hesha lay back on the bed. He was too weak to defend himself properly. The Nosferatu might have nursed him along this far, but merely to find out what he knew. This Calebros was obviously a suspicious one—and Hesha had no proof to offer of his innocence. If the sewer rats suspected him of harmful designs, his convalescence would ultimately prove short and unrewarding. *Nonthreatening*, he thought. That was his only hope. There were other paths to ruin, Hesha recognized—paths from which he would be powerless to detour once upon them. If the Nosferatu had turned on him, and Vegel's death had been a trap, then Hesha didn't stand a chance anyway.

"Erich Vegel's death," Calebros said, breaking the deepening silence and seeming to guess Hesha's thoughts, "was, we believe, an accident. Not his actual death, of course—whatever Sabbat pack he ran into certainly did what they did to him intentionally—but the circumstances leading to his death were not of our design."

Calebros paused. "Did Vegel contact you at all after entering the High Museum?"

Hesha shook his head. He, in fact, had tried to call Vegel that night, but somehow had only reached Victoria Ash on Vegel's cell phone.

"We arranged for you to receive the invitation to Ms. Ash's party," Calebros said. "We discovered the whereabouts of an object you have sought for many years, and we thought to turn it over to you. We have not forgotten the service you rendered us at Bombay."

Hesha nodded his understanding.

"Prince Bennison's Elysium seemed the perfect opportunity. You see, the Eye of Hazimel was hidden within one of the statues Ms. Ash had acquired and which would be on display."

Only with great effort did Hesha maintain his air of weariness. The Eye of Hazimel. He'd held it in his hand just…several nights ago, however many he wasn't exactly sure. It had been given to Vegel? Then Hesha had lost it not once but *twice*.

"The Eye was delivered to Vegel," Calebros said, "and he was given an escape route from the trouble we expected. The trouble we expected, unfortunately, was not the trouble we got." The Nosferatu crumpled up the receipt tape he'd been reading earlier and stuffed it into a pocket. "Or at least it wasn't *all* we got. We were expecting a Sabbat raid on the High Museum. Perfect opportunity to hand over the Eye to your man. What we got was an all-out attack. War. And what Vegel got was dead."

Hesha lay on his back and, to an observer's view, listened impassively. Within, he was not so placid. A knot was forming within the atrophied organ that had long ago been his stomach. The knot had begun with the news that both he and Vegel had held—and *lost*—the Eye. But the knot was growing.

The news of Vegel's destruction—an event that Hesha had assumed, though unconfirmed, weeks ago—was merely the outermost layer of information, the outer skin of an onion, and Hesha was nothing if not skilled at peeling away layers. If Calebros's account was to be believed, then the fact beneath Vegel's death was that someone, some Nosferatu somewhere down the line, had miscalculated. And badly. Someone had made unwarranted assumptions, and those assumptions had been passed along the lines of communication. Those higher-ups in a position to do so—maybe Calebros himself—had failed or been unable to detect the erroneous assumptions. For most clans, an embarrassment. For the Nosferatu, who made themselves useful to other clans and thereby *survived* through collecting and bartering information, a dangerous blow to their credibility.

Peel away a layer. What was the mistake about? The Sabbat raid was in fact a full frontal assault on the American Camarilla, and now the Nosferatu had more to worry about than a credibility issue. The sect they supported was on the verge of being annihilated from a large portion of the continent. Survival was suddenly much less abstract. Although, in truth, if any Camarilla clan were to survive the dissolution of the sect, the unobtrusive sewer rats would certainly have the best chance.

Peel away another layer. The Nosferatu had thought a Sabbat raid was going to strike Prince Bennison's Elysium, yet they had said nothing. Surely the benefit of chaos in which to complete a transaction with Hesha's retainer was not great enough a reason to undertake such a risk. The Nosferatu unquestionably had other schemes at work. The question that remained was, what? What profit was important enough to risk the enmity of a prince and possibly charges of treachery from the rest of the Camarilla?

Peel away another layer. Why should a Nosferatu elder—a being well-acquainted with the power of inference and deduction—share such information with a Setite? This was where Hesha's stomach began to curdle. Why, indeed? The most likely reason was to find out what the Setite knew, and in this case—with the Setite in question barely strong enough to sit up and take nourishment, much less defend himself—there seemed to be every likelihood that the Setite would never leave this place. That the knowledge, in short, would die with him.

"We found his clothes later," Calebros said.

Hesha's mind switched back to Vegel.

"And then his body, some distance away," Calebros continued. "One-eyed corpse, drained of blood, starting to turn to dust. We're virtually certain that the body was his."

Hesha felt that each new detail was a scorpion tossed among his ragged bedclothes, another piece of information that would never leave that room. Why tell him so much otherwise? But then the other possible answer dawned upon him. Calebros was attempting to convince him, to persuade him that there'd been no foul play on the part of the sewer rats. And why would the Nosferatu bother to convince someone he was simply going to destroy?

"So you say," Hesha said painfully. If his goodwill still mattered here, he was not completely helpless, he realized, although words were his only defense. He fought the urge to sit up and gauge Calebros's expression. The disarranged features would be too difficult to read anyway. There was only a long pause for Hesha to measure.

"I cannot think of a way to prove this to you," Calebros said finally.

Hesha nodded and cleared his throat again. "In Calcutta…I met with Michel, the Tremere. Owed me a favor. I was tracking the Eye…someone who was seeing *through* the Eye. Assamite got to Michel before I learned anything. I destroyed the Assamite. Your source tell you that?"

Calebros did not answer but merely continued to watch, and to listen.

"As for…Kindred population of entire Bengal region," Hesha went on, though his voice was again growing weak, "flattered that you would blame that on me…but far beyond my capabilities." Hesha was seized by a fit of coughing. His throat and chest burned.

After a few moments, the fit passed. "I cannot

think of a way to prove this to you," he added, mimicking Calebros's own words. "You know my true title. The Assamites are as much a threat to my responsibilities as the Sabbat. Perhaps more so."

The two elders, Setite and Nosferatu, sat in silence for some time. They stared into the darkness, each weighing suspicion against fact. For Hesha, the questions were moot. Even if he disbelieved Calebros—and what the Nosferatu said seemed likely enough—he was in the care of the sewer rats, and his safety depended upon their good graces.

Eventually, Calebros spoke: "It seems we each have our story. We each also have no way to prove our own or to disprove the other's."

"So it seems."

"It would also seem that it is in my clan's best interest for the Eye to pass to less...shall we say, *conspicuous* ownership than that of the present time. Fewer questions about how it got out and about. You remain interested in possessing it?"

"I do."

Calebros paused for a moment. "Then I see no reason that our cooperation should not continue."

"Nor do I."

"I should think not."

Through the darkness, Hesha thought he could see what might be a smile upon the Nosferatu's face.

"We do not forget our debts, Hesha, Prophet of Typhon."

The Setite did not miss the hint of warning, but chose to address Calebros's tone of gratitude. "You and your people have done me great service."

"Trust me," Calebros said, his voice conveying

none of the words' irony. "Preserving your mere existence is hardly on par with the debt of Bombay or the value of the Eye. I would be pleased, though, if you would consider it partial repayment for the loss of your friend, Vegel, in Atlanta. Chance worked against us there; it worked against you at St. John's."

"Perhaps it will work for us, soon enough," Hesha suggested. "Thank you, all the same."

"You'll be wanting to contact your retainers, then." From somewhere amidst the folds of his robes, the Nosferatu produced a cellular phone. "Your favorite weapon, I believe. Certainly mightier than the sword, in some hands."

The phone was oversized and flat, with huge yellow-green glowing buttons—the type of headset manufactured for the disabled, a designation not lacking in application to Hesha at the moment.

"Can you see to dial?" asked his host. The Setite peered through ragged eyelids at the glowing grid, and hissed assent. He lifted his hands—only the left obeyed him—and began picking out one of Janet's direct numbers with one fingerbone.

"Do you mind?" Calebros gestured to another extension—a black, two-piece bakelite telephone—and picked up the receiver.

Hesha tried to smile. "I would be more offended, I think, if I were no longer worth spying upon...."

"Listen, you said find a fence, and I did," Ramona said crossly. "If you don't like him, then you can find the next one, okay?" She threw her body into corner of the backseat of the cab. She was angry and directing her pointed words at Khalil, but she didn't miss the protective glances Sarat was aiming in the mirror at her from the driver's seat. She didn't like that one bit. "Or maybe Sarat can find one for you." She grunted in finality and lowered her eyes to her lap, but the fierce energy didn't leave her body.

Khalil wasn't ready to stop being mad, but he knew that Ramona was done arguing, and he didn't want to push the Gangrel over the edge. At least until he was sure she couldn't help him any more. On the other hand, she couldn't be allowed the last word. He curled his lip and softly snarled at her, "Well, it's a sorry fence that can't afford our goods, says they are too hot if he could, and doesn't know if he could find buyers even if they weren't so hot."

Ramona continued to stare sullenly at the floorboards, and Khalil was content to have shut her up after ten minutes of arguing. Another ten minutes passed in silence as Sarat made his way back into the city.

Khalil scanned skyscrapers with the ridiculous notion of spotting the fence that would make him wealthy. He figured he must have a hundred thousand dollars or more in stolen goods in the trunk, and the realization that it might all be essentially worthless after all ate at him like a carrion beetle attacking rotting flesh.

Then, as Sarat coasted to a stop at a traffic light in the city, a jovial asshole standing in the middle of the busy street practically shoved a bundle of roses through Khalil's half-open window.

The man chimed, "Roses for the pretty lady?"

Khalil's impulse was to slash the fool's throat, but a number of thoughts sprang to his mind and persuaded him to stay his hand. The fact that he would have a corpse dragging from his cab in the middle of New York City was not one of the deterrents that occurred to him.

First, he thought of Mary. The image of her with a rose clenched in her teeth while she danced sensuously those long years ago in Delhi was among the handful of genuinely emotional memories Khalil possessed. Even so, part of the allure of that image was how like blood dripping from her mouth before a packed house of kine that rose had seemed. Khalil had never laughed to so hard as then, and that's how he'd met Mary: She'd come to him later to ask what about her dance was so amusing.

And the roses also struck Khalil as an opportunity to seduce Ramona back to him. She was so damn quiet all the time, and that either meant she knew shit, or she knew a hell of a lot more than she was sharing. Until shown otherwise, he would have to assume the latter.

So Khalil smiled invitingly at the man, and said, "Sure, pal. How much for the dozen?"

"Only twenty bucks," said the man, now looking past Khalil at Ramona. "She's a pretty one; good move gettin' the flowers."

Khalil looked back at the man and said, "We just had a silly spat and I want her to know that it's no big deal. I was the one being an ass."

Meanwhile, the Ravnos fished in his back pocket where he'd stuck the Yellow Pages ad for Madama Alexandria. Without looking directly at the tearsheet, Khalil read the address to Sarat and then he handed the torn yellow paper to the flower seller. Khalil smiled magnanimously. "Keep the rest, pal, to pay for some flowers for your own sweetheart." He then took the flowers from the man, pulled one from the bunch and passed the remainder to Ramona with a flourish.

When she mutely accepted the roses, Khalil again had to fight back an impulse to gut her and be rid of her. Instead, he just sighed, and said, "Shit, what's a guy gotta do?"

When the light changed and Sarat pulled away, Ramona said, "What was all that? You gave him a page out of the phone book for the roses."

"Ramona," Khalil sighed again, "that's why you need to stick with me. So many tricks you got no clue about. A little twinkle of my nose and I made him see that yellow sheet as a US $50 bill."

He stretched forward toward Sarat, "You get that address?"

Sarat tossed the reply over his shoulder, "On our way, boss."

"Good." Khalil looked back to Ramona. "Sorry to filch one of your roses. We're going to go see Mary."

Ramona rustled the tissue paper that wrapped the roses and said, "Yeah, okay. Anyway, I still have a dozen."

"Huh?" Khalil looked at her. "I took one."

"Must've been a baker's dozen." Ramona spread out the roses.

Khalil made more than a pretense of counting them; he touched every single one and made certain of the number. "Damn. Shit like this doesn't happen randomly, don't you understand? This is bad…bad, what do you call it here, mojo? Damn it all."

They both sat silently for a moment, as Sarat glanced nervously back in the mirror at his blood master.

Finally, Khalil said, "Something bad is going to happen."

A few minutes later, Sarat whistled and said, "Something bad already has, boss. I'm sorry, but it already has."

Khalil and Ramona both became instantly alert. Ahead of the cab, they saw a diminishing plume of smoke trailing away from the charred husk of a building. A trio of fire trucks was still parked in the road, but traffic was being let through now. Now that there was nothing left to save.

Sarat confirmed, "That's the address you gave me, boss."

The cabby began to slow as he neared the wrecked building. It was completely demolished. The street was soaked and rivulets of water still flowed away from the burned building and into a storm grate. Firemen were everywhere, rolling hoses and packing equipment.

Suddenly, Khalil demanded, "Move it, Sarat. Get this car rolling. Not too fast, but don't stick around." The Ravnos then sank down in his seat and pressed Ramona to do the same.

In the fashion typical of New York cabs, Sarat slipped his car into the end of a pack being let through one direction before waiting cars facing the other way were allowed through. Several honks and Bronx cheers hailed the passing cab.

Still crouched in his seat, Khalil said, "Damn it all, Mary. Looks like someone's decided to settle some scores around here."

The apartment door slammed open against the wall, and Khalil slammed in after it. "Damn it! Why do I even *bother?*" He stomped across the living room and threw the small canvas sack he was carrying down onto the kitchen counter. A few pieces of gold and gem-laden jewelry slid out of the bag.

Ramona, vaguely bored, leaned against a bookshelf. "Let me guess," she said. "Your bright idea to try Sammy's Pawn 'n' Gun wasn't much help."

"That idiot wouldn't recognize the crown jewels if somebody stuffed them up his ass! And believe me, I was tempted." Khalil continued stomping around the apartment, picking up and slamming back down various of Liz's possessions.

Liz sat on the couch, studiously not looking at Khalil or acknowledging his presence in any way.

"I don't see why you need so much money, anyway," Ramona said.

"I need it because I need it!" Khalil raged, caught off guard by the strength of his own frustration and anger. "And I would remind you that *I'm* the one who knows what's going on around here! I know you go out and sniff around, but I don't see you finding the Eye."

It wasn't a healthy habit—yelling at a Gangrel who might well rip his head off. To soothe himself, he grabbed a book from a shelf—some god-awful, boring-looking archeology text—and began to rip pages out and sift them across the floor.

With each page he tore, a small amount of control returned to him.

"Besides," Khalil added after quite a few pages, "do you want to stay in this dump forever? What a mess." He indicated the now-sizable pile of torn and crumpled paper on the floor around him. Ramona, he knew, was the one he should have been trying to placate, but Khalil couldn't take his eyes off Elizabeth—sitting there chained to the couch and trying not to cringe with every page he ripped from the binding. Khalil dropped the book. He took another from the shelf and began tearing. His nostrils flared. The Ventrue blood he'd tasted was sweet, but he could smell Liz's—and it was sweeter still.

Khalil stared relentlessly at Elizabeth. "You'd be amazed how well a leech can set himself up if there's only enough money in the bank...." Half to Ramona, half to himself, he said, "Her sugar daddy's that rich. Those pasty-faced hens I snatched my pretty baubles from—they're that rich. You want to hire an army to avenge your wrongs? Buy a blood bank and never have to hunt again? Start a cult to worship the ground your immortal feet walk on?" He sneered and rubbed his fingers together in front of the Gangrel's face. "You can do *anything* with money, Ramona."

The Ravnos turned suddenly, threw down the book, and grabbed the sack from the counter. He brandished it at his prisoner. "Tell me how to sell these!" He threw the bag at her feet, spraying jewelry and gold figurines and watches across the floor. "You must know how!"

Liz's quiet, gold-brown eyes rose slowly from the stolen treasures. She opened her mouth, hesitated, and then said softly, "I won't." She looked at Ramona, and then at him. "Find your own crook."

Khalil, again rigid with anger and false hunger, literally shook with temper. "What's this?"

"Death to tyrants," whispered Elizabeth. *Gods!* thought Khalil. She was goading him with the fact that she *knew* he wasn't his own man. But he was now. He was working on his own terms. He planned to do *everything* on his own terms from now on.

"You want me to go back to Rutherford House?" the Ravnos shouted. "I could see Amy again; I could ask *her*." He snatched up her photograph and shattered the frame under Elizabeth's nose. She flinched. "I think she'd tell me, if I asked her hard enough." Shards of glass covered the Setite and the couch now. Khalil tore the picture to shreds and let the pieces fall into his captive's lap.

"Fred Summers, in Tribeca," said the girl at last, staring at the shreds of film stock. "He has…a reputation…."

Khalil, completely calm in an instant, smiled and patted her patronizingly on the head. "That's a good snake." He turned away toward the phone books.

Elizabeth, carefully collecting the pieces of Amy and the shards of glass, her chains rattling quietly, caught sight of Ramona in her peripheral vision. The girl was surprised, angry, and unhappy. She glared at Khalil; she twice moved as if to help

Liz clean up. Elizabeth placed the strips of picture into a nearby notebook, closed it, and drooped submissively. She saw Ramona's jaw clench tightly, and she settled in, content with her progress.

The click of the bolt seemed loud as thunder, and the creaking hinges more piercing than Ramona had ever noticed before. She had left when Khalil went out earlier that evening for his late appointment in Tribeca, but she'd doubled back before too long.

She shut and locked the door; she pressed her back against it. Elizabeth was sitting on the couch. Watching. Her chains were looped around and through the old radiator as well as a column.

"Who are you?" Ramona asked quietly.

Liz sat and continued to watch the Gangrel for half a minute before answering. "Elizabeth Ariadne Dimitros."

Ramona shook her head. "That's just a name—a mortal name. It doesn't mean anything anymore."

Liz's gaze hardened. But then she sighed, and her eyes slowly closed. She seemed to deflate with the sigh. All the fight went out of her, all the defiance that was her impenetrable armor against Khalil. "You're right," she said quietly.

The Gangrel took a step closer. "I'm Ramona Tanner-childe. I…" she struggled to find the words that defined her. "I saw the Eye destroy my clanmates."

Elizabeth's eyes opened, but she did not speak.

"Why are you here? How did this…" Ramona moved closer, bent down and rattled the chain on the floor, "happen?"

Elizabeth's gaze was hard again. She started to say something, stopped, started again. "Why are you working with Khalil?"

"That thing—the Eye—it's in the city. At least it was. He said he could find it."

"And you believe him?"

Ramona didn't answer.

"You saw it destroy your clanmates," Liz said.

"Yes."

"You couldn't stop it?"

"No." Ramona shook her head. *I was too afraid,* she thought.

"And you think Khalil can?"

Ramona stood back up. She pawed at the chain with her misshapen foot, then shrugged. "Maybe. Worth a shot. I can't just walk away." *Not again.* She turned away from Liz and began poking around at some of the odds and ends on the work table—some of the odds and ends *beneath* the clutter of paint rollers, clothes, and random pieces of gold jewelry that Khalil had left scattered all around.

"I believe you," Liz said after a while.

Ramona nodded. "Good." She hadn't really considered that *her* word would be in question. "Khalil said that you wanted to get back with this dude Hesha."

Silence. Ramona continued to look around the apartment. Minutes passed.

"No," Liz said eventually. "If you and Khalil find Hesha, please don't say anything about me. Let him think I'm dead. Really dead." But it was her words that were dead. Lifeless.

Ramona recognized that numbness—the wall that held back pain too great to face. Worse pain than what Khalil had caused Liz.

"He left me for the sun," Liz said. "These are his." She rattled the manacles.

"Why?"

"Punishment. For rebelling against him. He was going to make another person into…into what we are. And this man, my friend, decided he would rather die than be this. So I let him. And Hesha came after me. He's used to getting what he wants. He changed me and left me as a sacrifice to Ra—to the sun. Khalil actually rescued me." She laughed dryly. "I'm not sure Khalil completely understands the situation. I think he expects Hesha to be *grateful* to him for sheltering me, or something."

"I don't think Khalil wants to make a deal with Hesha," Ramona said. "He wants to kill him."

Liz chuckled. "Khalil? Kill Hesha? Won't happen. Hesha's too smart, too organized, too…too damned *perfect*."

"He's hired the Sabbat to do it."

That seemed to puzzle Liz. She didn't recognize "Sabbat." Ramona felt some slight satisfaction in finally finding someone who seemed to know even less than she did about what they had become. Liz lapsed into her protective silence again. Ramona continued to look around the apartment—to really *look*—and for the first time she could see what it was like before Khalil's destructive energy had transformed it into a prison. It had been a home. Liz's home.

Ramona worked her way back around to the couch. She bent down again and ran her fingers over Liz's chains.

"There are bolt-cutters on the shelf in my workshop," Liz said quietly, almost in a whisper.

"I know," Ramona said. "I saw them." She couldn't look at the pleading eyes. Instead, the

Gangrel stood and walked over to the work table. She stared at the bolt-cutters and thought about the chains that imprisoned Liz—and about the Eye.

"He'd know I helped you escape," Ramona said. She could taste the guilt, but it was not as powerful as the guilt over the deaths of her clanmates. "I still need what he knows."

"What he *might* know," Liz said pointedly.

"What he might know. I'm sorry."

Ramona began to rustle through the debris on the work table. She ignored the large bolt-cutters but gathered up other, smaller, metal tools—several looked like dentist's picks; one was some kind of file—and carried them over to Liz.

"These were in the sofa, down in the cracks beneath the cushions. Before any of this ever happened. Right?"

Liz nodded gratefully. "I never was a very good housekeeper." Ramona spread the tools across a cushion. Liz took one of the picks and began working at the keyhole of the manacle around her left wrist, while the Gangrel filed away at a chain link that could be covered if Khalil returned.

Monday, 30 August 1999, 10:40 PM
Morehead Park, Brooklyn
New York City, New York

The hunt. Ramona had found that a good stalk was the best way to keep her mind off things she didn't want to think about—things, and people. This was the second night running that she had made a point of staying away from the apartment...away from Liz. Ramona couldn't face her. The manacles had proven too damned tough. Neither woman had been able to pick the locks, and the small file hadn't been much help against the sturdy metal. Ramona had left promising to find a better, stronger file.

And she hadn't been back.

Tonight was another hot summer night. Ramona could smell mortal sweat, mortal blood. That was what she was trying to concentrate on—not the memory of Liz's proud but pleading eyes.

Ramona muttered curses under her breath. She'd had more luck distracting herself last night, but this time she wasn't actually hungry. She was just going through the motions. And it wasn't working.

The damnable fact of the matter was that she still might be able to learn something from Khalil. But was that possibility worth Liz's freedom? Ramona's dead demanded vengeance, and there was still the chance that her sire Tanner had survived—somehow. But was this the way to go about doing what had to be done?

Ramona cursed again. She cursed herself for indecision. She cursed Tanner for making her a predator. She cursed Khalil for the different type of predator that he was. She cursed Liz for being a victim—for getting in the way.

The hunt. The smell of blood. Ramona forced herself to concentrate. This park, where she had spent the past day submerged within the earth, was not crowded. There was, however, a woman sitting alone on a bench. *Stupid.* Ramona would have preferred a man, like last night: She had fed on a pimp who would need many days to recover before he abused his girls again. But maybe this woman, so unconcerned with her own self-preservation that she was alone in a park in New York City at night, deserved a scare. Maybe she'd be more careful next time.

Ramona could almost taste the blood as she silently approached the woman from behind. Conscious will began to give way to the instincts of the hunt.

Then the woman stood. She turned toward the Gangrel and looked directly at her. Ramona was crouched to spring—to cut off any scream before it was given voice—but the woman's mouth was already open, not to scream but to *speak:*

"Ramona!" the stranger said, less calmly perhaps than she might have liked.

Ramona froze. She'd thought the woman was mortal but now wasn't sure. The Gangrel frantically tried to look in every direction at once. Sabbat ambush? She'd run into them before, and Khalil had begged for their attention....

"Ramona, we need to talk to you," the woman said quickly. "My *employer* wants to talk with you."

The woman—short, darkly complected, dark hair—was breathing rapidly. *Breathing,* Ramona realized. Mortal after all. And scared—or at least fighting a rush of adrenaline. Then Ramona noticed something else. Above the excited breathing and the pounding heart, another sound caught her ear—a buzzing...no, a voice, now that she knew what to listen for. A voice, but it didn't sound right. It was very faint and...electronic.

Ramona looked more closely at the woman, and saw the tiny earphone. Someone else was talking to the woman. Whoever that someone was, he or she had warned the woman of Ramona's approach. An unaided mortal wouldn't have heard her.

"Your boss," Ramona said, looking around again and trying pierce the shadows. "Who's that?"

"Hesha Ruhadze."

Ramona kept scanning the darkness, but even her penetrating vision could find no one. "Hesha, huh." At least it wasn't the Sabbat—if this woman was telling the truth. But it didn't have to be Sabbat to be bad. Hesha might have heard that Khalil was spilling his secrets to the Sabbat; Hesha might consider Ramona an accomplice to that spilling. "Is he the little voice in your ear?"

The woman blanched. The buzzing resumed, fast and furious. "Uh, no.... Not exactly."

"Who is it then?"

The buzzing increased. Someone was clearly *very* concerned about what the woman was going to say next. "Just friends, here to make sure I return safely."

Ramona hesitated. Despite her best efforts, she still couldn't pinpoint the "friends." She supposed that, if they were going to attack her, there would have been no use in the woman talking to her. They could have ambushed her blind. "Tell them to come out where I can see them."

More very intense buzzing. "No," the woman said.

"I mean, no…they won't." The woman put a finger to her earphone and listened with a pained expression. "But they're willing to guarantee your safe passage if you come speak with Hesha."

"I don't accept guarantees from people I don't know."

The woman frowned as the buzzing erupted again. She yanked the receiver from her ear and let the device dangle from a wire tucked into her collar. The buzzing sounded very angry.

"My name is Pauline Miles. I work for Hesha. My friends are Nosferatu. They—*and Hesha*—guarantee your safety."

Ramona felt that she was out of her league somehow. Nosferatu. Khalil had met with them. Camarilla. The Gangrel were part of the Camarilla. *If* all this was on the level…

"Okay," Ramona said finally. Judging from the unabated angry buzzing spewing from the earphone, Pauline had pissed off somebody, and majorly.

Ramona gave her big-time points for that.

Khalil didn't have time to grow impatient waiting for a phone call this night. In fact, he was rather perturbed that it came so soon. The sun had just set and the Ravnos opened his eyes and stretched the kinks of a motionless sleep out of his limbs when it rang. He looked about him fretfully, certain that he was being spied upon for such precise timing to be possible.

He also glanced at the suitcase on the floor. It was still chained to the old radiator, and its lock seemed intact as well. It made him regret this phone call even more, because what he really wanted to do was count again the cash stashed therein and gloat.

Liz had proven her weight in blood with that fence tip the other night, and last night, Khalil had profited greatly. Perhaps the snake could now serve her worth in blood twice over: once for blood money and the second for her purer strain of Cainite blood. He smiled at the thought of breaking her as he had that Ventrue princess. Liz was another snotty Western woman who needed a good, and permanent, lesson.

The singsong of the phone continued and Khalil dashed away the haze of his sleep by rapidly shaking his head. Then he picked it up and pressed the RECEIVE button.

"Uh huh?" said the Ravnos into the tiny receiver portion of the cellular phone.

"Khalil Ravana?" said a voice the Ravnos recognized as the Nosferatu he knew as Mike. "You were right, Ravnos, there is a coming storm. I believe we may need your umbrella."

Khalil smiled. He pulled the phone away from his face a moment, afraid his smile was so loud that Mike might hear it. *Suckers*, the *shilmulo* thought. He had them right where he wanted them. Right where he'd maneuvered them. He put the phone back to his mouth.

He tried to be diplomatic, even though he and Mike both knew Khalil had the upper hand here. Well, he could afford to be diplomatic *because* they both knew who had the upper hand. "I'm sorry to hear of your troubles. I can, of course, be reasonable in my requests for payment."

Khalil smiled broadly again. He didn't need some crumbling, thousand-year-old Cainite buried in the slime of Calcutta to manipulate silly vampires with ease. This whole thing about the power of the elders and the control they exerted on the world was obviously overrated. So he couldn't choke someone halfway around the world like his once-upon-a-time master had done to him when last he'd spoken with Mike. Who needed that in a world with cell phones and computers? Brains could trump blood, in this day and age.

Khalil congratulated himself on being one of the new breed, the better breed, of vampire.

Mike had said something.

Khalil paused and then asked, "What was that, Mike? The connection was a little fuzzy for a minute there."

Still sounding so damn polite that Khalil figured the sewer rats must be feeling caught over a barrel, Mike repeated, "I said that we're looking now for that snake you're after, and we have some good leads. Good enough leads that I think we should set a meeting for tomorrow night. I'll have solid information for you by then."

Khalil shook his head. Pity the poor Nosferatu, he thought. So desperate for the cure that they were arranging meetings before they even had anything to provide in return. But that was okay, because Khalil had other plans now.

"Mike? Don't worry about the snake. I think I have the information I require on that count already. No, I think we're just talking a cash transaction here. I've got quality info. Surely your kind has enough cash stashed away to make the price right."

Mike stuttered a moment. "So you just want to sell the…umbrella?"

Khalil said, "Sure, but it comes high, Mike. It'll cost you…a million dollars."

"Whoa," Mike exclaimed. "We're not talking rupees here, you know."

Khalil hesitated, a little fazed by the exchange calculations in his head. "Half a million."

"Please. I'd think more like a quarter of a million would be more than reasonable."

"Well, sure, but we're talking no ordinary umbrella here," Khalil countered. "We're talking one-of-a-kind, supernatural umbrella."

Mike said, "For that much money, we should be able to buy a perfectly good raincoat elsewhere. How about I send someone to meet you tomorrow night, with a quarter of a million dollars? Ten o'clock okay?"

Khalil was silent for a moment, a little rattled, acting as if he was considering it. "Yes, that will do. Your lackey can meet me in Times Square. I'm sure you've got something like ten thousand tunnels radiating throughout the city from that spot."

"Something like that."

Khalil disconnected.

Ramona opened the door. Her eyes met Liz's and saw relief.

"Khalil?" Ramona called.

Liz shook her head. "He's out. I don't know where."

Ramona nodded. She locked the door behind her and moved quickly to the couch, where Liz was still chained. Liz immediately reached between the cushions and pulled out one of the picks and began working at her manacles again.

"I'm afraid I'll never make much of a burglar," Liz said. "An old lock on a door is one thing, but these—these were purely made *not* to be picked. Did you get another file?"

"I got better." Ramona held aloft a key.

Liz's jaw dropped. "Where in the world…?" But her wide-eyed amazement turned instantly to suspicion. "Hesha. The chains were his. You found him. He gave you the key." Ramona offered the key, but Liz refused to take it. She wouldn't touch it, or even look at it. "Whatever he told you was a lie."

"Look. I don't know about any of that," Ramona said. "But I do know…" she grabbed Liz's wrist and fit the key into the slot on the manacle. The key turned. *Click.*

Liz stared at her free hand but didn't seem to see it. She spoke very rapidly: "You can't trust him, Ramona. If he helps you, it's only because he gets something out of it. He wants me back—for what I know, for my expertise...and the dreams...not because he cares. Because he doesn't. He doesn't care about anyone. He just uses...people, things...."

Ramona clicked open the manacle around Liz's left ankle. The Gangrel tried all the locks to make sure the key worked for each. "Hey, baby. Earth to Liz. Don't matter what Hesha wants. You're free."

Liz stared desperately back and forth from the open manacles to her rescuer. Red tears began to form in her eyes. "He put me here. Now he lets me loose. He always gets what he wants," she said softly.

Ramona grabbed Liz by the arm. "Hey. What'd you tell me about your friend that Hesha wanted, that he wanted to make like us? And you didn't let it happen. You remember that?"

Liz blinked and nodded. A single tear of blood ran down her cheek.

"That wasn't Hesha getting what he wanted," Ramona said.

"No," Liz said, her voice gaining confidence. "Thompson got what he wanted. Not Hesha."

"It was *you*." Ramona shook Liz a little. "*You* got what *you* wanted. Hesha might be The Man, but you're The *Woman*. Right? *Right*?"

Liz nodded. For the first time in many nights, she smiled and even laughed a little. Ramona smiled too. This woman was going to make it. Somehow, she was going to make it. Maybe Ramona could never bring back Zhavon, but Liz was going to make it.

But the worry was not completely gone from Liz's face. "Don't let him control you," she said through more tears and dying laughter.

"Hey, the only way Hesha gets what he wants is I get what I want." But Ramona knew it wouldn't be quite that simple, and she wondered about the bargain to which she'd agreed.

But there was no more time for that. Footsteps. The stairs.

"*Khalil*," Ramona said. She took the key, pressed it into Liz's hand— "Hide this. *Now.*" —and then began fastening the manacles again. "He's got a meeting tomorrow night," she explained. "That's the time to go. Okay?"

The words took a moment to sink in. Liz was clearly despondent at seeing the chains locked back in place. But then she nodded. She wiped the tears as Ramona moved to the other side of the room, and they prepared to face Khalil.

Tuesday, 31 August 1999, 9:45 PM
Times Square
New York City, New York

Khalil stood facing one of the many tacky window displays along the western side of Times Square. The raucous and seedy sex shops and porn theatres were of some interest, as were a handful of items in the window displays themselves, but what really interested the Ravnos was the glittering bauble of his own future.

He was sure his Nosferatu contact was already here somewhere too, but Khalil had come early, both to scout the terrain before he met his contact, and also to let the Nosferatu know how cool and in control he was. It would make them think twice before trying to double-cross him.

So in the eerie neon red of a scripted sign that said merely "Condoms," the *shilmulo* smoothed his inky black eyebrows so they stood at crisp points. He continued to groom himself casually until his beard and moustache and curled hair were all in proper order. Then he began to pat down his new black clothing—so ultrahip, so ooh-la-la—but he pulled up short for the briefest second before nonchalantly continuing his task.

Inside, though, he began to sweat a river. Reflected in the window that served as Khalil's mirror was the Sabbat vampire, Jean-Paul. The tight smile the man flashed spoke volumes as he strode a few final steps to stand behind Khalil.

Khalil knew this was trouble.

"Well, well, who have we here?" Jean-Paul leered at him in the glass.

Perhaps the crowd here would make violence impossible. Khalil dashed that hope. First, it was Times Square. Second, Times Square was in New York, a city where the bystanders might turn a rape into a gangbang.

Not that his Calcutta was the most savory place either, but....

Khalil tried to sound relaxed, insouciant. "Jean-Paul. Good feeding in this area? Or do you have other business here?"

Jean-Paul merely smiled again, glacially, and said, "Other business, to be sure, Ravnos."

Khalil continued to focus his gaze on the Sabbat. Without moving his eyes, he was able to gather some movement in the periphery of his vision. The news was not good. The menagerie Khalil had labeled that night in the club revealed itself. The shark, swimming slowly but clearly smelling blood. The cat, stepping softly, and with a predatory gleam in its eye. The monkey now quiet, studying of its victim. Even the little dog was there, although its tail was no longer between its legs. Not a good sign, at all.

Jean-Paul's cold smirk became even more pronounced. "We've come to...spectate. Seems like it's been open season on you Ravnos lately."

Uh, oh, thought Khalil. He *was* in trouble. He continued tidying his clothes, straightening the beaded onyx and silver necklace to display it against the black of his shirt. "What exactly do you mean?"

Jean-Paul assumed a faux-concerned expression and said, "That's exactly what I mean. Here the only other two Ravnos we can even find in the city have both gone missing—the Camarilla unfortunately beat us to the gypsy fortune-teller—and nothing has happened. *Rien*. No reprisals. Isn't that strange?"

Khalil finally turned around. "Not really, you piece of filth," he said, squinting directly into Jean-Paul's eyes, though only for a second. It was dangerous to let such gazes linger among the Kindred.

Jean-Paul's expression darkened, but Khalil continued. "No, we're just waiting to see who thinks they can take advantage of us, and then we'll have words with every single one of you assholes, one at time and completely at our leisure. So persist at your own risk, Jean-Paul. And that's the only warning you get. Which is one more than usual, but you did point me toward that yummy Ventrue chick, so I have a soft spot for you and your mangy crew here."

And Khalil made a dash for it. The animals had fairly well encircled him, but the Ravnos crafted a brief illusion of himself standing where he had in fact been standing, so that when he moved, he also seemed to remain standing. The visual trick lasted but a split-second, but it was enough to confuse the beasts, and Khalil managed to tumble and roll through the legs of the shark.

Khalil was on his feet again and running when he heard the cat's voice. "There he goes."

"Why weren't you watching him? After him, fools!" demanded Jean-Paul, who also took up pursuit.

Khalil was wiry and quick, and crowd-wise from mortal and immortal years among the throngs of Calcutta, but those were his only advantages. He had not yet scouted the area very carefully, and he was fearful of making a wrong turn. He didn't have much time to think, though, because the cat and the squirty little dog were both quite fast. They immediately began to narrow the gap.

After making a few twists and turns, Khalil suddenly broke into the street and ran across six lanes of traffic, immediately after a red light changed to green. He wove through the as-yet-unmoving traffic on his side of the street and dashed across the other side before those cars cleared the intersection and overtook him. He timed it just right. Several cars blared horns at him as he skirted them. He didn't look back to see how the Sabbat fared. He just kept running, zigging and zagging through every sidestreet or alley that he could find.

But this giddy rush led him directly into trouble: He found himself at a dead-end. Of sorts, at least. He faced a chainlink fence—twenty feet high and topped with barbed wire. The alleyway continued on the other side and rejoined a busy street, where more headlights and turn signals flashed.

Khalil started to scale the fence but realized that he wouldn't have time—his lead wasn't enough; he would be clawed down from behind. Just then, he thought he heard a number of footfalls echoing behind him. There was no time to dither.

He pressed himself against a wall and dropped the veil of illusion over himself. Crouched low, he now appeared to be a pile of rotting refuse. For the sake of verisimilitude, he added a conjured stench to the illusion as well.

And then the Sabbat were upon the scene.

"Damn," hissed the cat as she slid to a stop at the fence.

Shark growled, "Did he go over?"

Cat was already partway up the fence. "What does it look like?"

Then Jean-Paul arrived. "Everyone over. Now! I want his blood!"

The others scrambled to comply. The cat slithered through the barbed wire, hopped down, and was off in pursuit. The others followed more cautiously, though both the shark and the dog cut themselves on the wire. The dog whined in pain, but the shark stoically accepted the wounds.

"Check all the grates and sewers," Jean-Paul called after his underlings as they rushed down the other side of the alley. Then he eased toward the fence as well, muttering a curse under his breath.

Glancing to make certain the other Sabbat were gone, Khalil rose from his deception and fell upon Jean-Paul from behind. The Ravnos flicked his left wrist and a slender blade dropped into his palm. With his other hand, he grabbed Jean-Paul by the throat. Khalil slammed the stiletto into his victim's back—stabbing and then digging to the side—over and over again.

Jean-Paul's eyes were wide with pain, fright, and fury. He strained against Khalil, but the Ravnos's grip was unbreakable. Khalil scraped his victim's face across the metal fence. Where the fence met the wall, he began slamming Jean-Paul's head against the bricks. The dull thuds filled the alleyway. Finally the skull gave way and the Sabbat crumpled to the ground.

The inert body had barely touched the pavement before Khalil pounced again. "Not so tough without your little army, are you?" He opened wide and sank his fangs into Jean-Paul's neck. A sweet rush of blood followed. His captive struggled reflexively, trying to break his grip. Khalil paused to hammer Jean-Paul's head into the pavement some more, until the writhing stopped.

Then Khalil drank…until there was nothing left.

Khalil was still feeling rosy-cheeked and aglow with energy as he sat across the table from the Nosferatu. His second diablerie. It was something he really could develop a taste for.

Was he perhaps looking too hungrily upon the sewer rats who sat around him now?

He was in the midst of reciting his personal recipe for the means to cure the wounds of the Eye of Hazimel. Somehow, none of his companions smelled quite right. Mike, typing away on his laptop, smelled like Mike and...something else. Another who looked like a walking corpse riddled with wounds and dangling bits of raw, seemingly half-healed flesh, smelled vaguely, weirdly familiar. The other two stank, period, but they were Nosferatu and the meeting was in a sewer tunnel, so this was no surprise.

But Khalil was feeling cocky, basking in the warmth of the blood, and the odors caused nothing more than a faint tremor of unease.

He continued, "So, apply a liberal dash of human spit to a poultice made of the mustard seed and sweet basil. The mustard will drive out the poisonous humors, and the basil will purify the flesh of the Eye's ill-intent. Bind that to the injury and leave it through the next full moon. Abracadabra— no more wound."

Mike asked, "The next full moon? Does it matter if that's the same night as the poultice is applied? Or should it be an entire lunar cycle later?"

Khalil considered a moment. "Better safe than sorry. I'd say the whole month. You don't want to play around with damage done by the Eye—it'll eat you up if you don't get it all."

Mike nodded and made another note. "Is that it?"

Khalil sat back from the table with a sly smile and spread his hands wide. "Unless you have other questions?"

Mike placed a briefcase on the table, opened it, and pushed it toward the Ravnos. Khalil flipped through the bills. He didn't want to linger long enough to count it exactly, but he figured there was enough here to satisfy a host of needs for some time to come. He closed the suitcase again with an approving nod, and stood up.

"Need a guide to find your way back out?" Mike asked.

Khalil said, "I know the way. See you around town."

He jauntily bowed to the monster and left the catacombs. Walking down the dripping tunnels, Khalil chuckled to himself. Surely his deception had worked. He was going to get out of here without giving them a damn thing, and with $250,000 in his hands. The Ravnos imagined the rats industriously conferring over the bogus information he had told them.

The fact was, Khalil had no intention of staying in New York a moment longer for them to figure out the scam. Well, maybe a few moments longer. Two more little visits, he'd promised himself, then he was out of town far richer, much stronger, and vastly more independent than when he'd entered.

Visit number one was back to the apartment and all that lovely Setite blood, just waiting for him.

Wednesday, 1 September 1999, 12:37 AM
Red Hook, Brooklyn
New York City, New York

Liz stared at the key. It rested beside her on the couch, torturing her—just as it had since that frozen moment when Ramona had held it aloft. Everything had seemed so unreal. Ramona had the key…*Hesha's* key…the manacles were open…the manacles that Hesha had placed on her the last time she'd seen him….

Not until Ramona snapped the metal bonds closed again had reality reasserted itself. Reality—imprisonment. Then Khalil had been back and the key hidden. Liz had been positive that he would find the key, that he would know about it somehow. All the rest of that morning, and tonight until he'd left, she'd lain there paralyzed by terror, unresponsive to her captor's snide comments and abusive questions. She'd grown expert over the weeks at ignoring him. He could still extort information from her when he wanted—he would threaten to harm Amy, or to let Liz herself starve—but there was nothing else he needed.

There was only his cold glare…his gaze of evil hunger.

Liz had forced herself to wait a full half-hour after he left before she pulled the key from its hiding place among the cushions. She'd placed it there beside her, gazing upon it like a holy relic. But like any gift of the divine, it laid bare her own deficiencies and fears.

Where would she go? She'd spent her every night of living death here…in her apartment…chained. She would have to find another haven against the sun. But Khalil had taken her money.

"Think, Liz. *Think*." Her own voice seemed strange at first, but it brought her back to herself, to her wits. Khalil had not found the key to her safety-deposit box. She kept two thousand dollars there—it was money she'd saved, telling herself that it was for a romantic getaway, for some planned spontaneity when that perfect man—*if* that perfect man—walked into her life.

Elizabeth laughed aloud, painfully. There would be no fairy-tale romance now, no passion-swept journey to Greece or Egypt.

"Dear God, *not* Egypt." She laughed again—could not stop, in fact. And then she was sobbing. She stopped *that* at once, angry with herself, wiping her tears and licking the blood from her hands before she realized what she was doing.

"Think," she said again, forcing calmness. She took a deep breath and tried not to notice how strange the sensation of air entering her lungs felt. She glanced at the clock—she'd wasted too much time already. Too much time tonight, dithering…too much time over the past weeks, being helpless.

She took the key and unlocked her left wrist, and the right. Then her ankles. As she rose from the couch, she was gripped by the fear—the near *certainty*—that Khalil would return any second. Liz hurried over to her desk—her war-horse, mighty, eight-hooved Sleipnir, had carried out one last heroic trust—and opened one of the side drawers. Khalil had not discovered the shallow false bottom. Only two flat items occupied that space: a letter containing the only kind words her father had ever seen fit to write to her, and the key to her safety-deposit box. Liz took them both and stuffed them into her pocket.

She paused to glance around the apartment, and her heart ached. Despite Khalil's ravages, there was still so much of *her* here—her books, her notes, her tools. How could she just leave it all? But there was no choice. Perhaps her imprisonment here had been useful in that one way: If she'd not been terrorized and abused, she might never have brought herself to leave all that was her old life.

Resolutely, Elizabeth strode to the door.

But as she reached for the first lock, it began to turn, seemingly of its own accord—a key used from the *outside*.

Liz faltered back a step in horror as the locks clicked open, one after another, and the door opened.

"Well, fuck you!" Khalil shouted at Liz, though she could not hear him. He swung the heavy chains he clutched into the side of the monstrous and monstrously ugly desk that crowded the room. Anger practically steamed from his eyes, and he hoarsely whispered, "Fine, just fine. I'll drink her bald black daddy's blood, and then she'll be *mine* to control. Snake bitch!"

He smashed the desk again with the chains.

Then he walked a bit and sat down on the couch, the chains and manacles that had once held Elizabeth A. Dimitros prisoner dangling at his feet. He tried to calm down, but he was defying a deep-seated urgency, a monster in his belly that raged at being denied the old blood Khalil had come to claim.

So Hesha's blood—as the pinnacle of achievement in the emancipation of Khalil Ravana—would have to do after all. And Khalil swore by the balls of the Rakshasa King that that time would not be too far off.

He'd returned moments before to find Liz gone. No Ramona either. The Gangrel hadn't been there when he could have used her, when the Sabbat was after him. Turned out he hadn't needed her anyway.

"Fuck her too! She's on her own from now on."

He should have devoured the snake bitch nights or weeks ago, but he'd thought there might have been time to gain power *and* go after Hesha.

Now Khalil was out of time. Hesha would have to wait for another night, and once he had that old snake's blood, Liz would frigging well do anything he demanded. Maybe it was even better this way. He could *really* take his time with her later.

As he sat and fumed, Khalil slowly began to notice something…something *odd*, something not quite right. He sat still and tried to determine what exactly had attracted his attention. There was nothing…but then there was something again.

Something in the shadows. *Someone* in the shadows—hiding. Or *not* hiding, as it turned out. Gradually, as Khalil concentrated on the matter, he could see the small, pitiful figure crouched in the darkness in the corner near the front door. The creature looked more mangy rat than human, with wrinkled rolls of flesh forming its body and a long-ish snout that apparently only contained two bucktoothed fangs.

"Your ugly friends decide they want their money back?" Khalil asked menacingly.

The Nosferatu—it was too grotesque to be anything else—started violently when Khalil spoke to it. It began to tremble, and suddenly Khalil could see it quite clearly. He began to understand. There had been times—before he'd grown so old and wise—that he'd been too distracted, or *frightened*, to perform the tricks like those that had saved his ass tonight. The little sewer rat, watching his savage fury, was having a similar problem, an attack of nerves, and not hiding too well.

"Bad timing," said Khalil.

The creature, frozen to the spot until now, took

that as its cue to flee. Khalil was on his feet just as quickly. He grabbed the chain and, blocking the way to the door, lashed at the Nosferatu. The heavy manacle on the end bashed the creature and drew blood from the sagging folds of skin. Khalil savored its squeal of pain. All the frustrated rage that he'd saved for Liz, he now turned loose on the discovered intruder.

"Did you let my snake loose?" Khalil snarled as his fury rose once again. He swung the chain. This time the manacle crushed one of the Kindred's wrists and tore a shielding hand away from its face as it cowered, squeaking. He swung the chain again. Probably this animal had nothing to do with Liz, Khalil knew in the back of his mind, but that made little difference really. Liz was gone. Ramona was gone. Hesha wasn't here. So the Nosferatu would bear the full brunt of Khalil's displeasure. Beyond all rational control at last, the Ravnos whipped it again and again, until the beast lay writhing in a pool of its own blood. The big eyes were largely swollen shut, but through slits it regarded Khalil.

Khalil stepped closer. "The wrong place and the wrong time," he said, shaking his head. Then Khalil stepped closer still.

Before long, the mange-ridden rat of a Nosferatu was no more than a pile of dust and memory. Khalil, sprawled on the floor, savored the pleasantly bloated sensation that had settled over him. He had feasted on three Kindred in the past two weeks—two that very night. Each had underestimated him—the Ventrue childe of privilege, Jean-Monsieur-Asshole-Paul, and the rat. It softened slightly the injury of Liz's escape.

"Ungrateful bitch," Khalil muttered, stretching out on a throw rug and rubbing his belly. "After everything I did for her…"

The best part, however, was yet to come. Maybe not right away. Khalil had seen enough of New York; he was ready to head for greener, quieter pastures. Pastures where not everyone wanted his hide. But some night, he would catch up with Hesha Ruhadze and then…*then* Khalil would taste Setite blood at last.

Do you plan to lie there until every other Nosferatu in the city realizes what you did to that pathetic creature?

Khalil slowly propped himself up on his elbows. He smiled, almost drunkenly, and wagged his finger at the air. "You don't tell me what to do anymore." His smile faded, however, and he stroked his mustache thoughtfully. "But you do have a point." He climbed to his feet. "No point in overstaying my welcome."

The briefcase—and all of that money—was safe, but Khalil still couldn't help scooping up the occasional stray ring or gem that he had scattered several nights ago in a fit of temper. While stuffing these tiny treasures into his pockets, he grew concerned about the sizeable, roughly body-shaped pile of dust still on the floor. If he was going to strategically withdraw from the city, sweeping ratboy's remnants under the rug might buy him a few more hours.

After a few minutes of casting about for a broom, Khalil had to settle for a Dust Buster, and he set to work. He'd barely sucked up one dusty leg when he realized that the door to the apartment was open—and that someone was standing in the doorway. A *very tall* someone.

Khalil whipped around, wielding the Dust Buster as he would his knife. The newcomer was wrapped from head to toe in rags and torn, disintegrating clothing. He—if it was a *he*—smelled of raw sewage. Despite that tiny reminder of Calcutta, Khalil was not pleased to see anyone—especially a Nosferatu.

"Let me guess," said the *shilmulo*, with a grin equally disarming and disingenuous. "I missed a spot." He carefully set down the Dust Buster.

The newcomer, just as carefully, began to unwrap the rags that all but covered his head and face. A few wraps was enough to reveal that this was no Nosferatu.

"*Hesha.*"

The Setite's glare moved from the incriminating dust to the empty shackles by the couch, and then back to Khalil. "If *you* have harmed her…"

Hesha didn't need to finish the sentence. Khalil could read the intent of his accuser's expression easily enough. A dozen lies flashed through Khalil's mind in seconds. Ironically, the truth seemed to be his best gambit this time.

"This?" Khalil gestured toward the remains at his feet. "This has nothing to do with your girlfriend. Nothing at all. Don't you worry yourself about a thing." As he spoke, Khalil nonchalantly sidled closer to the mammoth old desk that occupied much of the nearest wall. He distractedly noticed Liz's fading scent, but at the moment, he was less concerned about the missing Setite than he was about the one standing in front of him.

"Me and Lizzie, we were tight…*are* tight." Khalil held up two crossed fingers. "You know, like *garam masala.*"

Hesha did not seem particularly soothed by the banter. Khalil had a knife tucked away in his jacket, of course, but he had serious doubts about attempting physical violence now that Hesha was readily available. Never mind the color in Khalil's cheeks, the flush of vigor from Kindred vitae. The Setite, in person, was so very—imposing.

A moment later, however, Khalil's spirits rose immeasurably. Behind Hesha, Ramona stepped through the open doorway. Khalil let the fawning manner drop away. He sneered and stood straight and tall.

"Ramona…" the *shilmulo* said triumphantly. He motioned with a finger across his throat.

Ramona leaned against the door frame and stared back at him.

Khalil's sneer froze in place. "Ramona, which part of—" he drew his finger across his throat again "—do you not understand?"

"She understands a great deal," Hesha said, moving forward ominously.

That was all Khalil needed to see.

With a defiant roar, the Ravnos turned and took hold of the large desk. He bodily lifted it off the floor and flung it at the nearest expanse of black glass. The painted picture window shattered. Khalil shot for the opening.

Hesha stepped to intervene, but his movements were hindered by his wrappings. Khalil was past him too quickly.

Ramona did not have that problem. In motion before the desk was fully through the window, she sprang across the room and landed squarely on Khalil…and passed completely through him. The lack of resistance cost her her balance, and she landed in a heap. Back on her feet in a second, she was ready to spring again…but at what? The tall window was intact. The desk still rested by the wall.

And Khalil was gone.

"This is not her," Hesha said, poking at the dust on the floor. "Calebros's boy. Mouse. I *told* them not to worry about the money."

"I'll take your word for it."

He seemed very subdued, Ramona thought. Maybe that was just because of the pain from moving about. He had pulled off more of the rags. Below his shoulders, he was still bandaged. Some of the gauze was dark with whatever was oozing from his body. Ramona hadn't watched as Pauline had pressed the burning turmeric root against some of Hesha's wounds. The Gangrel felt that she'd done enough by telling them how to cure the injuries from the Eye. Her own encounter with the turmeric had been horrible enough. She didn't even want to think about the same treatment being applied to all of Hesha's face, to his head, to most of the rest of his body. Ramona cringed.

Hesha made his way to a chair and sat heavily. What treatment he had undergone had left him weakened. Mild tremors gripped his body every few minutes.

"Where is she?" Hesha asked. For a second or two, Ramona thought his pained expression might be from something deeper than physical pain, but then his cool façade was back in place.

"Don't know." That was true as far as it went. Ramona didn't know, didn't want to know. The deal had been that Hesha would make sure Liz was freed. He'd given Ramona the key as a sign of good faith.

"At the very least," he had said, "you can free her yourself." Apparently he hadn't expected Ramona to take him up on that. But Liz had been clear that she didn't want anything else to do with Hesha—even if she'd said it somewhat wistfully. Ramona didn't trust Hesha enough to take a chance on what he might do to Liz. That poor girl had been through enough—too much—already. But Ramona *did* trust Hesha, even on first meeting, more than she had come to trust Khalil. So she'd gone back and settled on the second part of the bargain with the Setite.

"You agree, now," Hesha said, not yet quite able to erase the hint of remorse in his voice, "that Khalil is not a reliable ally?"

Ramona shrugged. "Not a real big surprise there." She had watched from nearby as Khalil had lied to the Nosferatu about how to heal wounds from the Eye. Even though they'd given him the money—Hesha's money—he'd lied.

"It is a valuable lesson," Hesha said.

"Two hundred fifty thousand bucks worth of valuable?"

For the first time that Ramona had seen, a smile crept across Hesha's face. "If you're able to help me find the Eye, it will be many times more valuable."

Ramona shrugged again. "It's your money."

Wednesday, 1 September 1999, 1:08 AM
In a car, somewhere in Brooklyn
New York City, New York

Elizabeth sat low enough in the passenger seat
that the shoulder strap of the seatbelt dug into her
chin. She couldn't help feeling that true escape
was impossible. Any moment, Khalil would bound
from the side of the road and reclaim her, or
Hesha…. No, she told herself. Hesha had never
returned for her. He'd sacrificed her to Ra.

The driver wouldn't look at her. He concentrated entirely on the road—much more so than
driving required. Even when he spoke, he kept his
eyes directed forward.

"Your friend, Amy, wants very much to see
you," Jordan Kettridge said.

Liz shook her head. "I can't. I can't see her.
Not after…everything."

Amy had honored Liz's request after the robbery and called, not the police, but Professor
Kettridge. She'd told him what little she knew and
given him Rutherford House's set of keys to the
apartment when he'd arrived from California.
Good old Amy. But Liz couldn't face her. Liz didn't
know if she'd *ever* be able to face Amy again. Not
for a long time. Liz knew that much.

"I understand," Kettridge said. His fingers were
tight around the steering wheel.

Liz watched him. She could tell he knew she
was looking at him, but still he peered forward as
if straining to see the road…only the road.

"I've...changed," Liz said at last. "I'm...one of them. Like Hesha." It was true...yet it wasn't true. She might need blood to survive, but she was not *like* Hesha.

"I know," Kettridge said, still watching the road. "I've changed too." He didn't sound as confident as Liz remembered. "I...see things. Things I only suspected before."

Liz believed him. She had seen it in his eyes when he'd opened the apartment door—relief at recognizing her, then sudden shock at somehow seeing *what* she was. He'd looked away, and he'd not met her eyes since those first moments.

"Why did you bring me, then?" Liz asked.

Finally Kettridge did look at her. He held her gaze for a long moment. When he looked back to the road, it was no longer in avoidance of her. "I don't know," he said. "I trust you. I *did* trust you. I don't think that's changed. Maybe it will."

Elizabeth felt the tears coming then. She couldn't stop them this time. Kettridge handed her a handkerchief that soon was dabbed from white to red. Several miles passed.

"What do I tell Amy?" Kettridge asked eventually.

"Nothing. Don't tell her that you found me. I'm dead to her." Liz buried her face in her hands. "Or tell her everything. I don't care. I don't want to think about any of this right now. I just want...I just want..."

She couldn't finish the sentence. She didn't know. She wanted to be with Hesha; she wanted never to see him again. She wanted her old life back. She wanted her *life* back.

"Just keep driving," Liz said quietly.

Kettridge nodded. And kept driving. Away from everything that Liz had ever known.

Tuesday, 12 October 1999, 3:25 AM
O'Hare Airport
Chicago, Illinois

"Go get the bags."

Sarat cheerfully did as he was told.

Mouth tightly closed, Khalil took in a deep breath and savored the smells of the city that was his new home—or at least the smells of the airport of the city that was his new home. He tried to ignore the fact that there really weren't many distinctive scents about. One American airport smelled much like another—disinfectant not quite covering the odor of stale grease in the closed food court, sweat of other passengers disembarking from the red-eye...

Red-eye—Khalil had taken that as a good omen, not that there was any question about his wanting to leave New York. Especially after more than a month holed up in the basement of a friend of Sarat's cousin's grocer. That city was...a little too hot.

And why might that be?

"Hey, talk to me nice and I might just do you a favor once in a while," Khalil said, much to the puzzlement of a bleary-eyed businessman standing nearby.

As Sarat hurried back with their three suitcases—one of his own and both of Khalil's—the *shilmulo* was awash in self-satisfaction, not the least reason for which being that he wasn't stuffed into a cramped little trunk this time through Chicago. He'd come to America with nothing, a slave, and by the sweat of his brow, he'd bettered his lot. Instinctively, he clutched his carry-on bag to his side. The upscale duffel was full of cash—cash that he'd earned, despite the attempt of the Nosferatu to steal it back, despite Hesha's little appearance.

"Hmph. I should have killed him and drunk his blood while I had the chance," Khalil said to himself.

The bleary-eyed businessman began noticeably to edge away. Khalil looked at him and smiled. The man froze and smiled back unconvincingly.

"Where to now, boss?" Sarat asked, also watching the businessman who, as soon as Khalil's attention was diverted, scurried away down the concourse.

"Where to? To find us a hotel. And tomorrow night, we start exploring the city. Think your cousin will like it here?"

"You said the winters are milder here than in New York?"

"Oh yeah," Khalil said. "Balmy."

Sarat grinned enthusiastically. "Then Prasad will like it. He has always said that New York is too cold."

"That's what I like to hear. We'll have your whole family here and shop set up within a week. I know they love curry here more than anything. Go find us a cab." Sarat hurried off as quickly as he could without dropping the luggage, and Khalil followed along at a more leisurely pace.

Like Chicago or not, what Sarat's family would not like was what they'd find when they pried up the floor in Sarat's room to pack Elder Brother Ghose. Instead of a vampire beaten into dormancy, there would be merely an old woven rug full of dust.

But it was for a good cause, Khalil thought, licking his lips.

And he didn't put up nearly the struggle that Hesha would have.

"I couldn't stay in that basement all night *every* night. And I got hungry. Besides, the snake had already lost his girlfriend. I was just giving him a break. I've got a big heart."

I'll keep that in mind.

"Yeah, you do that."

Khalil was a family man now. He'd made Ghose's family—like the former Ravnos's blood—his own, and as long as Khalil's blood flowed in their veins, they wouldn't complain too loudly about dear departed Ghose.

Ahead, at curbside just beyond the glass-faced terminal, Sarat had secured a cab. Still clutching his duffel bag tightly, Khalil climbed in and prepared to enjoy his new city, his new wealth, his new freedom.

Far beneath Calcutta, finger tips that were little more than bone covered with a thin veneer of skin tapped against one another. Hazimel, were he given to physical displays of emotion, might have smiled in the darkness, there upon his throne of hewn rock.

The maggot Khalil had performed admirably. The woman with the temper, the Gangrel, might still lead Hesha to the Eye. It had only been a matter of time before Khalil, with his bluster and deception, had alienated her, had driven her to the service of the snake. So predictable. There was no longer any need for the young *shilmulo* to remain in that city.

Enjoy the nights of your youth, Khalil, Hazimel thought. *Let yourself believe that you could break my hold so easily—for that is what you want to believe. Hoard the treasures of the flesh, if that is what makes you feel safe.*

Then Hazimel did, at last, smile. And he laughed—but he remembered little of laughter. The sound that emanated from perhaps the eldest surviving Ravnos, to mortal ears, would have resembled more closely the fruits of torture than mirth. But to him, the sound was sweet.

about the author

Kathleen Ryan has worked for, with, and around White Wolf Publishing since 1993. Her first fiction pieces, about a young mage named Amanda, appeared as book-openers in **Mage: The Ascension**, first edition. Through cajolery and threats she has managed to get an Amanda piece in every major **Mage** release since then, wrangled all the fun parts of **Tradition Book: Euthanatos** for herself, and snuck most of **Changing Breed Book: Kitsune** into the back of **Hengeyokai: Shapeshifters of the East**. **Clan Novel: Setite** was her first novel-length published work. She would like to thank her family, the Rescue Party, John Steele, and Stewart Wieck for helping her get through **Clan Novel: Ravnos**, her second.

The Vampire Clan Novel Series......................

Clan Novel: Toreador
These artists are the most sophisticated of the Kindred.

Clan Novel: Tzimisce
Fleshcrafters, experts of the arcane, and the most cruel of Sabbat vampires.

Clan Novel: Gangrel
Feral shapeshifters distanced from the society of the Kindred.

Clan Novel: Setite
The much-loathed serpentine masters of moral and spiritual corruption.

Clan Novel: Ventrue
The most political of vampires, they lead the Camarilla.

Clan Novel: Lasombra
The leaders of the Sabbat and the most Machiavellian of all Kindred.

Clan Novel: Assamite
The most feared clan, for they are assassins of both vampires and mortals.

Clan Novel: Ravnos
These devilish gypsies are not welcomed by the Camarilla, nor tolerated by the Sabbat.

Clan Novel: Malkavian
Thought insane by other Kindred, they know that within madness lies wisdom.

Clan Novel: Giovanni
Still a respected part of the mortal world, this mercantile clan is also home to necromancers.

Clan Novel: Brujah
Street-punks and rebels, they are aggressive and vengeful in defense of their beliefs.

Clan Novel: Tremere
The most magical of the clans and the most tightly organized.

Clan Novel: Nosferatu
Horrific to behold, these sneaks know more secrets than the other clans—secrets that will only be revealed in this, the last of the **Vampire Clan Novels**.

..........................continues.

The American Camarilla is reeling. Can they take advantage of the death of Cardinal Monçada to turn the tide back against the Sabbat, who have grabbed vast tracts of the Eastern United States? Despite the apparent efforts of Hazimel himself, the Eye of Hazimel is again in the hands of a once-pitiful Toreador named Leopold. Whose influence could be greater than that of the Methuselah from whom the Eye originated?

Some characters have yet to be introduced, while the stars of previous books will still return. Victoria, Hesha, Ramona, Jan, Vykos and others have ambitions and goals to realize.

The end date of each book continues to press the timeline forward, and the plot only thickens as you learn more. The series chronologically continues in **Clan Novel: Malkavian** and **Clan Novel: Giovanni**. Excerpts of these two exciting novels are on the following pages.

CLAN NOVEL: MALKAVIAN
ISBN 1-56504-819-9
WW#11108
$5.99 U.S.

CLAN NOVEL: GIOVANNI
ISBN 1-56504-826-1
WW#11109
$5.99 U.S.

The General had a sixth sense about ambushes.

Perhaps it was a result of centuries of experience. Or the equivalent of a mortal's entire lifespan—days and nights—spent engaged in actual battle. Or perhaps it was simply the knowledge from having escaped them in the past.

The General had survived in the face of long odds many times before. Of course, the odds were not quite so long as kine historians would record and praise and believe. And in any event, surviving was a far different matter than winning, but such was the nature of the General's own peculiar sense of pleasure that he found something possibly only precisely described as arousing about the loss. Young men cut down around him. Their dreams flying on new wings just as their blood sought solace in the ground.

And for years afterward he could wryly enjoy the difference between the heroic stories of the soldiers' last moments and the sullied truth to which he was witness. At the Alamo. At the fall of Constantinople. At Little Big Horn. At Roanoke.

And so, so long ago at Thermopylae where it all began, though the General would not admit that to himself now. Perhaps could not, for the less a Malkavian recalls of his beginning the better. The terrors the Sabbat inflict upon their newly spawned kind are rumored to be terrible, but what could possibly be more ruinous than the Embrace of a man devoid of sanity at the hands of one devoid of compassion? Not all Malkavian Embraces are so terrible, of course, but to call this one, at least, merely inhuman would play lightly with the facts.

As the General made a spectacle of himself and clambered naked up the immense sculpture of *Count Ugolino and His Sons*, he wondered at his sanity. Not just because an ambush seemed so unlikely here tonight, though the nerves in his recently regrown tongue tingled with the likelihood of conflict, but because he seemed so in control of himself just now. His actions premeditated and directed. His purpose of finding safety, while still remaining within the probable confines of the likely struggle, so clear.

And *that* was what made him absolutely certain that death would be his dance partner in the chamber of art tonight. For nothing gave him a greater thrill than seeing others struggle for life, with the exception of seeing others struggle for life and fail. That moment when defeat and death registers on the faces of the doomed was so absolute a reflection of the General's own soul that he craved to view it, and better to view it without than to contemplate it within. That moment when a being—mortal or vampiric—enters a slow-motion state as the last ticks of its life's clock tock

by stewart wieck

away and this internally infinite time can be given to contemplation of what is being lost.

That preternatural awareness was the same sort that fueled the General's search for safety. He could already feel a noose constricting around the High Museum. It choked the vigor and energy from the assemblage and made the sights and sounds crisper and brighter.

The General could not ignore these signs.

So from within the sculpture of the cannibal count—the count who would devour his own children—the General beamed a smile at the crowd he entertained and that would soon itself be consumed.

It was supposedly a celebration of the Summer Solstice, an ironic holiday for the Kindred to commemorate; but such infantile humor did not easily desert the recently dead. Victoria Ash, the party's hostess, was not new among the Kindred, but she was a Toreador. With her kind, this variety of foolishness persisted even longer. Or so they made it seem, at least, and the General usually sided with the "at least" viewpoint. Especially so in the case of Ms. Ash. She was an adept Kindred, the General concluded.

Nevertheless, he relished seeing her lovely face paralyzed with anguish. Aye, her most of all, he decided, though for no good reason.

As he watched Victoria speak with guest after guest—a truly young Ventrue, then an encounter with the Brujah primogen and the

Malkavian prince, then an intriguing Setite and eventually the late-arriving Brujah archon—the General changed his mind. He sometimes liked to pick a hero, and tonight his hero would be Victoria Ash. Oh, certainly, she would be harmed, but the General decided that she would escape. He wasn't entirely sure of the rationale for this change of heart, but it was something in which he'd indulged in the past. Lone survivors could be as interesting as mass slaughter.

The General laughed and the plaster mouth of the count cracked a bit. He wondered if this sentiment suggested there was something noble still in him.

He purposefully soured his thought and face.

He hoped it meant nothing of the sort. However, his mind was made up, and short of sacrificing himself to the slaughter too, Victoria Ash would escape this night. If he leapt from his hiding place and waded through the inevitable conflict for his own salvation, then he would make certain she was ushered to the same safety he sought.

So for a while longer the General watched the Kindred play their meaningless games. Anything these Kindred did this night would be for naught. The sole exception was departure, and the General noted with interest when the Setite with whom Victoria had spoken and a Nosferatu the General knew as Rolph both left the party slightly before midnight.

He braced himself then for a reckoning within

this chamber, but he knew as he prepared that the time was not yet. However, the urgency of that departure confused him. Perhaps it was simply his anticipation making him edgy. One would think that centuries would bring patience. Especially centuries spent largely in torpor in this or that mountain or patch of earth.

When a darkness so thick and sudden it almost seemed to have flooded the room like a raging river overcame the party, the General was actually surprised. It was a delicious feeling, being startled like that, and one he'd not felt for a long, long time.

The cries and screams were indeed muffled by the odd darkness, and the General realized before someone sounded the nature of the threat that the Lasombra were surely behind this. The Lasombra and their Sabbat allies. It was an ambush of their hated Camarilla foes, a group to which the General's own bloodline belonged. The General decided that he would wait a moment longer before joining the fray. He at least needed to attenuate his vision to the virtual absence of light.

The slaughter that ensued was grisly and brutal. And swift. So fast that it could be completed in such time only by beings who were more than mortal. And the General didn't budge from his position. At first he convinced himself that it was not fear that held him back; rather it was prudence that held him in check.

But as the massacre unfolded and gouts of blood washed the white floors and walls, the General admitted that he liked much better being the sole Kindred among a pack of kine when such slaughters took place. His safety was much more assured, in fact virtually guaranteed, in such circumstances. Even so, he still did not truly register fear, and he still found ample time to watch the trembles of such work their way across the mouths and faces and eventually into the eyes of a score of Kindred whose undead lives were being snuffed in a heartbeat.

In fact, as his pride overcame the wound his hesitation inflicted, the General began to take a mad delight in this carnage. He used his powers to keep the battle clear of the statue within which he'd found refuge, and the weak-minded Sabbat warriors could not dispute his efforts. He then became so overwhelmed attempting to observe all the details of the struggle that he nearly lost his chosen co-survivor to an obscene creature which bashed her with a fleshy appendage.

He felt her mind grasping about for assistance, but she was so alarmed and confused that she could scarcely have called her own name aloud, let alone determine who might save her. So the General helped her. It was a little matter for such an aged Malkavian as himself to give voice to the terror and chaos of her thoughts. The voice still had no spoken component, of course, and such would not have been heard over the din of the battle in any event. It summoned assistance nevertheless.

by stewart wieck

A young Toreador the General had spied regarding Victoria with great fondness earlier was close at hand. No hero he, but he would act more quickly by virtue of his proximity than the General might from afar, so it was he who kicked at the head of the beast and saved the Toreador primogen.

The General continued to watch as the young Toreador was hauled away by a tentacle formed of darkness. Meanwhile, Victoria slipped from beneath her would-be mauler and found brief refuge within a small room formed of the temporary room dividers used to break the wide-open space of the top floor of the High Museum.

She did not, however, achieve this glassine asylum without the notice of others. A wounded war ghoul seeking easy prey noted the woman's escape and plodded forward on legs as massive as the pillars on any nearby plantation home. Blood oozed from a trio of severed limbs, but the freakish creature still sported four arms and all were tipped with jagged claws.

There were no other saviors for Victoria Ash this time; in fact, there was almost no one at all. The only Camarilla vampires still battling were Prince Benison and the Brujah archon Julius. What an odd couple they made!

The General acted swiftly. Still naked, he pulled himself from the statue and streaked into the path of the war ghoul. The beast barely had time to register the General's assault before the blood-flushed Malkavian was upon him. Blood served to augment the General's strength to untold levels, and the force of his blow was such that no mortal or even ghouled mortal could withstand it. The Tzimisce masters who'd stitched the war ghoul together had not accounted for a blow so terrible as this.

As if he were battering down a door with his fists and forearms, the General piledrivered into the ghoul's chest, and the beast hurtled backward and crashed into some of its kind already feasting on the streams of Camarilla blood.

Without pausing, the General threw aside one of the dividers and prepared to scoop Victoria Ash into his arms and carry her to safety. But she was not within.

The General muttered, "Crafty bitch." The trap door in the floor was apparent to him, but it would probably escape the notice of the enemy for some time, if not indefinitely.

The General pirouetted and returned to his sculpted sanctuary. The war ghoul he'd struck had not regained its feet and the others had not noticed him, so all would be well. The rush of the battle throbbed in the General's ears, but he knew his life would be forfeit if he attempted to escape now.

So he watched and listened.

Thursday, 15 July 1999, 1:27 AM
Seasons Restaurant, Bostonian Hotel
Boston, Massachusetts

"So, you're proposing what, exactly?" Isabel looked sternly at the Kindred before her. He had been sent from Baltimore at the behest of Jan Pieterzoon to entreat Giovanni support against the Sabbat. His name was something French, or maybe Canadian, but his English certainly didn't have any accent.

"Recognition of the Giovanni claim to Boston," replied the agent. "The Camarilla will formally acknowledge the supremacy of Clan Giovanni in Boston and its immediate environs. That is, in exchange for the support of the present members of the clan against the Sabbat's efforts along the eastern seaboard. It's in your best interests, you know."

"Don't patronize us, you fucking pindick," barked Chas from across the table. This *de facto* meeting had convened at the last minute, by request of Francis Milliner.

Francis was the eldest member of the Milliner family, the Boston branch of the Giovanni. Isabel believed him to be more than a bit paranoid, but she indulged him. Much had recently taken place in Boston, including the execution of one of the most dangerous loose cannons ever known to the clan. Genevra Giovanni had been a Sabbat sympathizer, having use for the Giovanni family only insofar as it served her immediate needs. Not that every Giovanni vampire—and probably every vampire, period—didn't harbor similar selfishness, but the open display had made her powerful enemies among the clan. Masterfully, the Milliners had hidden her elimination beneath a veil of organized-crime violence. Isabel had to give Francis credit—he had crafted an almost century-long ruse to use as a front for whatever untoward events befell him and his brood, and had not thought twice about playing it out to take Genevra out of the picture. For his foresight and cleverness, the elders of the clan decided to allow him to drink the heart's blood of the rogue, bringing him closer to the power of the elders themselves. Who knows how many other contingency plans Milliner had up his sleeve?

To that end, Isabel had little interest in talking details with a second-rate yes man. Francis was the man with the plan, but she was his smokescreen, she knew. The Camarilla probably didn't even know that it was Milliners and not Giovanni who exercised the most influence in Boston. Outside a few individuals, everyone knew that the Giovanni were the preeminent power there. Of course, the Milliners *were* Giovanni, but such semantic games were the coin of the Kindred realm. Misdirection and subterfuge could take a Kindred much farther than brute force, and Isabel was walking, unliving proof of that.

"Chas, please. Settle down," Isabel remarked. He was still headstrong, ostensibly here to deal with the Benito Giovanni affair, and a liability to this discussion. Chas was a testament to the fact that sometimes nasty and brutish did get the job done, particularly in America. He wasn't especially strong, powerful or clever, but he had a mean streak a mile wide and less and less reservation nightly against showing it to a rival. That had begun to show through—his eyes had sunk in the few weeks since Isabel had met him, and his once-full lips had been pulled back into a perpetual growl or sneer. His hands were always white-knuckled, as if only by the most persistent concentration could he keep the Beast in check. Isabel knew: Chas was bound to snap soon. She had planned to play her cards right, however, and unleash Chas when it was most convenient, watching him go down in a blaze of glory that would no doubt take a few others with him. The key was to do it subtly, however—again, discretion made sure one need not keep escalating her efforts—and to make sure his inevitable kamikaze took place visible only to Kindred eyes and nowhere she'd have to call upon cover-up favors among the media, police, etc.

Still, he had a point. The liaison sneered at Chas, who bristled visibly.

"But don't let Chas's lack of couth mislead you—I'm sorry, what was your name again?" She put the diplomat in his place.

The guest's eyes narrowed to slits, regarding Isabel coldly. "Gauthier. Jacques Gauthier. Childe of Paul Levesque, childe of Shlomo Baruch, childe of Christianne Foy, childe of Vidal Jar—"

"Yes, yes," Isabel interrupted, "very impressive. Archbishop of Canterbury, extract of vanilla, Milk of Magnesia, and so the old joke goes. We realize that you're here to represent the Camarilla's interests and that you're supposed to butter us up and make this seem like the most fantastic deal ever to fall into our laps.

"But let me offer you my counterposition. Your approval means nothing to us. Your high-handed 'recognition of sovereignty' and other quasipolitical jingoism won't work in this room. You're not dealing with rank neonates. Your Camarilla is not a government, nor is it a military body. It is a simple social convention, a contract supported by its members in the interests of furthering its own ends. Quite frankly, it is a civil sinecure with which bored, effete elders play games and delude themselves. Am I to believe that if we could not reach an agreement in this room, that before the next dawn Boston would face a liveried phalanx of Camarilla shock troops? It's more likely that a few rowdy insurgents of your sect would swagger among Boston's Kindred like a mob of drunken soccer hooligans for a few nights until routed by the very same Kindred whose havens they disturb.

by Justin Achilli

"Your recognition means nothing. Your support means nothing. Your sect is incapable of maintaining the quiet influence it has along this entire coast of one of the most affluent nations in the world, just as it has proven powerless against the unknown Kindred of the East sweeping in from the West Coast. Oh, Jacques Gauthier, don't be so shocked—I've looked into matters. I wouldn't dream of entertaining an envoy such as yourself without knowing the full ramifications of the relations you propose.

"When weighed against other options, the only benefit that a loose agreement of support provides is in the hope that the Giovanni of Boston could simply turn their backs on the whole matter and allow the Sabbat and Camarilla fanatics to shred each other in the streets. How does that sound? Is that answer satisfactory?"

Jacques had risen from his seat, his mouth open wide, his head turned slightly downward and his teeth clenched. At Isabel's side, Chas twitched, undead veins bulging, like an epileptic bound to his chair in the throes of seizure.

"Do not presume that we are so powerless, Isabel Giovanni," retorted Jacques. "The Camarilla is not a military organization, as you say; but to believe that renders us powerless is pure folly. Neither is the Sabbat a military power. But these are not battles fought exclusively in the trenches. For every brawling fool who sees this solely as a matter of martiality, three more Kindred behind him make their moves through quieter channels. This is a war of influence, and the resources of the Camarilla are orders of magnitude more than the resources of Clan Giovanni. We are merely interested in minimizing and localizing the influence of our enemies—and your enemies as well—the Sabbat."

"The resources of the Camarilla! Absurd. The Camarilla has no resources! The only power it wields is that which is voluntarily afforded to it by its members. Your sect is far more fractious and selfishly motivated than you would have us think. The Camarilla does nothing as an entity, and you know it."

"Nor does Clan Giovanni, by that rationale," countered Gauthier.

"True, but Clan Giovanni in this case is a community of Boston's Kindred. We will more than certainly protect our own interests, and put aside our personal grudges when faced with a greater opposition. Whether that opposition is Sabbat or Camarilla—or both—is irrelevant. I know the man who has sent you here. I know Jan Pieterzoon. He has made quite a name for himself among the Kindred, and I suspect he may one night find himself among the—what do you call them? archons and justiciars?—of the Camarilla. But he will not do it by playing the role of firebrand. Rather, he will master the game of politics, promising one thing, delivering another and then convincing those beneath him that what they wanted in the first place was what he actually delivered.

"I know that Boston is only part of Pieterzoon's larger move at this stage, but I'm not going to pretend to know what cards he still holds in his hand. Jan is a much more proficient plotter than I will ever be, but I am far better at seeing the secrets within. Pieterzoon and those like him depend upon Kindred like me to provide the pieces with which they play. I—we, the Giovanni of Boston—may be pawns in that game, but we know that we are pawns. And a pawn that turns against the side that pushes it forward is a dangerous piece, indeed." Isabel stood straight up, arms crossed high over her chest, staring imperiously at Jacques.

Gauthier showed no sign of backing down, however. Pieterzoon had charged him with this negotiation—warned him that the Giovanni were deadly as vipers in their nest—and expected no failure. "You're speaking in metaphors, Isabel. You're occluding the issue. This is not a game, as you want to rush to reduce it to. Pawns and pieces and chess allusions are the stuff of florid fiction, and we're dealing in matters quite tangible. We need your help. In return, we are willing to leave Boston be. You will not receive such a plain or sincere offer from the Sabbat, as their dominance of the East Coast attests. It may be that you are truly prepared to weather the storm. But I have no reason to suspect that you would prefer to stand against this conflict if we offer you a chance to avoid it altogether."

"It would seem, then, Jacques, that we are at an impasse for the time being. I will take the details of your proposed alliance back and peruse them. You know where to reach me. I suggest we meet again in a few nights to finalize the nature of the relationship—should I decide one exists."

"What the fuck were you doing in there?" Chas asked Isabel as they left the building, headed for the silver Audi coupe she had borrowed for the trip. Normally, the car had only a one-point-eight-liter four-cylinder, but Isabel had arranged to "preview" one of next year's upgrade prototypes with the six-cylinder.

"Quiet down, Chas. And don't speak to me like that or I'll have your tongue. Literally."

Isabel disdained driving, so she handed the keys to Chas. The pair climbed into the car, which was slung low to the ground. She preferred luxury cars, of course, for their amenities, but in a city that was about to be torn apart by three rival factions, speed and maneuverability were preferable to cabriolet leather.

"But there's no way you're going to cut a deal with the Sabbat, right?"

"Are you out of your mind, Chas?"

"No, but why were you busting his balls so hard?"

"Who says I have to throw in with anyone?

And who says the Milliners would honor it if I agreed to it?"

"But isn't that why you're here, Isabel? To negotiate the deal?"

"I'm here because Francis Milliner asked for me. I'm here to get the most out of this little venture with the least investment on my part or the Milliners'. Why are *you* here, Chas?"

"Benito thing."

"That's right. So why don't you worry about that and I'll worry about this, okay? Have you made any progress on Benito's disappearance?"

"No," Chas had started to scowl, his hands gripping the steering wheel with a new fervor.

"Were you expecting to get something out of that meeting?"

"I figured maybe they'd offer some information about Benito as part of the deal."

"And maybe they will, Chas. Now you see? Putting Jacques over as many barrels as I can means that if he really wants this support arrangement to go through, he's got to give me what I want. Pieterzoon wouldn't suggest this unless it was necessary, so I know I've got a lot of leverage. And Pieterzoon didn't want to come himself, so he sent that little lickspittle so it would look like this is no big deal. Therefore he thinks I think this is nothing. But that's not what I think, get it?" She smiled. Chas was playing the same game of "she thinks I think" with her, and she had called him on it, if only by allusion.

The Audi swung around a corner, its wide tires grabbing the road and holding tight as the chassis rolled low to keep the turn radius tight.

"In the meantime, Chas, I've got a side project for you. It'll teach you some fundamental investigation skills."

"Whoah, hang on. I'm not here for you on this deal. I'm still working for Frankie Gee."

"Yes, well, you need the practice. I'll bill Frankie later."

Chas sighed pointedly, as if to remind Isabel that since he didn't breathe, he meant something by it.

"That's my boy. So tomorrow night, you find out what you can about Jacques Gauthier. And tell me who calls the shots for the Sabbat in this city."

"I already know part two. It's Max Lowell."

"How do you know that?"

"Shit, my haven's in New York. Boston's just a shot up the road. Frankie's moved more stuff through Lowell than I care to think about. Fuck, if this shit comes down to a shootout, it'll probably be with Frankie's guns."

Isabel looked unwaveringly at Chas.

"See," he said with a smirk, "I'm not so stupid as I pretend."

Nope, Chas thought to himself as he boarded the T to ride back to his hotel, *I'm not so stupid at all*. And when he arrived, he dialed Frankie's number—the one with the **# area code.

by justin achilli

next: Malkavian

FROM CLAN NOVEL: GIOVANNI